DEBBIE MACOMBER

The Perfect Mismatch

The First Man You Meet and *Hasty Wedding*

/// MIRA

//MIRA™

ISBN-13: 978-0-7783-6849-6

The Perfect Mismatch

Copyright © 2025 by Harlequin Enterprises ULC

The First Man You Meet
First published in 1992. This edition published in 2025.
Copyright © 1992 by Debbie Macomber

Hasty Wedding
First published in 1993. This edition published in 2025.
Copyright © 1993 by Debbie Macomber

Recycling programs
for this product may
not exist in your area.

For questions and comments about the quality of this book, please contact us
at CustomerService@Harlequin.com.

TM is a trademark of Harlequin Enterprises ULC.

Mira
22 Adelaide St. West, 41st Floor
Toronto, Ontario M5H 4E3, Canada
MIRABooks.com

Printed in U.S.A.

Also available from Debbie Macomber and MIRA

CONTENTS

THE FIRST MAN YOU MEET

One

It had been one of those days.

One of those nightmarish days in which nothing had gone right. Nothing. Shelly Hansen told herself she should have seen the writing on the wall that morning when she tripped over the laces of her high-top purple running shoes as she hurried from the parking lot to her dinky office. She'd torn a hole in the knee of her brand-new pants and limped ingloriously into her building. The day had gone steadily downhill from there, with a package lost by the courier and—worst of all—the discovery that her bank account was overdrawn because a client's check had bounced.

By the time she returned to her apartment that evening she was in a black mood. All she needed to make her day complete was to have her mother pop in unannounced with a man in tow, convinced she'd found the perfect mate for Shelly.

She could only hope that wouldn't happen, but it was exactly the kind of thing Shelly had come to expect from her dear, sweet *desperate* mother. Shelly was twenty-eight now and still single, and her mother tended to view her unmarried status as a situation to be remedied. Since her father had decided not to retire, and her two brothers were both living out of state, Shelly had become the focus of her mother's obsessions. Marriage, closely followed by grandchildren, were the first and second items on Faith Hansen's agenda for her only daughter.

Never mind that Shelly felt content with her life just the way it was. Never mind that she wasn't interested in marriage and children…at least not yet. That time would come, she was sure, not now, but someday soon—or rather, some *year* soon.

For the moment, Shelly was absorbed in her career. She was proud of her work as a video producer, although she continually suffered the cash-flow problems of the self-employed. Her relaxation DVDs—seascapes, mountain scenes, a flickering fire in a brick fireplace, all with a background of classical music—were selling well. Her cat-sitting DVD had recently caught the attention of a major distributor, and she couldn't help believing she was on the brink of real success.

That was the good news.

Her mother hounding her to get married was the bad.

Tossing her woven Mexican bag and striped blue jacket onto the sofa, Shelly ventured into the kitchen and sorted through the packages in her freezer until she found something that halfway appealed to her for dinner. The frozen entrée was in the microwave when the doorbell chimed.

Her mother. The way her day was going, it *had* to be her mother. Groaning inwardly, she decided she'd be polite but insistent. Friendly but determined, and if her mother began talking about husbands, Shelly would simply change the subject.

But it wasn't Faith Hansen who stood outside her door. It was Elvira Livingston, the building manager, a warm, delightful but insatiably curious older woman.

"Good evening, dear," Mrs. Livingston greeted her. She wore heavy gold earrings and a billowing, bright yellow dress, quite typical attire. She clutched a large box protectively in both hands. "The postman dropped this off. He asked if I'd give it to you."

"For me, Mrs. L.?" Perhaps today wasn't a total loss, after all.

Elvira nodded, holding the package as though she wasn't entirely sure she should surrender it until she got every bit of relevant data. "The return address is California. Know anyone by the name of Millicent Bannister?"

"Aunt Milly?" Shelly hadn't heard from her mother's aunt in years.

"The package is insured," Mrs. Livingston noted, shifting the box just enough to examine the label again.

Shelly held out her hands to receive the package, but her landlady apparently didn't notice.

"I had to sign for it." This, too, seemed to be of great importance. "And there's a letter attached," Mrs. Livingston added.

Shelly had the impression that the only way she'd ever get her hands on the parcel was to let Mrs. Livingston open it first.

"I certainly appreciate all the trouble you've gone to," Shelly said, gripping the sides of the box and giving a firm tug. Mrs. Livingston released the package reluctantly. "Uh, thanks, Mrs. L. I'll talk to you soon."

The older woman's face fell with disappointment as Shelly began to close the door. Obviously, she was hoping for an invitation to stay. But Shelly wasn't in the mood for company, especially not the meddlesome, if well-meaning, Elvira Livingston.

Shelly sighed. This was what she got for renting an apartment with "character." She could be living in a modern town house with a sauna, pool and workout room in a suburban neighborhood. Instead she'd opted for a brick two-story apartment building in the heart of Seattle. The radiators hissed at all hours of the night in perfect harmony with the plumbing that groaned and creaked. But Shelly loved the polished hardwood floors, the high ceilings with their delicate crystal light fixtures and the bay windows that overlooked Puget Sound. She could do without the sauna and other amenities, even if it meant occasionally dealing with an eccentric busybody like Mrs. Livingston.

Eagerly she carried the package into the kitchen and set it on her table. Although she wondered what Aunt Milly had sent her, she carefully peeled the letter free, then just as carefully removed the plain brown wrapper.

The box was an old one, she noticed, the cardboard heavier than that currently used by stores. Shelly gently pried off the lid. She found layers of tissue paper wrapped around...a dress. Shelly pushed aside the paper and lifted the garment from its box. She gasped in surprise as the long white dress gracefully unfolded.

This wasn't just any dress. It was a wedding dress, an exquisitely sewn lace-and-satin wedding dress.

Surely it couldn't have been Aunt Milly's... No, that couldn't be... It wasn't possible.

Anxious now, her heart racing, Shelly refolded the dress and placed it back in the box. She reached for the envelope and saw that her hands were trembling as she tore it open.

My Dearest Shelly,

I trust this letter finds you happy and well. You've frequently been in my thoughts the past few days. I suppose you could blame Dr. Phil for that. Though now that I think about it, it may have been Oprah. As you'll have gathered, I often watch those talk shows these days. John would have disapproved, but he's been gone eight years now. Of course, if I wanted to, I'd watch them if he were still alive. John could disapprove all he wanted, but it wouldn't do him a bit of good. Never did. He knew it and loved me, anyway.

I imagine you're wondering why I'm mailing you my wedding dress and what Dr. Phil and Oprah have to do with it. (Yes, that is indeed my infamous wedding dress.) I suspect the sight of it has put the fear of God into you. I wish I could've been there to see your face when you realized what I was sending you. No doubt you're familiar with the story; everyone in the family's known about it for years. Since you're fated to marry the first man you meet once the dress is in your hands, your instinct is probably to burn the thing immediately!

Now that I reconsider, I'm certain it was Dr. Phil. He had a show recently featuring pets as companions to the elderly, lifting their spirits and the like. The man being interviewed brought along a cute little Scottish terrier and that was when the old seamstress drifted into my mind. Her name was Mrs. McDonald—or was it McDonnell? At any rate, I must have fallen asleep, because the next thing I knew the six-o'clock news was on.

While I slept I had a dream about you. This was no ordinary dream, either. I saw you plain as day, standing beside a tall young man, your blue eyes bright and shining. You were so happy, so truly in love. But what astonished me was the wedding dress you were wearing.

Mine.

The very dress the old Scottish woman sewed for me all those years ago. It seemed to me I was receiving a message of some sort and that I'd best not ignore it. Neither should you! You're about to embark on the grandest adventure of your life, my dear. Keep me informed!

Believe me, Shelly, I know what you're thinking. I well remember my own thoughts the day that seamstress handed me the wedding dress. I'd ordered something completely different from her—a simple evening gown—so I was shocked to say the least. Marriage was the *last* thing on my mind! I had a career, back in the days when it was rare for a woman to attend college, let alone graduate from law school.

You and I are a great deal alike, Shelly. We value our independence. It takes a special kind of man to be married to women like us. And you, my dear niece, are about to meet that one special man just the way I did.

All my love,
Aunt Milly

P.S. You're only the second person to wear the dress. Never before have I felt anything like this. Perhaps it's the beginning of a new tradition!

With hands that trembled even more fiercely now, Shelly folded the letter and slid it back into the envelope. Her heart was pounding, and she could feel the sweat beading her forehead.

The phone rang then, and more from instinct than any desire to talk, Shelly picked up the receiver.

"Hello." It hadn't dawned on her until that moment that the caller might be her mother, wanting to bring over a man for her to meet. Any man her mother introduced would only add to the growing nightmare, but—

"Shelly, it's Jill. Are you all right? You sound… strange."

"Jill." Shelly was so relieved that her knees went weak. "Thank heaven it's you."

"What's wrong?"

Shelly hardly knew where to begin. "My aunt Milly's wedding dress just arrived. I realize that won't mean anything to you unless you've heard the family legend about my aunt Milly and uncle John."

"I haven't."

"Of course you haven't, otherwise you'd understand what I'm going through," Shelly snapped, then felt guilty for being short-tempered with her best friend. Making an effort to compose herself, she explained, "I've just been mailed a wedding dress—one that's been in my family for over sixty years—with the clear understanding that I'll be wearing it soon myself."

"You didn't even tell me you were dating anyone." Jill hadn't managed to disguise the hurt in her voice.

"I'm *not!* And I'm not getting married, either. If anyone should know that, it's you."

"Then your aunt intends you to wear it when you do get married."

"There's more to it than that," Shelly cried. "Listen. Aunt Milly—who's really my mother's aunt, a few years older than my grandmother—became an attorney just after the Second World War. She worked hard to earn her law degree and had decided to dedicate her life to her career."

"In other words, she'd planned never to marry."

"Exactly."

"But apparently she did."

"Yes, and the story of how that happened has been in the family for years. It seems Aunt Milly had all her clothes professionally made. As the story goes, she took some lovely white material to an old Scottish woman who had a reputation as the best seamstress around. Milly needed an evening dress for some formal event that was coming up—business-related, of course. The woman took her measurements and told her the dress would be finished by the end of the week."

"And?" Jill prompted when Shelly hesitated.

"And…when Milly returned for the dress the old woman sat her down with a cup of tea."

"The dress wasn't ready?"

"Oh, it was ready, all right, only it wasn't the dress Aunt Milly had ordered. The Scottish woman said she was gifted with the 'sight.'"

"She was clairvoyant?"

"So she claimed," Shelly said, breathing in deeply. "The old woman told my aunt that when she began the dress a vision came to her. A clear vision that involved Milly. This vision showed Milly getting married. The old woman was so convinced of it that she turned what was supposed to be a simple evening dress into an elaborate wedding gown, with layers of satin and lace and lots of pearls."

"It sounds beautiful," Jill said with a sigh.

"Of course it's beautiful—but don't you see?"

"See what?"

It was all Shelly could do not to groan with frustration. "The woman insisted my aunt Milly would marry within the year. It happened, too, just the way that seamstress said, right down to the last detail."

Jill sighed again. "That's the most romantic story I've heard in ages."

"It isn't romance," Shelly argued, "it's fate interrupting one's life! It's being a...pawn! It's destiny whether you like it or not. I know that seems crazy, but I've grown up hearing this story. It was as though my aunt Milly didn't have any choice in the matter."

"And your aunt Milly mailed you the dress?"

"Yes," Shelly wailed. "*Now* do you understand why I'm upset?"

"Frankly, no. Come on, Shelly, it's just an old dress. You're overreacting. You make it sound as if you're going to marry the next man you meet."

Shelly gasped audibly. "How'd you know?" she whispered.

"Know what?"

"That's *exactly* what happened to Aunt Milly. That's part of the legend. She tried to refuse the dress, but the seamstress wouldn't take it back, nor would she accept payment. When Aunt Milly left the dress shop, she had car problems and needed a mechanic. My uncle John was that mechanic. And Aunt Milly married him. She married *the first man she met,* just like the seamstress said."

Two

"Shelly, that doesn't mean *you're* going to marry the next man you meet," Jill stated calmly, far too calmly to suit Shelly.

Perhaps Jill didn't recognize a crisis when she came across one. They were talking about fate here. Predestination. Okay, maybe, just maybe, she was being a bit melodramatic, but after the ghastly day she'd had, who could blame her?

"Aunt Milly came right out and said I'm going to get married soon," Shelly said. "According to the family legend, the first man you meet when you get the dress is the man you'll marry."

"It's just coincidence," Jill reassured her. "Your aunt probably would've met her husband *without* the dress. It would've happened anyway. And don't forget, she's an old woman now," Jill continued soothingly. "I know this wonderful old lady who comes into the pharmacy every few weeks and she always insists *I'm* going to get married soon. I smile and nod and fill her prescription. She means well, and I'm sure your aunt Milly does, too. She just wants you to be happy, the way she was.

But I think it's silly to take any of this prediction nonsense seriously."

Shelly exhaled sharply. Jill was right; Aunt Milly was a lovely woman who had Shelly's happiness at heart. She'd had a long, blissful marriage herself and wanted the same for her great-niece. But Shelly had plans and goals, none of which included meeting and marrying a stranger.

The story of Aunt Milly's wedding dress had been handed down through the family. Shelly had first heard it as a child and had loved it. She'd ranked the story of her aunt Milly and uncle John with her favorite fairy tales of Cinderella and Sleeping Beauty, barely able to distinguish truth from fantasy. However, she was an adult now. Her heart and her life weren't going to be ruled by something as whimsical as a "magic" wedding dress or a fanciful legend.

"You're absolutely right," Shelly announced emphatically. "The whole thing is ridiculous. Just because this wedding dress supposedly conjured up a husband for my aunt Milly sixty-plus years ago doesn't mean it's going to do the same thing for me, no matter what she claims."

"Well, thank goodness you're finally being sensible about this."

"No one bothered to ask me what I thought before shipping off a so-called magic wedding gown. I don't want to get married yet, so I certainly don't need the dress. It was a nice gesture, but unnecessary."

"Exactly," Jill agreed.

"I'm not interested in playing déjà voodoo." She paused to laugh at her own joke.

Jill chuckled, too. "I wouldn't be, either."

Shelly felt greatly relieved, and the tight muscles

along the back of her neck began to relax. Jill was, as usual, full of practical advice. Aunt Milly was a wonderful old lady, and the legend was a delightful bit of family lore, but it would be laughable to take any of this seriously.

"How about meeting me for lunch tomorrow?" Jill suggested. "It's been ages since we got together."

"Sounds good to me," Shelly said. Although they'd been close friends since college, it took some effort on both their parts these days to make time in their hectic lives to see each other. "When and where?"

"How about the mall?" Jill asked. "That would be easiest for me since I'm scheduled to work tomorrow. I can get off a few minutes before twelve."

"Great. I'll see you at noon at Patrick's," Shelly promised. Meeting her friend for lunch was just the antidote she needed after her terrible day. But what did she expect on Friday, April thirteenth?

Shelly overslept, then got stuck in a traffic jam on her way to meet Jill the following morning. She detested being late, although she often was. Rather than fight for a convenient parking spot in the vast lot that surrounded the mall, she took the first available space and rushed over to the nearest entrance. Patrick's, a cozy, charming restaurant on the mall's upper level, was deservedly popular for business lunches. Shelly had eaten there often and especially enjoyed the spinach-and-shrimp salad.

A glance at her watch told her it was already after twelve, and not wanting to keep Jill waiting, she hurried toward the escalator, weaving her way through the crowd.

Her mind must have been on the salad she intended

to order instead of the escalator because the moment she placed her foot on the first tread, she lost her balance.

"Oh…oh!" Swinging both arms out in a futile attempt to remain upright, she groped at thin air. She tried frantically to catch herself as she fell backward.

Landing in someone's arms shocked her as much as having lost her balance. Incredulous, she twisted around to thank her rescuer but this proved to be a mistake. Her action caught the man off guard, and before he could prevent it, they went crashing to the floor. Once again Shelly expected to experience pain. Instead, her waist was surrounded by arms that were surprisingly strong. His grip was firm but gentle, protective. As they fell, he maneuvered himself to take the brunt of the impact when they landed. Sprawled as she was above him, Shelly found herself staring down at the most attractive man she'd ever seen. Her heart thrummed. Her breath caught. Her body froze.

For a moment neither of them spoke. A crowd had gathered around them before Shelly managed to speak. When she did, her voice was weak and breathless. "Are you all right? I'm so sorry…"

"I'm fine. What about you?"

"Fine. I think."

She lay cushioned by his solid chest, their faces mere inches apart. Shelly's long hair fell forward, framing his face. He smelled of mint and some clean-scented soap. Her gaze wandered curiously over his features; at such close range she could see the tiny lines that fanned out from the edges of his sapphire-blue eyes, as well as the grooves that bracketed his mouth. His nose was classically straight, his mouth full and sensuous. At least his lower lip was. It didn't take her long to recognize that this man was uncompromisingly male. His eyes held hers reluctantly, as if he, too, was caught in the same powerful trance.

Neither of them moved, and although Shelly was convinced the breathless sensation she felt was a result of the fall, she couldn't seem to breathe properly even now.

"Miss, are you hurt?"

Reluctantly, Shelly looked up to find a security guard standing over her.

"Um… I don't think so."

"Sir?"

"I'm fine."

The arms that were holding hers securely began to loosen.

"If we could have you both sit over here for a moment," the guard instructed, pointing at a bench. "We have an ambulance on the way."

"An ambulance? But I told you I'm okay," she said.

The guard helped Shelly to her feet. Her legs were shaky and her breathing still uncertain, but otherwise she was unhurt.

"Officer, there's really no need," the man who'd fallen with her protested.

"Mall policy," the guard said. He hooked his thumbs into the wide leather belt and rocked back on his feet. "It's standard procedure to have all accident victims checked immediately."

"If you're worried about a lawsuit—"

"I don't make the rules," the guard interrupted her rescuer. "I just see that they're carried out. Now, if you'd sit over here, the medical team will arrive in a couple of minutes."

"I don't have time to wait," Shelly insisted. "I'm meeting someone." She glanced longingly at the upper level, wondering how she could get word of her delay to Jill. Needless to say, she'd forgotten her cell—could anything else go wrong? It didn't reassure her to notice the number of people clustered by the railing, staring down at her. Her little escapade had attracted quite a bit of attention.

"I've got an appointment, as well," the man said, looking pointedly at his watch.

The security guard ignored their protests. He removed a small notebook from his shirt pocket and flipped it open. "Your names, please."

"Shelly Hansen."

"Mark Brady."

He wrote down the information and a brief account of how they happened to fall.

"I won't have to go to the hospital, will I?" Shelly demanded.

"That depends," the guard answered.

This whole thing was ridiculous. She was perfectly fine. A little shaken, true, but uninjured. She suddenly realized that she hadn't thanked this man—Mark, was it?

"I'm terribly sorry about all this," she said. "I can't thank you enough for catching me."

"In the future, you might be more careful." Mark glanced at his watch a second time.

"I will be. But if it ever happens again, might I suggest you just let me fall?" This delay was inconvenient, but that wasn't any reason to be quick-tempered. She studied her rescuer and shook her head slightly, wondering why she'd been so impressed. He looked as if he'd stepped off Planet Nerd. Dark blue suit and tie, crisp white shirt, polished loafer-type shoes. This guy was as original as cooked oatmeal. About as personable, too.

If she was giving him the once-over, she discovered he was eyeing her, too. Apparently he was equally unimpressed. Her sweatshirt was a fluorescent orange and her jeans as tight as a second skin. Her ankle-high boots were black, her socks the same shade of orange as the sweatshirt. Her hair cascaded about her shoulders in a layer of dark frothy curls. Mark was scowling in obvious disapproval.

The wide glass doors at the mall entrance opened, and two paramedics hurried inside. Seconds later, when the ambulance arrived, two more medical people entered the building. Shelly was mortified that such a minor accident would result in all this scrutiny.

The first paramedic knelt in front of her while the second concentrated on Mark. Before she completely understood what was happening, her shoe was off and the man was examining her ankle. Mark, too, was being examined, a stethoscope pressed over his heart. He didn't seem to appreciate the procedures any more than she did.

It wasn't until he stood up that she realized how tall he was. Close to six-five, she guessed. A good match for her own five feet ten inches, she thought automatically.

It hit her then. Bull's-eye. Aunt Milly's letter had mentioned her standing beside a tall young man. Mark Brady was tall. Very tall. Taller than just about any man she'd ever met.

Aunt Milly's letter had also said something about Shelly's blue eyes. She'd ignored it at the time, but her eyes weren't blue. They were hazel. Mark had blue eyes, though. The kind of vivid blue eyes women generally found striking... Nor could she forget her initial reaction to him. She'd been attracted. Highly attracted. It'd been a long time since a man had interested her this much. Until he stood up, anyway. When she got a good look at him, she'd known immediately that they had nothing in common. She'd bet he didn't own a single article of clothing that wasn't blue, black or tan. Mark Brady was clearly a man without imagination or flair.

On a sudden thought, she glanced worriedly at his left hand. No wedding ring. Closing her eyes, she sagged against the back of the bench and groaned.

"Miss?" The paramedic was studying her closely.

"Excuse me," she said, straightening. She jerked impatiently on Mark's suit jacket. He was involved in a conversation with the ambulance attendant who was interviewing him and didn't turn around.

"Excuse me," she said again, louder this time.

"Yes?" Mark turned to face her, frowning impatiently.

Now that she had his attention, she wasn't sure she should continue. "This may seem like an odd question, but, uh...are you married?"

He frowned again. "No."

"Oh, no," Shelly moaned and slumped forward. "I was afraid of that."

"I beg your pardon?"

"Do you have a girlfriend? I mean, you're a good-looking guy. There's got to be someone important in your life. Anyone? Please, just think. Surely there's someone?" She knew she was beginning to sound desperate, but she couldn't help it. Aunt Milly's letter was echoing in her mind, and last night's logic had disappeared.

The four paramedics, as well as Mark, were staring at her. "Are you sure you don't want to come to the hospital and talk to a doctor?" one of them asked.

Shelly nodded. "I'm sure." Then before she could stop herself, she blurted out, "What do you do for a living?"

"I'm a CPA," he answered wearily.

"An accountant," she muttered. She should've guessed. He was obviously as staid and conventional as he looked. And as boring. The kind of man who'd probably never even heard of DVDs for entertaining bored house cats. He probably wouldn't be interested in purchasing one, either.

Her aunt Milly *couldn't* have seen Mark and Shelly together in her dream. Not Mark Brady. The two of them were completely ill-suited. A relationship wouldn't last five minutes! Abruptly she reminded herself that she wasn't supposed to be taking Milly's prediction seriously.

"May I go?" she asked the paramedic. "I'm not even bruised."

"Yes, but you'll need to sign here."

Shelly did so without bothering to read the statement. Mark, however, seemed to peruse every sentence. He would, of course.

"Uh, Mark…" Shelly hesitated, and Mark glanced in her direction.

"Thank you," she said simply.

"You're welcome."

Still she delayed leaving.

"Is there anything else?"

She didn't know quite how to say this, but she felt the need too strongly to ignore it. "Don't take offense—I'm sure you're a really great guy—but I just want you to know I'm not interested in marriage right now."

Three

Jill was seated at the table, doodling on the paper place mat, when Shelly arrived. "What kept you?" she asked. "I've been here for almost half an hour."

"I—I fell off the escalator."

Jill's eyes widened in alarm. "My goodness, are you all right?"

Shelly nodded sheepishly. "I'm fine."

"Shouldn't you see a doctor?"

"I already have," she said, avoiding eye contact with her friend. "Well, sort of. The security guard called in the paramedics."

"No wonder you're late."

"I would've been, anyway," Shelly admitted as she reached for a menu, although she knew what she was going to order—the same thing she always did.

"This has really got you flustered, hasn't it?"

"It's more than the fall," Shelly explained, lowering the menu. "It's the man who caught me."

Jill arched her eyebrows jokingly. "Aha! I should have guessed there was a man involved."

"You might try to understand how I felt," Shelly said

reproachfully. "Especially since I haven't recovered from receiving Aunt Milly's wedding dress yet."

"Don't tell me you're still worried about that first-man-you-meet nonsense."

"Of course not. That would be ridiculous. It's just… it's just I can't help feeling there might be *something* to that silly wedding dress."

"Then mail it back."

"I can't," Shelly said, slapping the menu down on the table. "Aunt Milly warned me not to. She didn't use exactly those words, mind you. She said I shouldn't ignore the dress. I mean, how can I? It's like an albatross around my neck."

"I still think you're overreacting."

"That's the crazy part. I *know* I am, but I can't seem to stop myself. I grew up hearing the legend of that wedding dress, and now it's in my possession. I've got a piece of family history hanging in the back of my closet. What if my mother hears about this?" She shuddered at the thought.

"So you hung the dress in your closet."

"I tried keeping it under my bed, but I couldn't sleep, so I finally got up and stuck it in the closet." She closed the menu and set it aside. "That bothered me, too. I tossed and turned half the night, then I remembered Aunt Milly had done the same thing when the seamstress gave her the dress."

"She put it under her bed?"

Shelly nodded slowly. "I seem to remember hearing that. She'd tried to refuse it, but the old woman insisted Aunt Milly take the gown home with her. By the time she got to her apartment she'd already met my uncle

John, although she still didn't know she was going to marry him."

Jill raised a skeptical eyebrow. "Then what? After she put it under her bed and couldn't sleep, I mean?"

"Well, she did the same thing I did," Shelly said. "She shoved it in her closet." Shelly felt as if she was confessing to a crime. "I didn't want the thing staring me in the face so I hung it in the back."

"Naturally." Jill was trying, unsuccessfully, to disguise a smile. Shelly could see how someone else might find her situation humorous, but she personally didn't think any of this was too amusing. Not when it was her life, her future, being tossed around like...like some cosmic football. At this rate, she'd be married by nightfall!

"That's not the worst of it," Shelly added. She exhaled slowly, wondering why her heart was still beating so fiercely.

"You mean there's more?"

She nodded. The waitress arrived just then and took their orders, returning quickly with glasses of iced tea. Shelly took a deep breath before she continued. "I literally fell into that man's—Mark Brady's—arms."

"How convenient."

"It's very nice of him to have broken my fall," she said sternly, "but I wish he hadn't."

"Shelly!"

"I mean it." She glanced around to make sure no one was listening, then whispered, "The man's an accountant."

Jill reacted in mock horror, covering her mouth with both hands. "No! An accountant?"

"Think about it. Could you honestly picture me married to an accountant?"

Jill mulled over the question for a moment. "Hmm, a CPA," she repeated slowly. "You still haven't memorized your multiplication tables, have you? You freeze up whenever you have to deal with numbers. No, I guess you're right, I can't see you with an accountant."

Shelly raised both hands, palms up, in a dramatic gesture. "I rest my case."

Jill reached for some bread, carefully selecting a whole-wheat roll. "Just because you fell into his arms doesn't mean you're going to marry him," she said in a matter-of-fact voice.

"I know that."

"Then what's the problem?"

"I can't make myself *believe* it," Shelly said. "I feel like one tiny pin fighting the force of a giant magnet."

"That's preposterous."

"I know," Shelly agreed readily. "I just wish I hadn't said anything to Mark."

Jill set the roll on her plate with exaggerated care. "You told him about your aunt Milly's wedding dress?"

"Of course not!" Shelly said. "I told him I couldn't marry him."

Jill's mouth dropped open. "You didn't! Did you?"

Shelly nodded. "I don't know what made me say anything so ludicrous. I can't imagine what he must think of me. Not that I plan on seeing him again, of course. Unless—"

"Unless what?"

Their lunches were served. Jill had ordered a hot spinach salad with slices of chicken. Shelly's spinach salad was piled high with shrimp, egg slices and black olives.

"Go on," Jill urged once the waitress had gone. "You don't plan on seeing Mark again unless—"

"Unless it's absolutely unavoidable."

"I take it this means your aunt Milly's first encounter with your uncle John wasn't her last." Jill giggled. "Silly me. Obviously it wasn't."

"No. Even though Aunt Milly didn't want to see him again. My uncle was a wonderful man, don't get me wrong, and he was perfect for Aunt Milly, as it turned out, but they were as different as night and day. Aunt Milly was a college graduate and Uncle John never completed high school."

Shelly sighed wistfully. At one time the story of their romance had been like her own personal fairy tale. But now she didn't find it nearly as enthralling. "He helped Milly fix her car the night it broke down. The very next day she was in court defending a client in a lawsuit—"

"Let me guess," Jill interrupted, "your uncle John was the man suing her client."

Shelly nodded. "Yes, and that was only the beginning. Every time they turned around they were bumping into each other."

"How soon after they met did they get married?"

This was the question Shelly had dreaded most. She closed her eyes and whispered, "Ten days."

"Ten days," Jill echoed with an incredulous look.

"I know. It seems that once they kissed, they both realized there wasn't any use fighting it."

"Did your aunt tell John about the seamstress and the wedding dress?"

Shelly shrugged. "I don't know, but my guess is she

didn't...at least not at first." She hadn't touched her salad yet and paused to savor a forkful of her favorite seafood. Then she said abruptly, "They eloped without telling anyone."

"Children?" Jill wanted to know.

"Three boys. My mother's cousins."

"What about granddaughters? You'd think your aunt Milly would want to hand the dress down to one of them."

"All three of her sons had boys themselves. I guess you could say I'm the closest she's got to a granddaughter."

"Ten days," Jill repeated. "That's really something."

Forking up another succulent shrimp, Shelly continued her story. "That old Scottish woman knew about the wedding even before the family did. When Aunt Milly and Uncle John returned from their honeymoon, there was a wedding card from the seamstress waiting for them."

Jill propped her elbows on the table and gazed at Shelly. "Tell me what Mark Brady looks like."

Shelly frowned, trying to form her impressions of him into some kind of reasonably articulate description. He was compelling in ways she didn't quite understand. She sensed that he was principled and headstrong, but what made her so sure of that, Shelly couldn't explain. "He's tall," she began slowly. "And he was wearing a suit."

"How tall?"

"Basketball-player tall. He must be about six-five."

"Brown hair?"

Shelly nodded. "With blue eyes. *Really* blue eyes. I don't think I've ever met a man with eyes that precise

color. They seemed to…" She hesitated, unsettled by
the emotion that stirred within her when she thought
about Mark. Although their encounter had been brief,
Shelly was left feeling oddly certain that she could trust
this man, trust him implicitly. It wasn't a sensation she
could remember experiencing with any other man. She
didn't like the feeling; it made her uncomfortable. Until
Jill had started asking her about Mark, Shelly didn't realize she'd experienced *any* emotion toward him—except for embarrassment, of course.

"Why do you want to know?" she asked.

Jill gave her a knowing grin. "Because if he's as tall
as you say, with dark brown hair and deep blue eyes,
and he's wearing a suit, he just walked into this restaurant."

"What?" Shelly felt her stomach sink. "Mark's here?
Mark Brady?"

"That's not so unusual, is it? This is, after all, the
same shopping mall where you, uh, met—" Jill made
a show of glancing at her watch "—thirty or so minutes ago."

"He's here." She reminded herself that Jill was right:
Mark's choosing to have lunch at Patrick's was just a
coincidence. Too bad she couldn't convince her racing
heart to believe that.

"He's on the other side of the room," Jill whispered.

"Has he seen me yet?"

"I don't think so."

Without being obvious—or at least Shelly hoped she
wasn't being obvious—she turned to look in his direction. At that same instant, Mark happened to look up.
Their eyes met. Despite herself, she gasped. Her hands
shook and she felt herself break out in a cold sweat.

Mark scowled and quickly looked away.

She couldn't blame him. He seemed surprised to see her there. Unpleasantly surprised.

"Well, is it him?" Jill demanded.

Shelly couldn't find her voice, so she answered with a nod.

"I thought it might be. What are you thinking?"

"That I've lost my appetite." Shelly doubted she'd be able to finish her lunch.

"You want my advice?" Jill asked, grinning broadly. "I don't have a lot of experience with magic wedding dresses, but I recently read a fascinating book on home remedies."

"Sure." At this point Shelly was feeling reckless enough to try just about anything.

"Garlic," Jill said solemnly. "Wear a garlic rope around your neck. Not only does it deter vampires and prevent colds, but it might ward off potential husbands conjured up by a magic wedding dress."

Four

Hard though she tried, Shelly had a difficult time ignoring Mark Brady. He sat there, stiff and unapproachable, at the other side of the small restaurant. Just as stiff and unapproachable as she was. Jill wanted to linger over her coffee before returning to her job at the Pay-Rite Pharmacy in the mall, but Shelly was eager to be on her way. The sooner she left, the sooner she could put this bothersome encounter behind her.

"Don't forget Morgan's baby shower on Tuesday night," Jill said as Shelly reached for her purse.

Shelly had completely forgotten about their friend's party, which was understandable given her present state of mind. Most of their college friends were married and several were now having babies. Rather than admit how absentminded she'd suddenly become, Shelly asked, "Do you want to drive over together?"

"Sure," Jill said. "I have to go directly from work so I'll stop off at your place and we can leave from there."

"I'll be ready." She tried to imagine their excitable classmate as a wife and mother. It was Morgan who'd gotten the entire dorm hooked on *Survivor*. Before anyone could figure out how it had occurred, all the girls were obsessed with the participants and their lives. It became as important as mealtimes to learn who'd been voted off and who'd won that week's challenges.

For no particular reason, Shelly thought of Aunt Milly's wedding dress—which seemed to have become her own private challenge. Sighing, she dropped her share of the bill and a tip on the table. "I'll see you Tuesday, then."

"Right. And, Shelly, don't look so worried. No enchanted wedding dress is going to interfere with your life—unless you allow it to."

Easy for Jill to say, since it wasn't *her* life and *her* great-aunt's wedding dress. Nevertheless, her advice was sound. Aunt Milly might have had some fanciful dream about Shelly's marrying a tall man with blue eyes, but that didn't mean it was going to happen, especially when Shelly was so determined that it wouldn't.

"You're absolutely right," she said emphatically. "I know I keep saying that, but…well, I seem to need reminding. So, thanks. Again." With a final wave, she wandered out of the restaurant, barely noticing the colorful shop windows as she passed them. As Jill had pointed out, Aunt Milly meant well, but the letter and the wedding dress shouldn't be taken too seriously.

Shelly knew exactly what kind of man she'd fall in love with, and he wouldn't bear any resemblance to Mark Brady. He'd be unconventional, and fervent about life, and as passionate as she was herself. Naturally, he'd appreciate her work and take pride in his own. He'd be a free spirit, like her. She'd prefer a man with gumption, too—someone who possessed initiative. It'd be nice if he was a little better at organizational skills than she was, but that wasn't a requirement.

With marriage so prominent in her mind, Shelly found herself standing in front of a jeweler's display window, studying a large assortment of wedding bands. She noticed one ring that stood out from the rest: three small rows of diamond chips, bracketed on each side by a thin band of gold. The ring was striking in its simplicity, its uncontrived beauty.

For the longest moment Shelly stared at the rings as she wove whimsical dreams around the happy bride and the tall groom. *Tall groom.* Her thoughts came to a skidding halt.

What on earth had come over her? She didn't know, but whatever it was, she didn't like it. Self-consciously she glanced around, fearful that someone was watching her. Well, a very specific someone, to be honest. Someone who definitely shouldn't see her gazing with open longing at a collection of absurdly high-priced wedding rings. Mark Brady.

With a sense of urgency, Shelly hurried toward the mall exit. It was all she could do to keep from breaking into a run. No matter how fast she walked, however, she couldn't shake the feeling that *he* was there, watching her. Twice she whirled around, convinced she'd see Mark Brady strolling behind her, sneering and making contemptuous remarks.

He wasn't there.

With profound relief, she arrived at the parking lot and located her car. She finally felt herself relax as she neared her apartment building. Once she'd parked her car, Shelly stopped in the lobby to collect her mail. As soon as she opened the small box, Mrs. Livingston's head poked out her door.

"Good afternoon, Shelly," she chirped, smiling at her expectantly.

It took Shelly a moment to realize that Mrs. L. must have been waiting to hear about the contents of her package.

"It's a lovely day," Shelly said conversationally, sorting through her mail. Two bills, a flyer and something from the Internal Revenue Service. The way her luck had been going, it was probably an audit notice. A quick inspection revealed exactly that. She closed her eyes and groaned inwardly.

"A lovely day indeed," Mrs. Livingston echoed cheerfully.

Muttering under her breath, Shelly stuffed the IRS notice back inside the envelope. When she looked up, she saw that the older woman was now standing in the hallway.

"I suppose you're wondering about the package," Shelly said resignedly, tucking her mail inside her purse. "It was a gift from my aunt Milly."

"Something from the past, I guess?" Mrs. Livingston asked.

"Why...yes. How'd you know?"

"I'd take whatever it is very, very seriously if I were you," Mrs. Livingston continued in a solemn voice. "Wizard wouldn't go anywhere near that box. Think what you want, but my cat's always had a sixth sense when it comes to this sort of thing."

"It's a dress, Mrs. L.," Shelly explained, hiding behind a false smile. "How am I supposed to take a dress seriously?" It was exactly what she'd vowed *not* to do.

Mrs. Livingston opened her apartment door and scooped the large black-and-white cat into her arms. "That I wouldn't know," she returned, her eyes narrowed. "All I can tell you is that Wizard felt skittish around that package. You don't suppose there's...magic in it, do you?"

Somehow Shelly managed a reply, although she felt certain it was unintelligible. Taking the stairs two at a time, she dashed into her apartment, leaning breathlessly against the door. Even Mrs. Livingston's cat knew there was something strange about Aunt Milly's wedding dress!

When Jill arrived late Tuesday afternoon, Shelly was ready and waiting for her, brightly wrapped baby gift in hand. She was eager to get out and socialize—eager to get out, period. Anything to escape another phone call from her mother, who'd recently heard from Aunt Milly. Now Faith Hansen was calling daily for updates on the romantic prospects in her daughter's life.

"Well?" Jill demanded as she entered the apartment. "Are you going to show it to me?"

"Show what to you?"

Jill gave her a look that seemed to question her intelligence. "The wedding dress, of course."

For several hours Shelly had succeeded in putting the dress out of her mind. "No," she said forcefully. "I want to forget about the whole thing."

"Met any tall blue-eyed men lately?" Jill couldn't resist asking.

"None," Shelly answered shortly. Checking her watch, she noted that they were early but suggested they leave, anyway. "Shall we go?"

"We've got lots of time," Jill countered, moving toward Shelly's bedroom. "Come on, it isn't going to hurt to let me look at the dress."

"Oh, all right," Shelly conceded ungraciously. Leading the way, she opened the closet door and reached into the back of the closet.

She brought out the lace-and-satin gown, holding it up for Jill's inspection. She'd hardly looked at the dress the day she'd received it, and now she was almost shocked by how beautiful it actually was.

The laughter drained from Jill's dark brown eyes as she stared at the gown. "Oh, Shelly, it's...lovely." She gently touched the Elizabethan sleeve and ran her finger along the delicate layer of pearls that decorated the cuff. The high neckline was also trimmed with an intricate design of pearls. "I don't know what I expected," Jill said in an awed whisper, "but certainly nothing as beautiful as this."

Shelly nodded wordlessly. The dress was far more exquisite than she'd realized. Her heart swelled with sudden emotion, and to her dismay, tears filled her eyes as she thought about the old Scottish woman who had so lovingly constructed the gown. Each pearl had been sewn into place by hand. She thought of her aunt Milly, as tall and statuesque as Shelly herself, wearing the dress. Then she recalled her uncle John, such a determined man, so wise and sensible. Shelly thought fondly of those two, who'd been so completely different, yet had loved each other so well....

For a moment neither she nor Jill spoke. "Have you tried it on?" Jill finally asked.

Shelly shook her head adamantly, not wanting her

friend to know how emotional she'd become. "Heavens, no, but you can if you want."

"I don't think I could resist if I were you," Jill whispered, obviously affected by the dress, too. "Just seeing it...makes me wish I was a bride myself."

"There's always Ralph," Shelly teased. Jill had been dating Ralph, a computer programmer, for several months, but Shelly couldn't understand what her friend saw in him.

Jill threw her an irritated look. "The dress is for you, not me."

"But I don't want it," Shelly insisted, though she was no longer sure what she felt. Not since she'd really examined the dress and allowed herself to remember the wonder of John and Milly's romance.

"You're sure you don't mind?" Jill asked, slipping off her shoes. "I mean, if you'd rather I didn't try it on, I'll understand."

"No, feel free." Shelly strove for a flippant air. "As far as I'm concerned, the dress is nothing but bad luck. It arrived on Friday the thirteenth. The next day I had that minor accident on the mall escalator. Now I'm being audited by the IRS."

It was as if Jill didn't hear. "I doubt it'll fit," she said as she cautiously removed the gown from the padded hanger. "I'm a good five inches shorter than you and heavier on top."

"Maybe the dress was meant for you in the first place," Shelly ventured. Perhaps Aunt Milly had been confused and it was Jill she'd viewed in her dream. After all, Milly's eyes weren't what they used to be....

"Does your mother know?" Jill asked as she stepped into the dress. She raised it over her hips and turned around to let Shelly fasten the buttons that ran down the back.

"That's another thing," Shelly moaned. "Mom's been calling me every day since I got the dress, wanting to know if I've met anyone special yet."

"What did you tell her?" Jill asked, looking at Shelly over her shoulder.

"What's there to tell?" she asked irritably.

"Well, you might have mentioned Mark."

"Mark," Shelly repeated. She shrugged elaborately. "I haven't given him a thought in days." Not strictly true, but she'd been *trying* not to think about him. Even if he was interested in her—and he'd made very clear that he wasn't—she couldn't imagine two more ill-suited people. "I haven't seen him since Saturday and I doubt I'll ever see him again."

"You're sure of that?"

"Positive."

"Well, what do you think?" Jill asked next, pirouetting slowly in front of her. "My hair's a mess and I've got hardly any makeup on, but…"

Shelly studied her friend and sighed audibly. Never had she seen Jill look lovelier. It was as if the dress had been made for her. "Absolutely enchanting. It fits like a dream."

"I feel like I *am* dreaming," Jill admitted softly. "Here," she said, turning around, "undo me before I start longing for a husband and 2.5 children."

"Don't forget the house with the white picket fence," Shelly teased, unfastening the buttons.

Jill slipped out of the dress. "Your turn," she said as she laid it carefully across the bed. "If it fits me, then

it can't possibly fit you. You've got the perfect excuse
to send it back to your aunt Milly."

"I...don't know." Shelly bit her lip. She felt an inex-
plicable urge to keep the dress, and at the same time
she would've willingly returned it to her aunt. Even
while she hesitated, Shelly found herself undressing.
She couldn't explain her sudden eagerness to try on
the wedding gown any more than she could fathom its
growing emotional appeal.

The dress slid easily over her hips. She turned around
so Jill could secure the back, then glanced at the mirror,
expecting to find the skirt miles too short. It would have
to be in order to fit Jill as perfectly as it had.

"Shelly," Jill whispered, then cupped her hand over
her mouth. "My goodness...you look beautiful...re-
ally beautiful."

That was what Shelly had felt the instant she'd seen
her friend in the dress. "Something's wrong," she said
once she found her voice. "Something's very wrong."

"No," Jill countered, "it's very right. It's as if the
dress was made for you."

"Then answer me this," Shelly whispered. "How is it
possible for the same dress to fit two women who wear
totally different sizes?"

Five

Shelly struggled to open the door of the Internal Revenue office, her arms weighed down with a huge box stuffed full of receipts and records for the audit. By bracing the box against the wall with her knee, she freed one hand to open the door. For the first time ever, she'd completed her tax return early—all by herself, too—and *this* was her reward. She grumbled righteously and bit her lip, more in anxiety than annoyance.

She'd just managed to grasp the door handle, when the door unexpectedly opened and she staggered into the room, nearly colliding with an end table. She did a quick pirouette, convinced she'd ruined a new pair of panty hose. With a heartfelt sigh, she set her box of records on the floor and sank into the first available chair, neatly arranging her unaccustomed skirt around her knees. Only then did she bother to look around. There was one other person in the large reception area.

Shelly's heart did a nosedive, landing in the pit of her stomach. The man who'd opened the door for her, the man sitting in this very waiting room, was none other than Mark Brady—the man she'd hoped to avoid for the rest of her natural life. She gave an involuntary gasp.

Mark was leafing through the dog-eared pages of a magazine when he happened to glance her way. The automatic smile faded from his face, and his eyes narrowed as if he strongly suspected Shelly had purposely arranged this meeting.

"What are you doing here?" Shelly demanded.

"I might ask you the same thing."

"I didn't follow you here, if that's what you're implying!"

"Listen, Ms….Hansen, I really couldn't care less." With that he returned to his magazine, but he raised his head again a moment later. "*You're* the person who blurted out to everyone within hearing distance that you weren't marrying me. As if I'd even asked! As if I even *knew* you!"

Shelly felt the heat rising up her neck and offered the first excuse she could think of. "I…was distraught."

"Obviously," he muttered from behind his magazine.

A few minutes of strained silence passed. Shelly shifted uncomfortably in her chair, checking her watch approximately every ten seconds. She was early for her appointment, but if this was where promptness got you, she'd prefer to be late.

"All right, I apologize," Shelly said when she couldn't tolerate the silence any longer. "What I said was ridiculous and…and out of turn—"

"Out of turn," Mark echoed, throwing the magazine down on the table. "I repeat—I don't even know you."

"I realize that."

He inhaled deeply, which drew her attention to his broad, muscular chest. She saw that he was as meticulously dressed as he'd been at their first encounter. His dark suit and silk tie, however conventional, added a touch of sophistication to his natural good looks.

"If there's anyone to blame for this it's Aunt Milly," Shelly said, more to herself than him.

"Aunt Milly?" Mark repeated, sounding unsure. He eyed her warily.

She'd said this much; she might as well launch into the whole ludicrous tale.

"Actually, it has more to do with the wedding dress than with my aunt Milly, although by now the two of them are inseparable in my mind. I don't usually dabble in this sort of thing, but I'm beginning to think there might be something supernatural about that silly dress, after all."

"Supernatural?"

"Magic, if you prefer."

"Magic in a wedding dress?" Mark gazed hopefully at the door that led to the inner offices of Internal Revenue, as though he was anxious to be called away.

"It's unbelievable, but the dress fits both Jill and me, which is virtually impossible. You saw Jill—she's the friend I was having lunch with last Saturday. I know we were halfway across the room from you, but you couldn't help noticing how much shorter she is than I am. We're completely different sizes."

Mark hurriedly reached for the magazine as if he wanted to shut her out before she said anything else.

"I know it seems crazy. I don't like this any better than I do, but I'm afraid you're the one Aunt Milly mentioned in her letter." Well, it was only fair to tell him that.

Mark glanced in her direction again, blue eyes suspicious. "Your aunt Milly mentioned me in a letter?"

"Not by name—but she said she had a clear vision of me in the wedding dress and I was standing with a tall man. She also referred to blue eyes. You're tall and you have blue eyes and the legend says I'm going to marry the first man I meet after receiving the dress."

"And I just happened to be that man?"

"Yes," Shelly cried. "*Now* do you understand why I was so disturbed when we met?"

"Not entirely," Mark said after a moment.

Shelly sighed loudly. How obtuse could the man be? "You're tall, aren't you? And you have blue eyes."

He flipped intently through the magazine, not looking at her as he spoke. "I really don't care what the letter said, nor am I concerned about this wedding dress you keep bringing up."

"Of course you don't care," Shelly said indignantly. "Why should you? It must all seem quite absurd to you. And I'm aware that I'm overreacting, but I do have a tendency to get emotional. If it helps any, I want you to know I'm happy with my life just the way it is. I don't want to get married—to anyone." When she'd finished, she drew in a deep breath and began leafing idly through a magazine, doing her utmost to ignore him.

Silence returned. Silences had always bothered Shelly. It was as if she felt personally responsible for filling them. "If you want something to be grateful about, you can thank your lucky stars I didn't mention you to my mother."

"Your mother," Mark repeated. "Does she know about Aunt Milly sending you this...dress?"

"Of course she does," Shelly answered, closing the

magazine. "She's phoned me every day since she heard, because she thinks I'm going to meet that special someone any minute."

"And you didn't say anything about me?"

"How could I? The instant I do that, she'll be calling the caterers."

"I see." The edges of his mouth lifted as though he was beginning to find the situation amusing. "She believes in the power of this dress, too?"

"Unfortunately, yes. You have to understand where my mother stands on the issue of marriage," Shelly continued, undaunted.

"I'm not sure I want to," Mark muttered under his breath.

Shelly disregarded his comment. "By age twenty-eight—my age now, coincidentally—Mom had been married for eight years and already had three children. She's convinced I'm letting the best years of my life slip away. There's nothing I can say to make her believe differently."

"Then I'll add my gratitude that you didn't mention me."

Mollified, Shelly nodded, then glanced at her watch. Her meeting was in ten minutes and she was nervous, since this was the first time she'd done her own taxes. She should have known there'd be a problem.

"I take it you're here for an audit?" Mark asked.

She nodded again, studying her tax return, sure she'd be in jail by nightfall without even understanding what she'd done wrong.

"Relax."

"How can I?"

"Have you knowingly hidden something from the

government? Lied about the income you received, or claimed expenditures you've never made?"

"Oh, no!"

"Then you don't have anything to worry about."

"I don't?" Shelly stared at him, envying his confidence. She'd been restless for days, worrying about this meeting. If it wasn't the wedding dress giving her nightmares, it was the audit.

"Don't volunteer any information unless they ask for it."

"All right."

"Did you prepare your own tax return?"

"Well, yes. It didn't seem that complicated, and well, this sounds silly but Jill bet me I couldn't do it. So I did. Back in February. You see, numbers tend to confuse me and I decided to accept the challenge, and..." She realized she was chattering, something she did when she was nervous. Forcing herself to stay quiet, she scanned her return for the hundredth time, wondering what she could have possibly done wrong.

"Do you want me to look it over for you?"

Shelly was surprised by his generosity. "If you wouldn't mind. Are you being audited yourself?"

Mark smiled and shook his head. "A client of mine is."

"Oh."

He crossed the room and sat next to her. When Shelly handed him her tax return, he quickly ran down the row of figures, then asked her several questions.

"I've got everything right here," she assured him, gesturing toward the carton she'd lugged in with her. "I really am careful about saving everything I should."

Mark gestured at the large cardboard box. "This is all for one year?"

"No," she admitted sheepishly. "I brought along everything I had for the past six years. I mean, it made sense at the time."

"That really wasn't necessary."

"I'd rather be safe than sorry," Shelly said with a shrug. She watched Mark as he scrutinized her return. At such close range, she saw that his eyes were even bluer than she'd thought. *Blue as the sky on a bright July afternoon...* Her heart felt heavy in her chest, and hard as she tried, she couldn't keep herself from staring.

Mark handed back her return. "Everything looks fine. I don't think you'll have a problem."

It was astonishing how relieved she felt at hearing that. No, at hearing that from *him*. Mark smiled at her and Shelly found herself responding readily with a smile of her own. The fluttery sensation returned to her stomach. She knew her eyes were wide and questioning and although she tried to look away, she couldn't do it.

Surprise mingled with gentleness on his face, as if he were seeing her for the first time, really seeing her. He liked what he saw—Shelly could read that in his eyes. Slowly his gaze traveled over her features, and she felt her pulse speed up. The letter she'd received from Aunt Milly flitted through her mind, but instead of dismissing the memory, she wondered, *Could there really be something to all this?*

Mark was the one to break eye contact. He stood abruptly and hurried back to his seat. "I don't think you have to worry."

"Yes, you told me."

"I mean about your aunt Milly's wedding dress."

"I don't have to worry?" Shelly repeated. She wasn't sure she understood.

"Not with me, at any rate."

"I don't quite follow...." If he was even half-aware of the way her heart was clamoring as they gazed into each other's eyes, he wouldn't be nearly as confident.

"I'm engaged."

"Engaged?" Shelly felt as though someone had slugged her in the stomach. Her first reaction was anger. "You couldn't have mentioned this sooner?" she snapped.

"It's not official yet. Janice hasn't picked out a diamond. Nor have we discussed our plans with her family."

The irritation faded, swallowed by an overwhelming sense of relief. "Engaged," she murmured, reminding herself that she really had no interest in marriage. And this proved there was no such thing as a "magic" wedding dress. If Mark was involved with Janice, he wouldn't be free to marry her. It was that simple. Shelly leaped to her feet and started to pace.

"Are you all right?" Mark asked. "You're looking pale."

She nodded and pressed her hands to her cheeks, which suddenly felt hot. "I'm so relieved," she whispered hoarsely. "You have no idea how relieved I am. You're engaged... My goodness, I feel like I've got a new lease on life."

"As I explained," Mark said, frowning, "it isn't official yet."

"That's okay. You're committed to someone else and that's all that matters. However—" she forced a smile

"—you might have said something sooner and saved me all this anxiety."

"You did ask that day at the mall, but I was more concerned with avoiding a scene than revealing the personal details of my life."

"I'm sorry about that."

"No problem."

Shelly settled back in the chair and crossed her legs, hoping to strike a relaxed pose. She even managed to skim a couple of magazines, although she barely knew what she was reading.

Finally, the receptionist opened the door and called her name. Eager to get this over with, Shelly stood, picking up the large box she'd brought with her. She paused on her way out of the reception area and turned to Mark. "I wish you and Janice every happiness," she said formally.

"Thank you," he answered, then grinned. "Same to you and whatever, uh, lucky guy the wedding dress finds you."

Six

She should be happy, Shelly told herself early the following morning. Not only had she survived the audit—in fact she'd come away with an unexpected refund—but she'd learned that Mark was practically engaged.

Yes, she should be dancing in the streets, singing in the aisles... Instead she'd been struggling with a strange melancholy ever since their last encounter. She seemed to have lost her usual vitality, her sense of fun.

Now it was Saturday, and for once she had no looming deadlines, no appointments, no pressing errands. Remembering the exhilaration and solace she'd felt when she recorded an ocean storm sequence recently, Shelly decided to see if she could recapture some of those feelings. She headed over to Long Beach, a resort town on the Washington coastline. The sky was clear and almost cloudless; the sun was bright and pleasantly warm—a perfect spring day. Once she drove onto the freeway, the miles sped past and two hours later she was standing on the sandy beach with the breeze riffling her long hair.

She walked around for a while, enjoying the sights and sounds—the chirping of the sea gulls, the salty spray of the Pacific Ocean and the scent of wind and sea. She was satisfied with her beach DVD and started to work out plans for a whole series—the ocean in different seasons, different moods. That would be something special, she thought, something unique.

She wandered down the beach, kicking at the sand with the toes of her running shoes. Tucking her fingertips in the pockets of her jeans, she breathed in the vivid freshness around her. After an hour or so, she made her way back to the concession stands, where she bought a hot dog and a cold drink.

Then, just because it looked like fun, she rented a moped.

She sped along the shore, thrilled with the sensation of freedom, reveling in the solitude and the roar of pounding surf.

The wind tossed her hair about her face until it was a confusion of curls. Shelly laughed aloud and listened as the galloping breeze carried off the sound.

Her motorized bike rushed forward, spitting sand in its wake. She felt reckless with exhilaration, as though there was nothing she couldn't do. It was that kind of afternoon. That kind of day.

When she least expected it, someone else on a moped raced past her. Shelly hadn't encountered anyone during her ride and this person took her by surprise. She glanced quickly over her shoulder, astonished by how far she'd traveled. The only other person she could see was the one who'd passed her.

To her surprise, the rider did an abrupt turnaround and headed back in her direction. With the sun in her eyes and the wind pelting her, Shelly slowed to a crawl and shaded her eyes with one hand.

It wasn't until he was nearly beside her that Shelly recognized the other rider.

Mark Brady.

She was so shocked that she allowed the engine to die, her feet dropping to the sand to maintain her balance. Mark appeared equally shocked. He braked abruptly.

"Shelly?" He seemed not to believe it was her.

Shelly shook her head and blinked a couple of times just to make sure she wasn't fantasizing. She certainly hadn't expected to encounter Mark Brady on a beach two hours out of Seattle. Mr. Conservative riding a moped! This time, though, he wasn't wearing a dark suit. He didn't have his briefcase with him, either. And he looked even handsomer than usual in worn jeans and a University of Washington sweatshirt.

"Mark?" She couldn't prevent the astonishment from creeping into her voice.

"What are you doing here?"

She heard the hostility in his tone and answered him coolly. "The same thing as you, apparently." She pushed the hair from her face, and the wind promptly blew it back.

Mark's blue eyes narrowed suspiciously. "You didn't happen to follow me, did you?"

"Follow you?" she repeated indignantly. She'd rarely been more insulted. "Follow you!" she said again, starting her moped and revving the engine. "May I remind you that I was on the beach first? If anyone was doing any following, it was *you* following me." She was breathless by the time she finished. "In fact, you're the last person I'd follow anywhere!"

Mark scowled at her. "The feeling's mutual. I'm not

in the mood for another story about your aunt Martha's damn wedding dress, either."

Shelly felt an unexpected flash of pain. "I was having a perfectly wonderful afternoon until you arrived," she said stiffly.

"I was having a good time myself," he muttered.

"Then I suggest we go our separate ways and forget we ever met."

Mark looked as if he was about to say something else, but Shelly was in no frame of mind to listen. She twisted the accelerator on the handlebar of her moped and took off down the beach. Although she knew she was being unreasonable, she was furious. Furious at the surge of joy she'd felt when she recognized him. Furious at Mark, because he didn't seem even a little pleased to see her. She bit her lower lip, remembering the comment he'd made about not wanting to hear any more about her "damn wedding dress." Now, that was just rude, she told herself righteously. She could *never* be interested in a man who was not only conventional but rude.

Squinting, Shelly hunched her shoulders against the wind, in a hurry now to return to the boardwalk. She hadn't meant to go nearly this far.

The wet, compact sand made for smooth, fast riding and Shelly stayed close to the water's edge in an effort to outdistance Mark. Not that he was likely to chase her, but she wanted to avoid any possibility of another embarrassing encounter.

Then it happened.

A large wave came in, sneaking its way up the sand, creating a thin, glistening sheen. Shelly hardly noticed as her front tire ripped through the water, spraying it out

on both sides. Then the moped's front wheel dipped pre-
cariously. One minute she was sailing down the beach
at breakneck speed and the next she was cartwheeling
over her handlebars.

She landed heavily in a patch of wet sand, too para-
lyzed with shock to know if she was hurt or not.

Before she could move, Mark was crouching at her
side. "Shelly? Are you all right?"

"I...don't know." Carefully she flexed one arm and
then the other. Sitting up, she tested each leg and didn't
feel pain there, either. Apparently she'd survived the
experience unscathed.

"You crazy fool!" he yelled, leaping to his feet.
"What are you trying to do, kill yourself?"

"Ah..." It was painful to breathe, otherwise she
would've answered him.

"Can you imagine what I thought when I saw you
flying through the air like that?"

"Good riddance?" she suggested.

Mark closed his eyes and shook his head. "I'm in
no mood for your jokes. Here, let me help you up." He
moved behind her, sliding his arms around her waist
and gently raising her.

"I'm fine," she protested the instant his arms surrounded her. The blood rushed to her head, but Shelly
didn't know if that was because of her tumble or because Mark was holding her. Even when she was on her
feet, he didn't release her.

"Are you sure you're not hurt?"

Shelly nodded, not trusting her voice. "I'm less confident about the moped, though." Her bike seemed to
be in worse shape than she was.

"It doesn't look good to me, either," Mark said. He finally dropped his arms and retrieved the moped, which was lying on its side, the waves lapping over it. There were regular hissing sounds as the cold water splashed against the heated muffler. Steam rose from the engine.

Mark did his best to start the bike, but to no avail. "I'm afraid it's hopelessly wet. It won't start now until it's had a chance to dry. A mechanic should check it over to be sure nothing's wrong."

Shelly agreed. There was no help for it; she was going to have to walk the bike back to the rental shop. No small feat when she considered she was about three miles down the beach.

"Thank you very much for stopping," she said a bit primly. "But as you can see I'm not hurt…."

"What do you think you're doing?" Mark asked as she began pushing the moped. It made for slow progress; the bulky machine was far more difficult to transport under her own power than she'd expected. At this rate, she'd be lucky to return it by nightfall.

"I'm taking the bike back to the place where I rented it."

"That's ridiculous."

"Do you have any better ideas?" she asked in a reasonable tone of voice. "I don't understand what you're doing here in the first place," she said, sounding far calmer than she felt. "You should be with Janet."

"Who?" he demanded. He tried to take the moped away from her and push it himself, but she wouldn't let go.

"The woman you're going to marry. Remember?"

"Her name is Janice and as I said before, the engagement's unofficial."

"That doesn't answer my question. You should be with her on a beautiful spring day like this."

Mark frowned. "Janice couldn't get away. She had an important meeting with a client—she's a lawyer. Listen, quit being so stubborn, I'm stronger than you. Let me push the bike."

Shelly hesitated; his offer was tempting. She hadn't gone more than a few feet and already her side ached. She pressed one hand against her hip and straightened, her decision made. "Thanks, but no thanks," she answered flatly. "By the way, it's Aunt Milly who sent me the wedding dress, not Aunt Martha, so if we're going to get names straight, let's start there."

Mark rolled his eyes skyward, as though he'd reached the end of his limited patience. "Fine, I'll apologize for what I said back there. I didn't mean to insult you."

"I didn't follow you," she said.

"I know, but I didn't follow you, either."

Shelly nodded, deciding she believed him.

"Then how do you explain that we've inadvertently bumped into each other twice in the last week?" Mark asked. "The odds of that happening have got to be phenomenal."

"I know it sounds crazy, but… I'm afraid it's the dress," Shelly mumbled.

"The wedding dress?" Mark repeated.

"I'm really embarrassed about all this. I'm not sure I believe any of it myself. And I do apologize, especially since there's been an apparent mix-up…."

"Why's that?" Mark asked.

"Well…because you're involved with Janice. I'm sure the two of you are a perfect match and you'll have a marvelous life together."

"What makes you assume that?"

His question caught her off guard. "Well, because… didn't you just tell me you're about to become officially engaged?"

"Yes," he muttered.

Although she was reluctant to admit it, Shelly found pushing the moped extremely taxing, so she stopped to rest for a moment. "Listen," she said a little breathlessly, "there's no need for you to walk with me. Why don't you just go on ahead?"

"There most definitely is a need," Mark answered sharply. He didn't seem too pleased with her suggestion. "I'm not going to desert you now."

"Oh, Mark, honestly, you don't have to be such a gentleman."

"You don't like gentlemen?"

"Of course I do—but it's one of the reasons you and I would never get along for any length of time. You're very sweet, don't get me wrong, but I don't need anyone to rescue me."

"Forgive me for saying so, but you *do* appear to need rescuing." The look he gave her implied that he was referring to more than the moped.

"I was the one foolish enough to get the engine wet," she said brightly, ignoring his comment. "So I should be the one to deal with the consequences."

Mark waited a moment, as if debating whether to continue arguing. "Fine, if that's the way you feel," he said finally, straddling his moped and starting the engine, which roared to life with sickening ease. "I hope you don't tire out too quickly."

"I'll be okay," she said, hardly able to believe he was actually going to abandon her.

"I hope you're right about that," he said, revving the engine.

"You...you could let someone know," she ventured. Maybe the rental agency would send someone out with a truck to find her.

"I'll see what I can do," he agreed, then grinning broadly, took off at top speed down the beach.

Although she'd made the suggestion that he go on without her, Shelly had assumed he wouldn't take it seriously. She'd said it more for the sake of dignity, of preserving her pride. She'd been enjoying his company, enjoying the banter between them.

As he vanished into the distance, Shelly squared her shoulders, determined to manage on her own—particularly since she didn't have any choice. She'd been dragging her moped along for perhaps ten minutes when she noticed another moped racing toward her. It didn't take her long to identify the rider, with his lithe, muscular build, as Mark. She picked up her pace, unreasonably pleased that he'd decided to return. He slowed as he approached her.

"Still eager to be rid of me?"

"No," she admitted, smiling half in relief, half in pleasure. "Can't you tell when a woman means something and when she's just being polite?"

"I guess not." He smiled back, apparently in a jovial mood. "Rest," he said, parking his own moped and taking hers. "A truck will be along any minute."

Shelly sank gratefully down on the lush sand. Mark lowered himself onto the beach beside her. She plucked several blades of grass and began weaving them industriously together. That way, she wouldn't have to look at him.

"Are you always this stubborn?" he asked.

"Yes," she said quietly, giving him a shy smile. Shelly couldn't remember being shy in her life. But something about Mark made her feel shaky inside, and oddly weak. An unfamiliar sensation, but she dared not analyze it, dared not examine it too closely. She turned away from him and closed her eyes, trying to picture Janice, the woman he was going to marry. Despite her usually creative imagination, Shelly couldn't seem to visualize her.

"Shelly, what's wrong?"

"Wrong?"

"It's not like you to be so quiet."

She grinned. They were barely more than acquaintances, and he already knew her. "Nothing."

"I think there must be." His finger against the side of her face guided her eyes toward him. Their lips were so close. Shelly's breath seemed to be caught in her throat as she stared helplessly into the bluest eyes she'd ever seen....

His forehead touched hers, then he angled his face, brushing her cheek. Shelly knew she should break away, but she couldn't make herself do it. Gently, deliberately, he pressed his mouth to hers, his lips warm and moist.

Shelly moaned at the shock of sensation. Her eyes drifted shut as his mouth moved hungrily over hers, and soon their arms were wrapped tightly around each other, their bodies straining close.

The sound of the approaching truck intruded into their private world and broke them apart. Mark's eyes met hers, then he scowled and glanced away. But Shelly didn't know whether he was angry with her or with himself. Probably her.

Seven

"Hey," Shelly said reassuringly, "don't look so concerned. It was just an ordinary, run-of-the-mill kiss." She stood and brushed the wet sand from her jeans. "Besides, it didn't mean anything."

Mark's scowl darkened. "Didn't mean anything?" he echoed.

"Of course it didn't! I mean, we were both wondering what it would be like, don't you think? Good grief, we seem to be running into each other every other day and it's only logical that we'd want to, you know, experiment."

"In other words, you think the kiss was just a means of satisfying our mutual curiosity?"

"Sure. All this nonsense about the wedding dress overcame our common sense, and we succumbed to temptation." Thank goodness Mark seemed to understand her rambling. Shelly's knees were shaking. It was a wonder she could still stand upright. Although she'd tried to minimize the effects of his kiss, it left her feeling as though she'd never been kissed before. Her entire body had been overwhelmed by a feeling of *rightness*.

Now all she felt was the crushing weight of confusion. She shouldn't be feeling any of these things for Mark. A CPA! An almost-engaged CPA, to boot.

"And was your curiosity satisfied?" he asked. His blue eyes probed.

"Uh…yes. And yours?"

"Yes," he muttered, but he was frowning again.

The kid from the rental agency leaped out of the truck and loaded Shelly's moped into the back. "You're not supposed to get the engine wet," he scolded. "It's in the rental agreement. You'll have to pay a fine."

Shelly nodded. She didn't have an excuse; she doubted the agency would accept her trying to escape Mark as a legitimate reason for damaging one of their vehicles.

Mark drove his moped, while Shelly got into the pickup's cab and rode silently down the long stretch of beach.

Shelly went to the office to deal with her fine and was surprised to find Mark waiting for her when she'd finished. "You hungry?" he asked in an offhand invitation.

"Uh…" She would've thought he'd be anxious to see the last of her.

"Good," he said immediately, not giving her a chance to reply. He grasped her elbow firmly as he led her to a nearby fish-and-chips stand. Shelly couldn't recall any other time a man had taken her elbow. Her first reaction was to object to what she considered an outdated gesture but she was surprised to find it oddly comforting, even pleasant.

They ordered their fish and chips, then carried the small baskets to a picnic table.

"I should've paid for my own," she said once they

were seated, feeling vaguely guilty that he'd paid for both meals. Janice might be the jealous type, and Shelly didn't want her to hear about this.

His eyes met hers, steady and direct. "When I ask you to join me, I pick up the bill."

Any argument she had vanished before it reached her lips.

After that, Shelly concentrated on her fish and chips, which were fresh and absolutely delicious. Mark seemed equally preoccupied with his meal.

"What brought you to the beach today?" Shelly asked, finishing the last few French fries in her basket. Perhaps if they could determine what had brought them both to a lonely stretch of beach two hours from Seattle, they might be able to figure out how they'd happened upon each other once more.

"I have a beach house here. After tax time I generally try to get away for a few days. I like to come down here and relax."

"I had no idea." She found it inordinately important that he understand she hadn't somehow managed to stalk him across the state. Their meeting was pure coincidence...again.

"Don't worry about it, Shelly. You couldn't possibly have known about the beach house or that I intended to be here today. I didn't know it myself until this morning."

Shelly suddenly wished Mark hadn't kissed her. Everything was becoming far too complicated.

"You're very talented," he told her out of the blue. "I bought one of your DVDs the other day."

"How'd you know what I do?" Shelly felt flustered

by his praise; she was at a complete loss to understand
why it meant so much to her.

"I saw it on the income tax form and I was curious
about your work."

"Curiosity seems to have gotten us both into trouble,"
she said.

Mark grinned, a shameless, irresistible grin. The kind
of grin that makes a woman forget all sorts of things.
Like the fact that he was practically engaged. And that
he was a tall, blue-eyed stranger who, according to Aunt
Milly's letter, would soon become her husband....

Shelly scrambled to her feet, hurrying toward the
beach. Mark followed.

"You shouldn't look at me like that," she said, her
voice soft and bewildered.

"You said it was just a kiss. Was it?"

"Yes," she lied boldly. "How could it be anything
more?"

"You tell me."

Shelly had no answers to give him.

"While you're at it, explain why we keep bumping
into each other or why I can't stop thinking about you."

"You can't?" She hadn't been able to stop thinking
about him, either, but she wasn't ready to admit it.

"No." He stood behind her, his hands caressing her
shoulders. Leisurely he stroked the length of her arms.
His touch was so light that she thought she was imagining it, and she felt both excited and afraid.

He turned her around and gazed at her lips. "If that
was just a run-of-the-mill kiss, then why do I feel the
need to do it again?"

"I don't know."

His lips brushed hers. Briefly, with a whisper-soft

touch, as though he was testing her response. Shelly closed her eyes and moaned. She didn't want to feel any of this. They were so far apart, such different people. Besides, *he* was involved with another woman and *she* was involved with her career.

When the kiss ended and he slowly released her, it was all Shelly could do to keep from sinking to the sand. "I have...to get back to Seattle," she managed to say, backing away from him. She turned and took four or five wobbly steps before she realized she was headed toward the Pacific Ocean.

"Shelly?"

"Yes?"

"Seattle is due north. If you continue going west, you'll eventually end up in Hawaii."

"Oh, yeah, right," she mumbled, reversing her direction, eager now to escape.

The first person Shelly called when she got home was Jill. "Can you come over?" she asked without preamble. She couldn't keep the panic out of her voice.

"Sure. What's wrong?"

"I saw Mark again."

"And?"

"Let me put it like this. We kissed and I haven't stopped trembling since."

Jill's romantic sigh came over the receiver. "This I've got to hear. I'll be there in ten minutes."

Actually it was closer to seven. Shelly had begun pacing the moment she got off the phone. She'd checked her watch repeatedly, waiting desperately for a dose of Jill's good sense.

"Shelly," Jill said, smiling as she breezed into the apartment, "what happened to your hair?"

Shelly smoothed down her curls. "I was at Long Beach."

"That's where you saw Mark? That's kind of a co-incidence, isn't it?"

"I saw him earlier in the week, too.... Remember I told you I was being audited by the IRS? Lo and behold, guess who was in their waiting room when I arrived?"

"I don't need to be a rocket scientist to figure that one out. Mark Brady!"

"Right." Shelly rubbed her damp palms along her jeans in agitation. They, at least, had finally dried.

"And?"

Shelly groaned. "Can't you see what's happening? This is the third time we've been thrown together in the past few days. I'd never seen the man before, and all of a sudden he's around every corner. Then the wedding dress fit. It fit you...and it fits me."

"I agree that's all rather odd, but I wouldn't put too much stock in it, if I were you."

"Put too much stock in it... Listen, Jill, no man's ever made me feel the way Mark does—all weak inside and, I don't know, special somehow. To be perfectly honest, I don't like it." She closed her eyes, hoping to chase away the memory of his touch, but it did no good. "You want to know the real kicker?" she asked abruptly, turning to face her friend. "He's engaged."

"Engaged," Jill echoed, her voice as startled as her expression.

"He keeps insisting it's not official yet. Nevertheless he's involved with someone else."

"But it was you he kissed," Jill pointed out.

"Don't remind me." Shelly covered her eyes with both hands. "I don't mind telling you, I find this whole thing unnerving."

"Obviously. Here," Jill said, directing Shelly toward the kitchen. "Now sit down. I'll make us some tea, then we can try to reason this out. Honestly, Shell, I don't think I've ever seen you so upset."

"I'm not upset!" she cried. "I'm confused. There's a big difference. I'm… I'm trapped." Despite all logic to the contrary, she couldn't help fearing that the entire course of her life was about to change because her aunt Milly had fallen asleep watching *Dr. Phil* one day and had some nonsensical dream.

"Trapped?" Jill said. "Aren't you being a bit dramatic?"

"I don't know anymore." Shelly rested her elbows on the table, buried her face in her hands and breathed in deeply. She had a tendency to become emotional, especially over family issues; she realized that. But this was different. This was scary.

"Calm down," Jill advised. "Once you think it through in a rational manner, you'll realize there's a perfectly ordinary explanation for everything."

Jill's serenity lent Shelly some badly needed confidence. "All right, you explain it."

"I can't," Jill admitted matter-of-factly, pouring boiling water into Shelly's teapot. "I'm not even going to try. My advice to you—once again—is to quit taking all of this so seriously. If a relationship develops between you and Mark, just enjoy it—provided the other woman's out of the picture, of course! But forget about that dress."

"Easy for you to say."

"That's true," Jill agreed. "But you're going to have to do it for your own peace of mind."

Shelly knew good advice when she heard it. "You're right. I'm leaping into the deep end unnecessarily."

"A dress can't make you do anything you don't want to do."

Shelly always counted on her friend's levelheadedness. Although Jill had given her basically the same advice several days earlier, Shelly needed to hear it again.

Jill prepared two cups of tea and carried them to the table. "Are you going to be all right now?"

Shelly nodded. "Of course. I just needed a friend to remind me that I was overreacting." She took a sip of tea, surprised by how much it revived her. "You're still planning to see *Jersey Boys* with me tomorrow afternoon, aren't you?"

The recent Broadway hit was showing locally, and Shelly and Jill had purchased their tickets several weeks earlier.

"That's not tomorrow, is it?" Jill looked stricken, her teacup poised midway to her mouth.

"Jill…"

"I promised I'd work for Sharon Belmont. She's got some family thing she has to attend. She was desperate and I completely forgot about the play. Oh, dear, you'll have to go without me."

"You're sure you can't get out of it?" Shelly couldn't help feeling disappointed.

"I'm sure. I'm really sorry, Shell."

Although frustrated that Jill couldn't come with her, Shelly decided to go to the theater alone. She wasn't pleased about it and, given her proclivity for running into Mark Brady, she didn't feel entirely convinced that this wasn't another attempt by the fates to regulate their lives.

However, if she stayed home, she'd be missing a wonderful show. Not only that, she'd be giving in to a nebulous and irrational fear, something she refused to do.

The following afternoon, Shelly dressed carefully, in the type of conservative outfit her mother would have approved of. Mark, too, would approve of her rose-colored linen dress with its matching jacket.... The minute the thought flashed through her head, she rejected it.

She was on her way out the door when her phone rang. For a split second she toyed with the idea of not answering. More than likely it was her mother, checking in to see if Shelly had met a prospective husband yet. Her calls had become more frequent and more urgent since Aunt Milly's dress had arrived.

But years of habit prompted her to reach for the phone.

"Shelly." Mark's voice came over the line. "I was about to leave for the afternoon's performance of *Jersey Boys*. Since we seem to have this tendency to run into each other everywhere we go, I thought I should probably clear it with you. If you're going to be there, I'll go another time."

Eight

"Actually I was planning to see it this afternoon myself," Shelly admitted hesitantly. "Jill had to cancel at the last minute."

"It seems Janice can't attend, either."

Hearing the other woman's name, the woman Mark loved, had a curious and unexpected effect on Shelly. Her heart sank, and she felt a sharp pang of disappointment. She rebounded quickly, however, forcing a lightness into her voice, a blitheness she didn't feel. "Mark, there's no need for you to miss the show. I'll call the ticket office and see about an exchange."

"No, I will," Mark said.

"That's ridiculous. Jill really wanted to see this musical and—"

"Would it really be so terrible if we both attended the same performance?"

"Uh…" The question caught Shelly unprepared. Mark was the one who'd suggested they avoid each other.

"What could it possibly hurt? You have your ticket and I have mine. It'd be absurd to let them go to waste because we're afraid of seeing each other again, don't you think?"

Forming a single, coherent thought seemed beyond Shelly at that moment. After her conversation with Jill the day before, followed by the pep talk she'd given herself, she'd recovered a degree of composure. Now, all of a sudden, she wasn't sure of anything.

"I don't think it should matter," she said finally, although it *did* matter.

"Good. Enjoy the show."

"You, too."

The theater was within walking distance of her apartment building, and Shelly left as soon as she'd finished talking to Mark. He was right. Just because they each had tickets to the same play was no reason for either of them to be penalized.

So Mark was going to see *Jersey Boys*. It wasn't the sort of production she would've thought he'd enjoy. But the man was full of surprises. Riding mopeds on the beach, kissing so spectacularly, and now this…

Shelly's mind was full of Mark as she hurried down the steep hill on Cherry Street. The theater was only a block away when she saw him. Her pulse soared and she didn't know if she should smile and wave or simply ignore him.

She didn't need to do either. He stood on the sidewalk, waiting for her.

"You're late," he said, glancing at his watch. "But then you traditionally are." His grin was wide and welcoming. "I can't see any reason not to watch the play together," he went on. "What do you say?"

"You're sure?"

"Positive." He offered her his arm, and she reflected

that it was the kind of old-fashioned courtesy she expected from Mark.

The usher seated them and smiled constantly as if to say they were a handsome couple. Shelly was tempted to explain that Mark was engaged to someone else; luckily she managed to hold her tongue. Minutes after they'd settled into their seats, the curtain rose.

The musical was as lively and as good as the reviews claimed, and Shelly enjoyed herself thoroughly. Throughout the performance, however, she was all too aware of Mark sitting next to her. She found herself wondering if he was equally aware of her. She also found herself wondering how long it would be before they "bumped" into each other again—and hoped it was soon.

By the end of the show, Shelly felt inspired and full of enthusiasm, eager to start a new project of her own. As she and Mark left the theater, she talked excitedly about her idea for the "ocean moods" series. He asked a few questions and even suggested some shots. Before she realized it, they were several blocks past the theater, headed in the opposite direction from her apartment. Shelly paused and glanced around.

"There's an excellent Chinese restaurant in this neighborhood," was all Mark said. Without giving her the opportunity to decline, he gently guided her toward the place he'd mentioned.

It was early for dinner, and they were seated immediately. Although they'd been talking comfortably during their walk, Shelly suddenly felt self-conscious. She played with her linen napkin, smoothing it across her lap.

"I'm not a big fan of musicals, so I hadn't expected to like the show as much as I did," he said after a while.

In that case, Shelly considered it a bit odd that he'd ordered tickets for this production, but perhaps he'd gotten them because Janice had wanted to see *Jersey Boys.*

"It's a little frightening the way we keep running across each other, isn't it?" she ventured.

"I can see how *you'd* find it disconcerting," Mark answered.

"You don't?"

Mark shrugged. "I haven't given it much thought."

"I'll admit all these…coincidences do throw me," she said, tracing the outline of a fire-breathing dragon on the menu cover. "But I'm learning to deal with it."

"So you feel you've been caught in something beyond your control?" Mark surprised her by asking.

Shelly lifted her gaze to his, struck by the intensity she read in his eyes. "No, not really. Well…a little, maybe. Do you?"

"It wasn't *my* aunt Milly who had the dream."

Shelly smiled and dropped her gaze. "No, but as my friend Jill reminded me recently, no sixty-year-old dress is going to dictate my life. Or yours," she felt obliged to add. Then she understood why he'd asked the question. "You must feel overwhelmed. All of a sudden I've been thrust into your life. There's no escaping me, is there?" she said wryly. "Every time you turn around, there I am."

"Are you going to stand up and tell everyone in the restaurant that you refuse to marry me?"

"No!" Shelly was shocked by his remark until she remembered she'd done exactly that the first time they met.

"If you can resist public declarations, then I think I can bear up under the pressure."

Shelly ignored his mild sarcasm. "I'm not interested in marriage yet," she told him solemnly—just in case he'd forgotten. "I'm satisfied with my life. And I'm too busy for a husband and family."

She hadn't noticed how forcefully she was speaking until she saw several people at other tables glancing in her direction. Instantly she lowered her voice. "Sorry, my views on marriage seem to be more fervent than I realized. But I'm not about to let either my mother or my aunt Milly determine when I decide to settle down and marry."

"Personally, I can't see you ever settling down," Mark said with a small grin. "You don't have to worry. When you're ready, you'll know it."

"Did you?" She hadn't meant to bring up Janice, but it seemed wise to remind him—and her—that there was someone else in his life.

Mark raised one shoulder casually. "More or less. I took a good, long look at my life and discovered I'd already achieved several of my professional goals. It was time to invest my energy in developing the personal aspects—marriage, children and the like."

Mark talked about marriage as if it were the next chapter in a book he was reading or part of a connect-the-dots picture. Shelly couldn't stop herself from frowning.

"You have a problem with that?"

"Not a problem, exactly. I happen to think of marriage a bit differently, that's all."

"In what way?"

He seemed genuinely interested, otherwise she

would've kept her opinions to herself. "People should fall in love," she said slowly. "I don't think it's necessary or even possible to plan for that. Love can be unexpected—it can take a couple by surprise, knock them both off their feet."

"You make falling in love sound like an accident—like tripping on the stairs or something."

Shelly smiled. "In some ways, I think that's how it should be. Marriage is one of the most important decisions in anyone's life, so it should be a *deeply felt* decision. It should feel inevitable. It's the union of two lives, after all. So you can't simply check your watch and announce 'it's time.'" She was suddenly concerned that she'd spoken out of turn and might have offended him, but one quick glance assured her that wasn't the case.

Mark leaned forward. "I would never have guessed it," he said.

"Guessed what?" She was beginning to feel a little foolish now.

"That a woman who gives the impression of being a scatterbrain is really quite reflective. Beneath those glow-in-the-dark sweatshirts lies a very romantic heart."

"I seem to get emotional about certain things," she responded, studying the menu, eager to change the subject. "I really like hot-and-sour soup. Have you ever tried it?"

Their conversation over dinner remained light and amusing. Shelly noticed that Mark avoided any more discussion of a personal nature, as did she.

After they'd finished their dinner and Mark had paid the bill, they strolled leisurely back toward the theater. Mark offered to drive her home when they reached his parked car, but Shelly declined. Her apartment was only a couple of blocks north and she preferred to walk.

Walk and think. Their time together had given her plenty to think about.

"Thank you for dinner," she said as he unlocked the car.

"You're welcome," he answered. "Well, good night for now," he said, grinning. "I suspect I'll be seeing you soon."

She grinned back. "Probably within a day or two. Maybe we should synchronize our schedules," she teased.

"That wouldn't bother you, would it? If we ran into each other, I mean."

"Oh, no. What about you?" She hated the way her voice rose expectantly with the question. She certainly wasn't *bothered* by the prospect of seeing him again. In fact, she was downright eager to see what tricks fate would play on them next.

Mark's eyes found hers then, and he slowly pocketed his car keys. His look was so potent, so full of emotion, that Shelly took a step in retreat. "I had a wonderful afternoon, a wonderful evening. Thanks again," she said nervously.

Mark didn't say a word as he continued to gaze at her.

"The play was great, wasn't it? And dinner…fabulous." Shelly's throat seemed to close as Mark stepped onto the curb and walked toward her.

The whole world came to an abrupt halt when she realized he intended to kiss her. *Not again,* her mind shouted. *Please hurry,* her heart sang.

Her heart tripped wildly as Mark lowered his head, his mouth seeking hers. Despite the fierce battle inside her, Shelly had to admit how much she wanted this kiss.

If for no other reason, she told herself, than to prove that the first time had been a fluke.

Only it happened again. But this kiss was a hundred times more compelling than the first one they'd shared. A hundred times more exciting.

Shelly wanted to cry out at the unfairness of it all. If a man's kiss was going to affect her like this, why did it have to be Mark Brady's?

He broke away from her reluctantly, his warm breath fanning her cheek. His eyes were filled with questions, filled with surprise. Shelly wasn't sure what her own eyes were saying to him. She didn't even want to know.

"Take care," he whispered as he turned away.

Shelly stayed home from work on Monday. She wasn't sick, just puzzled and confused. Nothing about her relationship with Mark made sense. He was everything she *didn't* want in a man—and everything she did.

Shelly didn't realize how despondent she was until she found herself standing barefoot in front of her closet, carrying on a conversation with Aunt Milly's wedding dress.

"I'll have you know I had a perfectly good life until you got here," she muttered. "Now my whole world's been turned upside down." She slammed the door shut, then jerked it open. "No wonder Mrs. Livingston's cat wouldn't go near you. You're *dangerous*."

Nine

"The show was great," Shelly told Jill over coffee Wednesday afternoon. She'd stopped off at PayRite, hoping Jill could get away for lunch. "Even Mark—"

"Mark?" Jill's coffee cup hit the saucer with a clang. "He went to see *Jersey Boys*?"

Shelly nodded sheepishly. "I guess I forgot to mention I ran into him, didn't I? Actually he called me first and since we both had plans to attend the same performance, we decided to go together."

"Is there anything else you haven't told me?" Jill's eyes narrowed astutely.

Shelly tried to hide her uneasiness behind a relaxed shrug, but how well she succeeded in fooling Jill remained to be seen. "We had dinner afterward…as friends. It didn't mean anything. I did tell you he's engaged, didn't I?"

"*Unofficially* engaged." Jill was studying her closely and Shelly felt uneasy under her scrutiny.

"We've been friends for a long time," Jill reminded her. "I know you, and I know there's something troubling you."

Shelly nodded. There was no point in hiding the truth from Jill. Her need to confide in a sympathetic, understanding person was the very reason for her impromptu visit to Jill's workplace. Lunch had been a convenient excuse.

"You won't believe this," Shelly said, cradling the coffee cup in both hands and keeping her gaze lowered. "I can hardly believe it myself."

"You're falling in love with Mark."

Shelly's eyes shot upward. "It's that obvious?"

"No," Jill said softly. "But you look like you're about to break into tears."

"If I wasn't so darn irritated I would. Good grief, think about it. Can you imagine two people less suited to each other? Mark is so…so responsible…"

"So are you."

"Not in the same way," Shelly argued. "He's so sincere and—"

"Shelly, so are you."

"Perhaps, but I'm such a scatterbrain." She grimaced as she remembered that was the very word Mark had used. "I'm disorganized and always late and I like to do things my own way. You know that better than most."

"I prefer to think of you as creative."

Shelly sent Jill a smile of appreciation. "That's the reason you're my best friend. I don't mind telling you, Jill, I'm worried. Mark Brady may be the Rock of Gibraltar, but I doubt he's got an original thought in his head. Everything's done by the book or according to a schedule."

"You need someone like Mark in your life," Jill returned. "Don't look so shocked. It's true. The two of you balance each other. He needs you because you're fun and crazy and imaginative, and you need him because he knows his multiplication tables by heart and will remind you when it's time for meals."

"The problem is, Mark's the type of man who'd expect a woman to *cook* those meals."

Jill chuckled.

"If the fates are determined to match me up with a man," Shelly moaned, "couldn't it be with someone other than an accountant?"

"Apparently not."

"What really angers me is that I allowed it to happen. The first time he kissed me—"

"He *kissed* you?" Jill feigned a look of horror.

Shelly ignored it. "Yes. Twice. It's only natural—our being curious about each other, don't you think?"

"I suppose," Jill said quickly, no longer teasing. "So tell me what happened."

"Fireworks bigger than the Fourth of July. I've never experienced the feelings I do with Mark, and all because of a kiss." She paused. "Well, two kisses."

"And does Mark feel the same thing?"

"I—I can't speak for him, but I assume it's equally disturbing for him. He certainly looked as if he'd been taken by surprise."

"How do you get along with him otherwise?"

"Fine, I guess." Shelly took a sip of her coffee. "I'm sure I amuse him. But someone like Mark isn't looking for a woman to entertain him, any more than I'm looking for a man to handle my finances."

"His opinion of you has mellowed, hasn't it?" Jill asked, then answered her own question. "There was a time when he thought you were more than a little bizarre, remember?"

Shelly did, all too well. "At first I thought he was totally unexciting, but I've altered my opinion of him, too."

"So what's the problem?"

"I don't *want* to fall in love," Shelly said pointedly. "I've got bigger plans for my life than to tie myself down to a committed relationship right now."

"Then don't. It shouldn't be that difficult. Decide what you want and disregard everything else. There's no law that says you have to fall in love this minute. For that matter, no one can regulate when and who you marry, either. Not even your aunt Milly."

Jill was saying everything Shelly wanted to hear. Everything she *needed* to hear. But it didn't make any difference; her heart was already involved. If she could forget she'd ever met Mark, she would. But it was too late. She was in love with him. With Mark, who was in love with someone else. Mark, who saw love and marriage as goals to be achieved within a certain time frame. He'd probably never done anything impulsive in his life.

A relationship between them would never last. If he wasn't smart enough to figure that out, she was. Something had to be done and soon, and Shelly knew it would be up to her to do it.

Shelly didn't have long to wait before she saw Mark again. They met at the main branch of the Seattle Public Library on Wednesday evening. She was returning ten overdue books. Six months overdue. The library had sent her three warnings, each progressively less friendly.

She was half-afraid the buzzer inside the library entrance would go off the moment she walked through the hallowed doors, and armed officers would haul her away.

"I wondered when we'd find each other again," Mark said, strolling up to her at the counter. She'd seen him almost immediately and tried to pretend she hadn't.

Shelly acknowledged him with a quick nod and ordered her heart to be still. She managed a slight smile. "Hello again," she said, drawing a checkbook out of her purse. At least she'd come prepared. The fine for the books was sure to be monstrous; in fact, it might be cheaper to buy them.

Mark set the two volumes he was borrowing on the counter. Shelly noted the titles—*Tools for Time Management* and *The State of the Language,* and groaned inwardly. To someone like her accountant friend, these books were probably easy reading. Her own tastes leaned more toward mystery and romance, with a little nonfiction thrown in.

"Have you got time for a cup of coffee?" Mark asked as she wrote out the check to pay her fine.

She was gladdened by the invitation, but knew she had to refuse it. Before he could say or do anything to change her mind, she shook her head. "Not tonight, thanks."

His smile faded as though her refusal had startled him. "You're busy?"

She nodded, smiling at the librarian as she handed over her check. The librarian smiled back. It had been a civilized exchange, Shelly thought, and her library card had't been confiscated, despite her transgressions.

"You've got a date waiting for you?"

It took Shelly a second to understand that Mark was referring to her refusal to join him for coffee.

"Not exactly." She turned away from the counter and headed toward the exit. To her surprise Mark followed her outside.

"Something's wrong," he said, standing at the top of the steps.

She stopped her descent and stood below him, looking up. Pretense had never suited Shelly; she was too innately honest to hide her feelings. "Mark, I think you're a very nice man—"

"But you don't want to marry me," he concluded for her. "I've heard that line before, remember? Actually, half the mall heard it, too."

"I've already apologized for that. It's just that...all right, if you must know, I'm beginning to like you... really like you, and frankly that terrifies me."

Her candid response seemed to unnerve him. He frowned and rubbed the side of his jaw. "I know what you mean. I'm beginning to like you, too."

"See!" she cried, raising both hands. "If we don't take care of this now, heaven only knows what could happen. It has the potential of ruining both our lives. We're mature adults, aren't we?" At the moment, though, she felt singularly lacking in maturity.

All her senses were clamoring, telling her to enjoy their brief time together, despite the consequences. It was what her heart wanted, but she couldn't allow her life to be ruled by her heart. Not when it came to Mark.

"Liking each other doesn't have to be a federal crime," he said, advancing one step toward her.

"You're right, of course, but I know myself too well. I could easily fall in love with you, Mark." She didn't dare admit she already had. "Before we knew it, we'd be spending more and more time with each other. We might even become seriously involved."

He remained suspiciously silent.

"You're a wonderful man. If my mother were to meet you she'd be shouting from the rooftops, she'd be so thrilled. For a while I might convince myself that we could really make something of this relationship. I might even consider taking cooking classes because you're the kind of man who'd expect a woman to know how to make a roast and mashed potatoes."

"It'd probably come in handy someday," he said.

"That's what I thought," she murmured, disheartened. "I'm not a traditional woman. I never will be. The only time I ever baked a pie I ended up throwing it in the garbage disposal—and it broke the disposal."

"A pie ruined your garbage disposal?" Mark repeated, then shook his head. "Never mind, don't bother explaining. It seems to me you're getting ahead of yourself here. You're talking as though coffee together means a lifetime commitment."

Shelly wasn't listening. "What about Janice?" she demanded. "*She's* the one you should be inviting to coffee, not me."

"What's Janice got to do with this?" he asked impatiently.

"Janice," Shelly snapped, her own temper short. "The woman you've decided to marry. Remember her? The love of your life? The woman you're unofficially engaged to marry."

"It's not unofficial anymore," Mark explained evenly.

"Oh, great, you're taking me out to dinner, kissing me and at the same time picking out engagement rings with another woman." She had to admit he'd never lied to her about his relationship with the faceless Janice. He'd been forthright about it from the beginning. But it hurt, really hurt, to learn that he was going ahead with his plans to marry Janice.

He was about to speak, but she forestalled him, struggling to force some enthusiasm into her voice. "Congratulations are in order. I wish you both the very best." With that she turned and bounded down the stairs, taking them recklessly fast.

"Shelly!"

She could hear Mark calling after her, but she ignored him, desperate to get away before the lump in her throat made it impossible to breathe. Tears had formed in her eyes and she cursed herself for being so ridiculous, for caring so much. Her vision blurred and she wiped a hand across her face, furious at her lack of control. This marriage was what she'd hoped would happen. What she wanted for Mark. *Wasn't it?*

"Shelly, for heaven's sake, will you wait?"

When she reached the bottom of the steps, Shelly moved into a side street, hoping to disappear in the crowd, praying Mark wouldn't pursue her.

She thought she'd escaped until a hand on her shoulder whirled her around.

"Shelly, please listen," Mark pleaded breathlessly, his shoulders heaving. "The engagement isn't official because there is no engagement. How could I possibly marry Janice after meeting you?"

Ten

"You broke off your engagement with Janice?" Shelly demanded furiously. Something inside, some reservoir of emotion, had burst wide-open. "You fool," she shouted. "You idiot!" Her eyes brimmed with tears, and deep in her heart she felt the stirrings of glad excitement. "That was the worst thing you could've done!"

"No," he said. "It was the smartest."

"How can you say that?" she wailed.

"Shelly?"

He reached for her as though to offer comfort, but Shelly jerked away and stepped back, freeing herself from his grasp. "Janice was perfect for you," she lamented.

"How do you know that?" he asked calmly and much too reasonably to suit Shelly. "You never met her."

"I didn't need to. I know she was right for you. You'd never have asked her to marry you if she wasn't."

"Janice is a wonderful woman and she'll make some man a good wife, but it won't be me."

"You're crazy to break off your engagement. Crazy!"

"No, I'm not," Mark returned confidently. "I'm absolutely certain I did the right thing. Do you know why?"

Shelly could only shake her head, wiping away the tears with the back of her hand. She was ecstatic—and yet she was so frightened. She loved him; she was sure of it. Then why had everything become so difficult and confused?

"What you said about love the other day changed my mind."

"You *listened* to me?" she cried in real horror. "Do I look like an expert on love? I've never been in love in my life!" Not counting what she felt for him, of course. She'd always thought love would clarify her life, not make it more complicated.

Mark paid no attention to her outburst. "You helped me understand that I was marrying Janice for the wrong reasons. I'd decided it was time to settle down. Janice had come to the same conclusion. She's thirty and figured if she was going to marry and have a family, the time was now. It wasn't a love match, and we both knew it."

"This is none of my business," Shelly said, frantically shaking her head as if to chase the words away. "I don't want to hear it."

"You *are* going to hear it," Mark insisted, clasping her elbows and gently drawing her closer. "You claimed people shouldn't plan love. It should take them by surprise, you said, and you were right. Janice and I are fond of each other, but—"

"There's nothing wrong with fond!"

His eyes widened. "No, there isn't," he agreed, "but Janice isn't a zany producer. I like spending time with you. I've come to realize there's a certain thrill in expecting the unexpected. Every minute with you is an adventure."

"A relationship between us would never last," Shelly insisted, drawing on the most sensible argument. "It would be fine for a while, but then we'd drift apart. We'd have to. In case you haven't noticed, we're nothing alike."

"Why wouldn't a relationship last?" Mark asked patiently.

"For all the reasons I listed before!" Mark was so endearing, and he was saying all the words she'd secretly longed to hear, but nothing could change the fundamental differences between them.

"So you aren't as adept in the kitchen as some women. I'm a fair cook."

"It's more than that."

"Of course it is," he concurred. "But there's nothing we can't overcome if we're willing to work together."

"You know what I think it is?" she said desperately, running her splayed fingers through her hair. "You're beginning to believe there's magic in Aunt Milly's wedding dress."

"Don't you?"

"No," she cried. "Not anymore. I did when I was a little girl… I loved the story of how Aunt Milly met Uncle John, but I'm not a child anymore, and what seemed so romantic then just seems unrealistic now."

"Shelly," Mark said in exasperation. "We don't need to do anything right away. All I'm suggesting is we give this thing between us a chance."

"There's nothing between us," she denied vehemently.

Mark's eyes narrowed. "You don't honestly believe that, do you?"

"Yes," she lied. "You're a nice guy, but—"

"If I hear any more of this nice-guy stuff I'm going to kiss you and we both know what'll happen then."

His gaze lowered to her mouth and she unconsciously moistened her lips with anticipation.

"I just might, anyway."

"No." The threat was real enough to make her retreat a couple of steps. If Mark kissed her, Shelly knew she'd be listening to her heart and not her head. And then *he'd* know...

"That's what I thought." His grin was downright boyish.

"I think we should both forget we ever met," she suggested next, aware even as she said it how ludicrous she sounded. Mark Brady had indelibly marked her life and no matter how much she denied it, she'd never forget him.

"Don't you remember that you threw yourself into my arms? *You* can conveniently choose to overlook the obvious, but unfortunately that won't work for me. I'm falling in love with you, Shelly."

She opened her mouth to argue that he couldn't possibly love her—not yet, not on such short acquaintance—but he pressed his finger to her lips, silencing her.

"At first I wasn't keen on the idea," he admitted, "but it's sort of grown on me since. I can see us ten years in the future and you know what? It's a pleasant picture. We're going to be very happy together."

"I need to think!" She placed her hands on either side of her head. Everything was happening much too quickly; she actually felt dizzy. "We'll leave it to fate... how does that sound?" she offered excitedly. It seemed like the perfect solution. "The next time we bump into each other, I'll have more of a grasp on my feelings. I'll know what we should do." She might also hibernate inside her apartment for a month, but she wasn't mentioning that.

"Nope." Mark slowly shook his head. "That won't work."

"Why not?" she asked. "We bump into each other practically every day."

"No, we don't."

He wasn't making any sense.

"*Jersey Boys* was a setup," he informed her. "I made sure we bumped into each other there."

"How? When?"

"The day at the beach I saw the ticket sticking out of your purse. Our meeting at the theater wasn't any accident."

Mark couldn't have shocked her more if he'd announced he was an alien from outer space. For the first time in recent memory, she was left speechless. "Tonight?" she asked when she could get the words out. "The library?"

"I'd decided to stop off at your apartment. I was prepared to make up some story about the wedding dress luring me into your building, but when I drove past, I saw you coming down the front steps loaded down with library books. It wasn't hard to figure out where you were headed. I found a parking space and waited for you inside."

"What about...the IRS office and the beach?" She didn't know how he'd managed *those* meetings.

Mark shook his head again and grinned. "Coincidence, unless you had anything to do with them. You didn't, did you?"

"Absolutely not," she replied indignantly.

Still grinning, he said, "I didn't really think you had."

Shelly started walking, her destination unclear. She felt too restless to continue standing there; unfortunately the one action that truly appealed to her was leaping into his arms.

Mark matched his own steps to hers.

"It's Aunt Milly's wedding dress, I know it is," Shelly mumbled under her breath. She'd tried to bring up the subject, but Mark had refused to listen. "You broke off an engagement because you believe fate's somehow thrown us together."

"No, Shelly, the dress doesn't have anything to do with how I feel," Mark said calmly.

"But you'd already decided to marry someone else!"

"I'm choosing my own destiny, which is to spend the rest of my life with you."

"You might have consulted me first. I have no intention of getting married...not for years and years."

"I'll wait."

"You can't do that," she cried. He didn't understand because he was too respectable and adorable and too much of a gentleman. The only thing that would work would be to heartlessly send him away.

She faced Mark, careful to wear just the right expression of remorse and regret. "This is all very flattering, but I don't love you. I'm sorry, Mark. You're the last person in the world I want to hurt."

For a moment Mark said nothing, then he shrugged and looked away. "You can't be any more direct than that, can you? There's no chance you'll ever fall in love with me?"

"None." Her breath fell harshly, painfully, from her lips. It shouldn't hurt this much to do the right thing. It shouldn't hurt to be noble. "You're very nice, but..."

"So you've said before."

Falteringly, as though the movement caused him pain, he lifted his hand to her face, his fingers caressing the curve of her jaw.

Until that moment, Shelly hadn't understood how fiercely proud Mark was. He could have dealt with every argument, calmed every doubt, answered every question, but there was nothing he could say when she denied all feeling for him.

"You mean it, don't you?" he asked huskily. He was standing so close that his breath warmed her face.

Shelly had schooled her features to reveal none of her clamoring emotions. His touch, so light, so potent, seemed to clog her throat with anguish, and she couldn't speak.

"If that's what you want—" he dropped his hand abruptly "—I won't trouble you again." With those words, he turned and walked away. Before she fully realized what he intended, Mark had disappeared around a corner.

"You let him go, you idiot!" she whispered to herself. A tear escaped and she smeared it across her cheek.

Mark meant what he'd said about not bothering her. He was a man of his word. He'd never try to see her again—and if they did happen upon each other, he'd pretend he didn't know her.

He might eventually decide to marry Janice. Hadn't he admitted he was fond of the other woman?

Shelly's heart clutched painfully inside her chest. Before she could stop herself, before she could question the wisdom of her actions, she ran after Mark.

She turned the corner and was halfway down the block when she realized he wasn't anywhere to be seen. She came to a skidding halt, then whirled around, wondering how he could possibly have gotten so far in such a short time.

Mark stepped out from the side of a building, hands on his hips, a cocky, jubilant smile on his face. "What took you so long?" he asked, holding out his arms.

Shelly didn't need a second invitation to throw herself into his embrace. His mouth feasted on hers, his kiss hungry and demanding, filled with enough emotion to last a lifetime.

Shelly slid her arms around his neck and stood on her tiptoes, giving herself completely to his kiss, to his love. All that mattered was being in his arms—exactly where she was supposed to be.

"I take it this means you love me, too?" he whispered close to her ear. His voice was rough with emotion.

Shelly nodded. "I'm so afraid."

"Don't be. I'm confident enough for both of us."

"This is crazy," she said, but she couldn't have moved out of his arms for the world. Breathing deeply, she buried her face in his chest.

"But it's a good kind of crazy."

"Aunt Milly saw us together in her dream. She wrote to me about a tall, blue-eyed man."

"Who knows if it was me or not?" Mark whispered into her hair and brushed his lips over her temple. "Who cares? If fate had anything to do with me finding you or if your aunt Milly's wedding dress is responsible, I can't say. Personally, I couldn't care less. I love you, Shelly, and I believe you love me, too."

She glanced up at this man who had altered the course of her life and smiled, her heart too full for words. "I do love you," she said when she could. "An accountant! In a suit! Hardly the husband I imagined for myself."

Mark chuckled. "I would never have guessed I'd fall head over heels in love with a woman who wears the type of clothes you do—but I did."

"I love you, too," Shelly said and closed her eyes.

The morning of her wedding day, Shelly couldn't sit still. Her mother was even worse, pacing in front of her, dabbing her eyes and sniffling.

"I can't believe my baby's getting married."

Shelly had to restrain herself from reminding her dear mother that less than a month before, she'd been desperate to marry her daughter off. Thank goodness Jill was there. Without her best friend to reassure her, Shelly didn't know what she would've done. While her mother fussed with the caterers, complained to the florists and fretted about who had a key to the kitchen in the reception hall, Jill led Shelly upstairs to her childhood bedroom and helped her dress. When Shelly was finished, Jill stood back to examine her.

"Well?" Shelly asked, smoothing her hand down the antique dress, loving the feel of the satin and lace against her fingers. It was probably her imagination but now that she was wearing the dress, really wearing it, she could almost feel its magic.

Tears gathered in Jill's eyes as she stared at her friend.

"That bad?" Shelly teased.

Jill pressed her fingers to her lips. "You're beautiful," she whispered. "Mark isn't going to believe his eyes when he sees you."

"Do you really think so?" Shelly hated sounding so insecure, but she wanted everything to be perfect today. She was crazy in love—and crazy enough to give her mother free rein planning her wedding. Crazy enough to go through with a formal wedding in the first place. If it'd been up to her, they would've eloped weeks ago. But Mark had wanted a proper wedding and her mother certainly wasn't going to be cheated out of this moment. So Shelly had gone along with it.

Mark and her mother had defeated most of her ideas. She'd wanted to hire clowns to entertain at the reception, but her mother didn't seem to think that was a good idea.

Shelly had never been that fond of white wedding cake, either. She'd suggested Cherries Jubilee instead, but Mark was afraid something might catch on fire and so in the interests of safety, Shelly had agreed to a traditional cake, decorated with pink roses.

A knock sounded on her bedroom door and Jill opened it. In walked Aunt Milly, looking absolutely delighted with herself.

She introduced herself to Jill, then turned to gaze lovingly at Shelly. "So I see the dress worked."

"It worked," Shelly agreed.

"You love him?"

Shelly nodded. "Enough to eat white wedding cake."

Milly laughed softly and sat on the edge of the bed. Her hair was gray and her face wrinkled, but her eyes were still blue and clear. It was difficult to tell that she was a woman well into her eighties. She clasped both of Shelly's hands in her own.

"Nervous?"

Shelly nodded again.

"I was, too, although I knew to the bottom of my heart that I'd made the right decision in marrying John."

"I feel the same way about Mark."

Aunt Milly hugged her tightly. "You're going to be very happy, my dear."

An hour later Shelly and Mark stood at the front of a packed church with Pastor Johnson, who'd known her most of her life. He smiled warmly as he spoke a few words, then asked Shelly to repeat her vows.

Linking hands with Mark, she raised her eyes to his. Everyone else faded away. Aunt Milly. Jill. Her mother. Her long-suffering dad. Her brothers and their wives. There were only the two of them. She felt a jolt of pure joy at the love that radiated from Mark's eyes. He stood tall and proud, his gaze holding hers, the love shining through without question, shining through for her to read. Shelly knew her eyes told him the same thing.

Later, Shelly couldn't remember speaking her vows, although she was sure she did. The words came directly from her heart. Directly from Mark's.

They'd been drawn to this place and this time by forces neither fully understood. Shelly wasn't entirely sure she believed Aunt Milly's wedding dress was responsible, but as Mark had said, it didn't matter. They were there out of love. She didn't know exactly when it had happened. Perhaps that day on the beach, when Mark first kissed her. Something had happened then, something that touched them both.

The love that began as a small spark had grown and flared to life until they'd been brought here, to stand before God and family, pledging their lives to each other. To love. To cherish. All the days of their lives.

* * * * *

HASTY WEDDING

Prologue

Why did it have to be her? Reed Tonasket asked himself as he strolled into the Tullue library. Clare Gilroy was standing at the front desk, a pair of reading glasses riding the bridge of her pert nose. She glanced up when he entered the front door, and as always, Reed experienced a familiar ache at the sight of her.

He guessed she was holding her breath, as though she were afraid. Not of him, but of what he might do. He had a reputation, well earned during his youth, as a rabble-rouser. Being half-Indian added flavor to the stories circulating town about him. Some were true, while others were fiction in the purest form.

His grandfather, in his great wisdom, had wanted Reed to appreciate the part of himself that was not Indian. From ages ten to twelve, Reed had attended school off the reservation. Until that time, Reed had thought of himself as part of the Tullue tribe, not white. He hadn't wanted to become like the white man, nor had he been eager to learn the ways of his mother's people. But his grandfather had spoken, and so Reed had attended the white man's school in town.

Those years had been the worst of his life. He'd fought every boy in the school who challenged him, and nearly everyone had. Usually he was obliged to take on two or three at a time. He defied his teachers, resisted authority and became the first boy ever expelled from the Tullue school district while still in grade school.

Perhaps it was his blunt Indian features that continued to feed the rumors, or the way he wore his thick black hair in heavy braids. It amused him that he caused such interest in Tullue, but frankly, he didn't understand it.

In reality he was pretty tame these days, but no one around town had seemed to notice. Certainly Clare Gilroy hadn't. Whenever he came into the library, she eyed him with concern, as though she suspected he was going to leap atop a bookcase and shout out a piercing war cry. Then again, Reed could be overreacting. He had a tendency to do that where Clare was concerned.

Reed longed to reveal his feelings for her, but words were not the Indian way. He couldn't think of how to tell Clare he was attracted to her and not sound like a fool. Nor was he convinced his love was strong enough to bridge their cultural differences. He was half-Indian and she was a beautiful Anglo.

Reed walked to the back of the library toward the mystery section. He could feel Clare's gaze follow him. It pleased him to know he had her attention if even for those few moments, which wasn't something likely to happen often.

Then why her? Why did he lie awake nights dreaming of holding her in his arms? Why was it Clare Gilroy he wanted more than any woman he'd ever known? He could find no logic for his desire.

Even now he had trouble remembering that he wasn't pure Indian. His blood was mixed, diluted by a mother who was blond and pure and sweet. She'd died when he was four, and the memories of her remained foggy and warm. He understood well his Indian heritage, but he'd ignored whatever part of him was white, the same way he ignored his desire for this uptight librarian.

If Reed had required an answer for his preoccupation with Clare, it was that she intrigued him. She presented a facade of being proper and untouchable. Yet he sensed a fire in her, an eagerness to break free of her self-imposed reserve. He saw in her a fragile spirit yearning to soar. In his mind he gave her the Indian name of Laughing Rainbow because he felt in her a deeply buried joy that was ready to burst to life and spill out into the full spectrum of colors. Colors so bright they would rival that of a rainbow.

That she was involved with Jack Kingston didn't set well with Reed. He'd waited, dreading the time he learned of their marriage. The white man wasn't right for her, but Reed could do nothing. He wasn't right for her, either. And so, like a green seventeen-year-old boy, he dreamed of making love with the one woman he knew he could never have.

One

"If Jack said he'd be here, then he will," Clare Gilroy insisted, although she wasn't the least bit convinced it was true.

Erin Davis, Clare's closest friend, glanced at her watch and sighed. "You're sure about that?"

"No," Clare admitted reluctantly, lowering her gaze. When it came to Jack, she wasn't sure of anything. Not anymore. Once she'd been so positive, so confident of their relationship, but she felt none of that assurance now. They'd been unofficially engaged for three years, and she was no closer to a commitment from Jack than the evening they'd first discussed the possibility of marriage.

Come to think of it, Jack never had actually proposed. As Clare recalled, they'd sort of drifted into a conversation about their future and the subject of marriage had come up. No doubt she was the one to raise it. Jack had suggested they think along those lines, and ever since then that was all he'd been doing. Thinking.

In the meantime, Clare was watching one friend after another marry, have children and get on with their lives. She loved Jack, honestly loved him…she must, otherwise she wouldn't have been so willing to wait for him to make up his mind.

"We'll give him five more minutes," Clare suggested, knowing Erin was anxious. This dinner party was important to her best friend. Although Erin and Gary were planning a Las Vegas wedding, they were meeting with family and friends for this dinner before flying to Nevada the following afternoon with Clare and Reed Tonasket, who was serving as Gary's best man.

"Five minutes is all we'll wait," Clare promised. No sooner had the words slipped from her lips than the telephone rang. She hurried into the kitchen, knowing even before she answered that it would be Jack.

She was right.

"Clare, I'm sorry, but it doesn't look like I'm going to be able to get away."

Disappointment swamped her. "You've known about this dinner for weeks. What do you mean you can't get away?"

"I'm sorry, babe, but Mr. Roth called and asked if I'd come over this evening to give him an estimate. We both know I can't afford to offend a member of the city council. Roth's got connections, and his account could be the boost I've been waiting for."

Clare said nothing.

"I'm doing this for us, babe," Jack continued. "If I can get this landscaping contract, it might lead to a project for the city."

Again Clare said nothing, gritting her teeth.

"Are you going to be angry again?" Jack asked, using just the right amount of indignation to irritate Clare even more. Jack had a habit of purposely doing something to upset her and then making it sound as if she

were being unreasonable. At times it seemed as though
he intentionally set out to annoy her.

"Why should I be angry?" she asked, knowing her
voice was brittle, and not caring. Not this time. "It's
only a dinner party to honor my best friend. Naturally
I'll enjoy attending it alone."

"Which brings up another thing," Jack said, his voice
tightening. "Rumor has it Gary Spencer's asked Reed
Tonasket to be his best man. That isn't true, is it?"

"Yes."

"I don't like the idea of you flying off to Vegas with
that Indian. It isn't good for your reputation."

"Really? Then why don't you come along?"

"You know I can't do that."

"Just like you can't make the dinner party?"

"You're in one of your moods, again, aren't you?
Honest to Pete, there's no reasoning with you when
you get like this. I'm working hard to get this business
on its feet and all you can do is complain. Fine, you go
ahead and be mad. Now if you'll excuse me, I've got
an appointment to keep."

Clare was still holding on to the receiver when the
line was disconnected. The drone in her ear continued
for several seconds before she set down the receiver.
Oh yes, she was in one of her moods again, Clare silently agreed. This sense of annoyance came over her
whenever another friend married, or delivered a baby.

She was thirty-two years old and sick and tired of
waiting for Jack's struggling business "to get on its
feet." She was tired of holding on to empty promises.

"That was Jack," Clare announced when she joined
Erin. As always, she kept her frustration and anger buried deep inside, not wanting her friend to know how

upset she was. "Something's come up and he won't be able to come with us after all."

Erin didn't say anything for a moment, but when she did, Clare had the impression there was a whole lot more her friend would have liked to have said. "We should leave then, don't you think?"

Clare agreed with a curt nod and forced herself to smile. "Here you are marrying for the second time, and I haven't managed to snare myself even one husband," Clare joked as they walked out the front door.

Clare had put a lot of stock into this evening, hoping that once Jack was around Erin and Gary he'd see how happy the two of them were. Both had been through disastrous first marriages, and after several years of being single and despairing of ever falling in love again, they'd met. Within eight months, they'd both known that this time, this marriage would be different.

Gary was the football coach for the local high school. Clare loved sports and each autumn made an attempt to attend as many of the home games as she could. In a town the size of Tullue, with a population of less than six thousand, football was a wonderful way to spend a Friday evening. Jack had gone with her a couple of times, although he wasn't nearly as interested in local sports the way she was.

Clare had inadvertently been responsible for Erin meeting Gary. Erin had stopped to talk to Clare after a game, and because she'd got held up, she'd met Gary on her way to the parking lot. The two had struck up a conversation and the relationship had snowballed from there. Although Erin had been her best friend since high school, Clare couldn't ever remember Erin being this happy.

The dinner party was being held at The Tides, which was the best restaurant in town. Until Jack's phone call, Clare had been looking forward to this evening, but now she could feel a headache coming on. One of the sinus ones she dreaded so much, where the pressure built up in her head until it felt as though a steel band was tightening around her forehead.

"It looks like everyone's here," Erin said animatedly as they pulled into the parking lot.

By everyone, Erin meant her mother and stepfather, her father and stepmother, and Gary's elderly aunt. His parents lived on the East Coast and weren't able to fly in. Following a short honeymoon in Vegas, Gary and Erin were heading east so Erin could meet his mother and father.

Naturally Reed Tonasket would be attending this dinner. It made sense that he'd have a date with him. That meant that Clare and Gary's maiden aunt would be the only ones without partners. Clare groaned inwardly. She'd smile, she decided, and get through the evening somehow. It wouldn't be the first time she was odd woman out.

The Tides had set aside their banquet area for the dinner. It was a small room overlooking the Strait of Juan De Fuca, the well-traveled waterway that separates Washington State from Vancouver Island in British Columbia. As Erin predicted, everyone had arrived and was waiting when the two of them walked in.

Gary stood and wrapped his arm around Erin's shoulders, leading her to the chair next to his own. The only other seat available was the one on the other side of Reed Tonasket.

Clare didn't hesitate; that would have been discourteous, and being rude to anyone was completely alien to her. It wasn't that she disliked Reed, or that she was prejudiced, but he intimidated her the same way he did most everyone in town. His size might have had something to do with her feelings. He was nearly six four, and built like a lumberjack. By contrast Clare was slender and nearly a foot shorter. Although it was only the middle of June and summer didn't officially arrive in the Pacific Northwest until August, Reed was tanned to a deep shade of bronze. Clare knew that like most of the Skyutes, he lived on the reservation. She'd heard that he carved totem poles, which were sold all around the country. But that was all she knew about him. Just enough to engage in polite conversation.

What troubled Clare most about Reed was the angry impatience she sensed in him. She was familiar with several Native Americans who frequented the library. They were graceful, charming people, but she found little of either quality in Reed Tonasket.

"Hello," she said, taking the seat beside him. Since they'd be spending the better part of two days in each other's company, it made sense to Clare that she make some effort to be cordial.

His dark eyes met hers, revealing no emotion. He nodded briefly, acknowledging her. "I'm Clare Gilroy," she said. He didn't give any indication he recognized her from the library, although he was a frequent patron.

"Yes, I know."

He wasn't exactly a stimulating conversationalist, Clare noted. "I... I wasn't sure you remembered me."

His eyes, so dark and bright, made her uncomfortable. They seemed to look straight into her soul. It was as if he knew everything there was to know about her already.

"Has everyone had a chance to introduce themselves?" Gary asked.

Reed nodded, and Clare wondered if not speaking was a habit of his; if that was the case, she was about to spend two very uncomfortable days in his company.

"You don't have a date?" Gary's aunt Wilma leaned across the table to ask Clare. "I seem to remember Gary saying something about you bringing your young man."

Clare could feel heat seeping into her face. "Jack... my date couldn't come at the last minute. He has his own business. He's been working very hard at getting it established." She didn't know why she felt the burning need to make excuses for Jack, but she did, speaking quickly so that the words ran into one another. "He got a call from an important man he's hoping will become a client and had to cancel. I'm sure he regrets missing the dinner, but it was just one of those things. It couldn't be helped." She realized as she finished that she was speaking to the entire table of guests.

"How unfortunate," Wilma Spencer murmured into the silence that followed Clare's explanation.

They were distracted by the waitress who delivered menus, and Clare was eternally grateful. She had little appetite and ordered a small dinner salad and a crab cake appetizer.

"That's all?" Reed questioned when she'd finished.

Flustered, Clare nodded. "I'm not very hungry."

His dark eyes, which had been so unreadable only a few minutes earlier, clearly revealed his opinion now. He was telling her, without uttering a word, that she was too thin.

Erin had been saying the same thing for weeks. Clare had defended her recent weight loss, claiming she was striving for an understated elegance, a fashionable thinness that suited her petite five-foot-four frame. Erin hadn't been fooled, and it was unlikely she was deceiving Reed Tonasket, either. Clare was unhappy, and growing more so every day as she battled her suspicions that Jack had no intention of ever marrying her.

"Look, the band's going to play," Erin said excitedly, looking with wide-eyed eagerness toward Gary. Their gazes met and held, and even from where she was sitting, Clare could feel the love they shared.

Love had taken her friends by surprise. They'd both been wary, afraid of repeating the mistakes of their first marriages. Even though it was apparent to everyone around them how perfectly suited they were, Erin and Gary had taken their time before admitting their feelings for one another.

Dinner was served, and the chatter around the table flowed smoothly. Clare found herself talking with Aunt Wilma, who at seventy-five was as spry as someone twenty years younger. The meal was festive, filled with shared chatter and tales of romance and rediscovered love.

Erin and Gary told of how they'd met following a football game, crediting Clare, who blushed when she became the focus of the group's attention. Funny, she had no problem linking up her friends with prospective husbands, but she couldn't find love and companionship herself.

Following the dinner, Reed stood and waited until the table had quieted before proposing a toast to the happy couple. Clare sipped her wine. Although she was happy for Erin and Gary, the lonely ache inside her intensified. Rarely had she felt more alone.

Dessert arrived, a flaming Cherries Jubilee that produced sighs of appreciation. Erin dished up small servings and passed them down the table, but it seemed Erin, who was looking longingly toward the band, was more interested in dancing than sampling dessert.

As soon as everyone had a plate, she reached for Gary's hand and led him onto the dance floor. Erin's parents and their prospective mates joined the wedding couple.

Soon everyone at the table was on the dance floor with the exception of Reed Tonasket, Clare and Aunt Wilma. The feeling of being excluded from the mainstream of happy couples had never felt more profound.

Aunt Wilma, bless her heart, kept her busy with small talk, although Clare answered in monosyllables, sloshing through a quagmire of self-pity. Reed hadn't exchanged more than a few words with her the entire evening, and the burden of carrying the conversation was beyond her just then.

"Would you care to dance?"

His invitation took her by surprise. It was all she could do not to ask if he meant to dance with *her*. His eyes held hers; the same dark eyes she'd found intimidating before were warm and intriguing now. Before she realized what she was doing, Clare nodded.

He held his hand out and guided her onto the crowded floor. The dance was a slow number, and he turned Clare gently into his arms as though he feared hurting her. His arms circled her, drawing her close to the solid length of his body. Soon she was wrapped in the shelter of his embrace, in the warm muskiness of this man.

They fit together as though they'd been made for each other, and her heart beat steadily against his chest. Together they moved smoothly, with none of the awkwardness that generally accompanies a couple the first time they dance together. Clare swallowed, surprised by how easily she adapted to his arms, by how right she felt being held by him. Even her headache, which had been pounding moments earlier, seemed to lessen.

Something was happening. Something Clare couldn't explain or define. They were closer, much closer than when they'd first started dancing, but Clare couldn't remember moving. Her heart was more than beating, oddly it seemed to be pounding out a rhythm that matched the hard staccato of Reed Tonasket's heart. His hold on her was firm, commanding, as if he had every right in the world to be this intimate.

A scary excitement filled her. Her body ached in a strange, embarrassing way. Her breathing went shallow as she battled these inappropriate sensations.

Reed's eyes found hers, and their gazes met and locked. Clare could feel the heat in him. It reached out and wrapped itself around her, enfolding her as effectively as if keeping her prisoner. For a wild moment she seemed incapable of breathing or swallowing.

Myriad feelings tingled to life, feelings she didn't want to feel, not now, not with this man when it should be Jack. Clare closed her eyes, concentrating instead on matching her steps with his. That didn't work, either; instead she felt every nuance of his intense, magnificent body. Battling down a bevy of fluttering, inarticulate feelings, she opened her eyes and stared into the distance.

Without speaking, Reed seemed to be commanding

her to look at him. Feeling the way she did, Clare decided it would be best to avoid eye contact. He may be able to hide his emotions, but she couldn't. Reed would know in an instant how confused and shaken she was.

The urge to look up at him was nearly overwhelming. She wasn't going to do it, she determined a second time. She didn't dare. Yet, the urge to do so grew stronger, more intense as his unspoken request seemed to draw her gaze upward.

No, she silently cried, I can't.

"You're not feeling well, are you?"

Despite her recent conviction, Clare's gaze shot to his. "How...how'd you know?"

"Headache?"

She nodded, amazed he could read her so accurately, unable to drag her gaze away. "I'll be better by morning."

"Yes," he agreed, and his lips grazed her temple as though to ease away the pain with his touch. The kiss was so gentle, so overwhelmingly sweet that tears sprang to her eyes.

With what felt like superhuman strength, she broke away. Color burned in her face, pinkening her cheeks. She felt jolted and dazed and for some odd reason... reprehensible to the very core of her being.

"I...have to go," Clare said abruptly. She needed to escape before she did something that would humiliate her. "I've got a million things to do before the flight tomorrow," she offered as an excuse. "Would you be kind enough to make my excuses to Erin and Gary for me?"

"Of course." He released her immediately and guided her back to the table. Clare swiftly gathered her purse, and with little more than a nod to Aunt Wilma, hurried out of the restaurant.

Clare didn't know what had prompted her to behave this way. She'd practically made a spectacle of herself. That was it. She wasn't herself, Clare mused, searching to find some excuse, some reassurance as she hurried out of the restaurant and into the parking lot.

The day had been a whirlwind of activity as she'd driven with Erin into Port Angeles, fifty miles east of Tullue, to shop for a new outfit for the honeymoon trip.

After such a hectic afternoon, Clare couldn't be blamed for indulging in a few unorthodox fantasies. Circumstances were further complicated by Jack's canceling at the last minute. But no matter what excuses she offered, when it came right down to it, Clare had to admit she was thoroughly fascinated by Reed Tonasket.

Not sexually fascinated…no, not that; Clare was the first to concede she was something of a puritan. Her experience was limited and what little she'd encountered had always been—she hated to admit—boring. But in Reed she sensed hunger, raw and primitive, as elemental as the man himself. Heaven help her, she was intrigued. That was only natural, wasn't it? Especially when she'd be spending the better part of two days in his company.

Reed's reputation with the ladies only added to her curiosity. Although Clare wasn't privy to a lot of what was said about him, she'd heard rumors. There were those who claimed no woman could refuse him. After experiencing his blatant sensuality, Clare tended to believe it.

Once she was home, Clare leaned against her door and turned the lock. Her heart was racing, and the headache had returned full force. Already the pressure was building up in her sinuses. Stress. These headaches came on whenever she was under an abnormal amount of anxiety.

She walked into her bedroom, ignoring the suitcase, which was spread open atop her mattress, and sat on the edge of the bed. Covering her face with both hands, her long brown hair fell forward. Impatiently she pushed it back, regretting now that Erin had convinced her to wear it down. She exhaled slowly, then breathed in a deep, calming breath. The last thing she needed now was one of her infamous headaches.

She lay back and closed her eyes, hoping to relax and let the tension drain out of her body. But when her head nestled against the pillow, Reed Tonasket leaped, full-bodied, into her imagination. He wore that knowing look, as if he were capable of reading her thoughts, capable of discerning how much he'd affected her.

The doorbell chimed and, groaning inwardly, Clare moved off the bed. Jack Kingston stood on the other side of the door, his handsome face bright with a smile. For a split second, Clare debated if she should let him inside.

He was always so persuasive, so convincing. She had every reason in the world to be angry with him, but if the past was anything to go by, before the end of the evening, she'd end up apologizing *to him*. It went like that. He'd hurt or disappoint her, and before the night was over, she was asking his forgiveness.

"Clare," he said, kissing her softly on the cheek as he casually strolled inside her home with the familiarity of a long-standing relationship. "I've got wonderful news."

"You're going to marry me," she said smoothly, crossing her arms. She didn't suggest he sit down, didn't offer him coffee. In fact she did nothing.

Her lack of welcome didn't appear to phase Jack,

who moved into her kitchen and opened her refrigerator, peering inside. "I'm starved," he announced, and reached for a cluster of seedless grapes.

Clare reluctantly followed him. "What's your news?"

Jack's brown eyes brightened. "It looks like Roth is going to give me the contract. He wanted to think about it overnight, which he says he does as standard procedure, but he was impressed with my ideas and the quotes I gave him. I like the man, he's got a good head on his shoulders. It wouldn't surprise me if he decided to run for mayor sometime in the future."

"Congratulations," Clare returned stiffly.

Jack hesitated and eyed her suspiciously. "Do I sense a bit of antagonism?"

"I'm sure you do. I just spent one of the most uncomfortable evenings of my life." But not for the reasons she was implying. It shook her that she could look at Jack and feel nothing. There'd been a time when she'd lived for those rare moments when he'd drop by unannounced, but those times had wilted and died for lack of nourishment. Perhaps for the first time, she saw Jack as he really was—self-centered and vain. If she let him, and so far she had, he'd string her along for years, feeding her blank promises, keeping her hopes alive. It astonished her that she hadn't realized it earlier.

"Aren't we being a bit selfish?" he asked, arching his thick eyebrows.

"Not this time," Clare answered smoothly. "If anyone was selfish it was you. This dinner's been planned for weeks—"

"I've got to put the business first," Jack interrupted calmly. "You know that. I don't blame you for being disappointed, but really, babe, when you think about it, I did it for us."

"For us?" The excuse was well-worn, and she'd grown sick of hearing it.

"Of course." He popped another grape into his mouth, not threatened by her words. "I don't enjoy working these long hours any more than you enjoy having me miss out on these social events that are so important to you. I hated not being there for your friends' dinner party this evening, but it was just one of those things. Someday all this hard work is going to pay off."

"What if I were to say I didn't want to marry you anymore?"

Jack's hand was halfway to his mouth. He paused, the grape poised before his lips. "Then I'd say you don't mean it. Come on, babe, you're talking nonsense."

"Actually I'm grateful you put off setting the wedding date. I seem to be a slow learner and it's taken me this long to realize we're nowhere near being compatible. Marriage between us would have been disastrous."

Jack stood immobile for a moment, as though he wasn't sure he should believe her. "Are you in one of your moods again?"

"Yes," she returned evenly, "I guess you might say I haven't recovered from 'my mood' earlier this evening."

"Clare…"

"Please don't say anything. I didn't know anyone could be so blind to the obvious."

"I want to marry you, Clare," Jack refuted adamantly, "but when the time's right. If you think you're going to pressure me into setting the date because you're angry, you're wrong. I'm not going to allow you to manipulate me."

"This isn't a pressure tactic, Jack. I'm serious, very serious. It's over."

"You don't mean it."

Arguing with him wouldn't help, she should have known that by now. With her arms crossed, she leaned against the refrigerator door. "You're wrong, Jack, I do mean it." Her voice faltered just a little—with regret, with sadness. She'd wasted three years of her life on Jack, when it should have been obvious after the first month how ill suited they were. Erin had tried to tell her, but Clare hadn't listened. She hadn't wanted to hear the truth.

Jack stalked to the far side of her kitchen, opened the cabinet door under her sink and tossed what remained of the grapes into the garbage. "You're trying to pressure me into marrying you, and I won't have it. If and when we marry, it'll be on my timetable, not yours."

"Whatever," she said, growing bored with their conversation. She wasn't going to change her mind, and wondered briefly how she could have endured the relationship this long.

"Come on, Clare, you're being unreasonable. I'm not going to put up with this. I said I'd marry you and I will, but I don't like being blackmailed into it."

"Jack," she said, growing impatient, "you're not listening to me. I've had a change of heart, I *don't* want to marry you. You're off the hook, so stop worrying about it."

"I hate it when you get in these moods of yours."

"This isn't a mood, Jack, it's D day. We're through, finished. In plain English, it's over."

"I refuse to allow you to back me into a corner."

"Goodbye, Jack."

His eyes rounded with surprise. "You don't mean this, Clare, I know you. You get all riled up about one thing or another and within a day or two you've forgotten all about it." Frustration layered his words.

"Not this time," she said without emotion as she led the way to her front door. She opened it and stood there waiting for him to exit.

Jack's eyes followed her across the living room floor, but he stood where he was, just outside her kitchen, as though he wasn't sure he could believe what was happening.

"Don't be hasty," he warned in a low voice. "We both know you don't mean it and that tomorrow you'll have a change of heart."

"I do mean it, Jack. It took me three years to wake up and smell the roses. I'm not exactly a fast study, am I?" she asked dryly.

"You're going to regret this."

Clare didn't answer.

Jack's gaze narrowed. "You're being unreasonable because of Erin and Gary getting married, aren't you? I swear I hate it when one of your friends asks you to be in their wedding party. It never fails. You become completely irrational. This time you've gone too far. It's over, Clare, you just remember that, because once I walk out that door, I'm never coming back, and that's final."

Once again, Clare decided it was best to say nothing.

"Don't try to phone me, either," Jack added, as he cut across her lawn to where he'd parked his pickup truck. "You've pushed me just a little too hard this time." He pulled open the door and leveled his gaze at her.

"Goodbye, Jack," she said evenly, then stepped back and closed the door.

Two

Clare had done it. She'd actually severed her ties with Jack. She wasn't sure what she expected to feel, certainly not this sense of release, of freedom, as though a heavy burden had been lifted from her shoulders.

For months, perhaps even years, she'd been wearing blinders when it came to Jack's faults and the unhealthy twists their relationship had taken. It'd bothered her, but she'd chosen to overlook their problems all in the name of love. And the promise of marriage.

At some point she'd cared deeply for Jack, but her feelings had died a slow, laborious death. So slow that she hadn't realized what was happening until she'd danced with Reed Tonasket. She would never have felt the things she did in Reed's arms if she truly loved Jack.

The memory was followed with an instant surge of renewed embarrassment. Groaning inwardly, Clare placed her hands over her reddening cheeks and closed her eyes. When he'd asked her to dance, Clare had fully expected to feel awkward in his arms. The last thing she'd anticipated was a full scale sensual awakening.

Reed had known what was happening, too. He must

have. It mortified her to recall the erotic way in which their bodies had responded to each other, as though they were longtime lovers. It'd flustered her so badly, she'd hurriedly left the restaurant, unable to cope with what had passed between them.

To complicate matters even more, they were due to see each other again in only an hour. It would have been so much better if she could have put some time and distance between last night and their next meeting. She needed time to gain perspective, to think this matter through. But the luxury of that was being taken away from her.

Within a short while Clare would be with Reed again. For the next two days they'd be sharing one another's company. To her dismay she hadn't given a single thought to how she'd spend her time with Reed following Erin and Gary's wedding. They'd be together almost exclusively from that point onward. Clare sincerely doubted that Erin and Gary would feel responsible for entertaining them the first hours of their honeymoon.

Jack had been concerned about her traveling with Reed. His apprehension was only token, she was sure, nevertheless, he'd made a point. Clare didn't know Reed, really know him that is. Until recently she'd viewed him as unruly and even a tad dangerous. Rumors about him had been floating around town for years, but Clare had never paid much attention to hearsay. To her way of thinking, not half of what was said could possibly be true. It couldn't be, otherwise Gary, who was decent and honorable wouldn't have asked Reed to stand up as his best man.

Clare wondered about the relationship between the two men. If she'd had her wits about her the night before, she would have asked Reed herself. It would have been a good place to start a conversation. But she'd been upset over Jack and hadn't made the effort to engage him.

Well, she needn't worry about Jack any longer, she reminded herself. He was out of her life. Once again she experienced a lighthearted, almost giddy sensation of relief. It was over, finally. Her life was her own once again.

Broken engagement aside, Clare now had to battle a growing sinus headache. There wasn't time to contact Dr. Brown for an appointment. She'd endured the problem for years and had several medications from leftover prescriptions. Gathering together what she had into one bottle, she downed a capsule, then placed what remained in her purse. Once she was home, she'd give the doctor's office a call and see about scheduling an appointment. It wasn't the best plan, but it was the most workable option available to her at the moment.

"Have I got everything?" Gary asked, slapping his hands against his suit pockets in frenzied movements. "I can't believe I'm this nervous."

Reed smiled patiently at his friend, amused.

"I feel like… I don't even know what I feel anymore. I'm about to get married and I swear I'm so nervous I'm breaking out in a cold sweat." Gary walked over to the hotel window that overlooked the Vegas strip, stuffed his hands into his pants pockets as he stared at the flat Nevada landscape. "It could be worse, I suppose, I could make an even bigger fool of myself and break into tears at the altar."

Once again Reed grinned at his friend. He'd known

Gary for several years and couldn't remember ever seeing him in such an agitated state. Often he'd admired Gary for his cool head and his calm, levelheaded manner. As a coach there were ample opportunities for his friend to allow his emotions to get away from him, but Reed had yet to see it happen. Until now, just before he was due to marry Erin Davis.

Love seemed to do that to a man, Reed noted. He wasn't all that educated in the emotion himself, and wondered if their situations were reversed how he'd react. If he were to marry Clare, would he be any less nervous? Reed didn't know, but it wasn't likely the situation would arise so he need not concern himself with it.

He'd spent the better part of the day with Clare Gilroy and they hadn't exchanged more than a handful of sentences. He would have liked to talk, but it was apparent Clare wasn't feeling well. She'd fallen asleep on the plane and had unknowingly rested her head against his shoulder. Reed had wanted to wrap his arm around her, shield her and make her as comfortable as possible in their cramped quarters. But he feared when she woke his actions would alarm her, and so he'd done nothing.

Clare Gilroy was off-limits to him, Reed reminded himself for the hundredth time in the past four hours. She was cultured, educated and refined. Reed was none of those things. They shared almost nothing in common except a thriving sensual awareness. She'd chosen to pretend otherwise, but the feelings were there whether she admitted it or not. They hadn't lessened from the night before, either. If anything they'd grown more intense.

The harshest agony Reed had ever endured had been holding Clare in his arms on the dance floor. It required every ounce of restraint he possessed not to crush her against him and kiss her the way he'd dreamed of doing for longer than he cared to admit.

He wasn't a fool. He knew what she was feeling. He knew what he was feeling. Their bodies had moved together, each action echoed instinctively by the other in an age-old ritual of desire.

It had terrified her, Reed realized, feeling the things she did. She'd broken away from him, rushed off the dance floor, and left the restaurant in a near panic.

He'd watched her closely when they'd met again that morning, looking for a sign, some indication of what she was feeling now. He hadn't been able to read her soft brown eyes. Her gaze had skirted away from his, and later, on the plane, he realized she was in pain. Whatever he read in her would be clouded by her discomfort.

"How do I look?" Gary asked, easing his finger along the inside of his starched white collar of his shirt. "Erin's the only woman in the world who could ever talk me into wearing a tuxedo."

"You're the one person in the world who could convince me to wear one," Reed echoed. Gary Spencer was his only Anglo friend. The two had met because of Reed's efforts with the Indian youths at the high school. He worked hard to preserve his people's culture, making it a point to pass on his skills as a totem pole carver to the next generation.

A couple of the Skyute boys had been a part of the football team and Reed had got to know Gary through them. The coach's insights into dealing with teenagers had impressed Reed, and when Derek, one of the youths, had got into trouble with the law, Gary had helped him. Reed was grateful, even if Derek wasn't.

"You look…" Gary paused, apparently searching for the right word.

"Different," Reed supplied.

"More than that."

"It's the braids." Or rather the lack of them. Reed had combed his hair back and tied it at the base of his neck. When he'd surveyed the results in the mirror, he'd been surprised himself. Removing the braids seemed to erase the part of him that was Indian. He was the same man on the inside, but the outside had decidedly changed. His skin was darker than most Anglos, but the bronze tone could have as easily been from a tanning booth as his heritage. With his hair pulled away from his face, he could be Italian as easily as Native American. For the first time he could see his mother's mark in his features. Somehow he looked less harsh, less austere.

"What's different is that you're…hell, I feel foolish even saying it, you're downright good-looking."

Reed scoffed and shook his head. "I don't trust the judgment of a man who's about to marry the woman he loves."

Gary rubbed his palms together. "I suppose you're right." Glancing at his wrist, he paced the length of the hotel room once again. "We've got fifteen minutes to kill. You want to go downstairs for a drink?"

Reed shook his head. "Not particularly."

"You're right," Gary agreed, "I need a clear head." He ran his fingers through his hair. "I wonder if Erin's having second thoughts."

"I doubt it."

"You don't think so?" he asked anxiously, then sighed. "I can't remember ever being this jittery."

"Any second thoughts yourself?" Reed asked. "Are

you sure you really want to marry Erin?" The question wasn't a serious one, but one intended to distract Gary and take his mind off the time.

Gary ceased his pacing and turned to face Reed. "I've never been more confident of anything in my life. Erin's the best thing that's ever happened to me."

"I thought so."

"I'd given up hope of ever finding a woman I'd want to marry," Gary continued, "and now that I have I'm so impatient to make her my wife I can hardly stand it."

"From what I've seen of Erin, I'd say she feels the same about being your bride."

"I want a houseful of children, too. I imagine that surprises you. Every time I think about Erin and me having a baby I get all mushy inside."

"That doesn't surprise me."

"What about you?" Gary asked. "Have you ever thought of marrying?"

"No," Reed answered honestly.

His quick response seemed to catch Gary by surprise. "Why not?"

"I'm half-white, half Indian."

"So?"

Reed didn't answer. He hadn't found acceptance in either world. Certainly not in the white man's society. He was looked upon as a hellion although he hadn't done anything in years to substantiate the rumors. With his father's people he was respected, mainly because of his art. He'd been reared by his grandfather, taught the Indian ways until they became as much a part of him as breathing. Nevertheless there was a distance between the tribal leaders from an incident that happened when he was a youth. He'd been passed over for an award he deserved, because he was only half-Indian. In some ways Reed was responsible for the rift, but not in all.

"Then you've never been in love," Gary said dismissively, and glanced at his watch. "I've waited six years for this day, and I should be a little more patient."

"Do you want to go to the chapel and wait there?"

Gary nodded. "Anything would be better than pacing this room."

The same way hotels around the world supplied room service and a variety of other amenities to their guests, Las Vegas provided a wedding chapel. Gary had made the arrangements for his and Erin's nuptials with the hotel staff weeks earlier. Following the ceremony, the four of them would share in an elegant dinner, and from there Gary and Erin would adjourn to the Honeymoon Suite. Reed would take Gary's room for the night and Clare would sleep in Erin's. They were scheduled to fly out early the following morning.

"I appreciate you coming down with us," Gary said as they headed out of the elevator.

"I was honored you asked."

"Oh, Erin," Clare whispered when her friend appeared. "I've never seen you look so beautiful."

"I'm going to cry… I know I'm going to make an absolute fool of myself and sob uncontrollably through the entire ceremony."

Clare smiled at her friend's words. "If anyone weeps it'll be me."

"How are you feeling?" Erin asked, studying her, her gaze revealing her concern.

"Much better," Clare assured her friend. "The headache's almost gone."

"Good." Erin nervously twisted the small bouquet of white rosebuds between her hands, closed her eyes and exhaled slowly.

By tacit agreement they made their way to the elevator and the wedding chapel. Clare's heart swelled with shared happiness. Jack claimed she got in one of her moods every time one of her friends married, and for months Clare had listened to him, believed him. Because he'd been so adamant, Clare hadn't recognized her own feelings.

She wasn't jealous of Erin, she was joyous. Despite tremendous odds, Erin and Gary had found each other, let go of their pasts, learned from their mistakes and were ready to try their hands at love again. Clare saw in them courage, strength and love, and she deeply admired them both.

Gary and Reed were standing outside the chapel, waiting. Clare's gaze was immediately drawn to Reed, and for an instant she didn't recognize him. He looked completely different, but, without staring, she couldn't figure out what it was that had changed. Her heart fluttered wildly as though she were the bride, and she lowered her gaze, fearing she might have been too obvious.

It was crazy, but she wondered what Reed thought when he first saw her. It didn't seem possible that he experienced the same wondrous sensation that had struck her. Her dress was a lovely shade of pale blue with a spray of tiny pearls spilling over the shoulders and across the yoke. Erin had chosen it for her, and it closely followed the shapely lines of Clare's breasts and slim hips. Clare became so involved with what was happening between her and Reed that she was only fleetingly aware of what was going on with Gary and Erin.

It seemed there was some paperwork that needed to be completed before they could proceed with the actual ceremony. Erin and Gary were busy with that, leaving Clare and Reed to their own devices.

"Is Erin as nervous as Gary?" Reed surprised her by asking. To the best of her memory it was the first time he'd initiated a conversation.

"A little. Erin's afraid she's going to end up weeping through the ceremony." How odd her voice sounded, as though it were coming from the bottom of a deep pit. Having Reed focus his gaze on added to her nervousness.

She was aware of everything around her, the tall white baskets filled with a wide array of colorful flowers, of gladiolas and irises, roses and baby's breath. Their soft scents lingered in the room, delicate and sweet.

Clare found the need to look at Reed irresistible, and she subtly centered her gaze on him. He was dressed in a black tuxedo, which complimented his dark looks. The petite pleats of the shirt front added a decidedly masculine accent.

"You'll need to sign here," Gary said, but Clare was so enraptured with Reed that she didn't realize he was speaking to her.

"Clare," Erin said gently, "we need you to sign these papers."

"Oh, of course," she faltered, embarrassed.

"If you're ready, we can begin the ceremony." The officiant reached for his Bible, and the four of them formed a semicircle in front of him.

Over the years, Clare had been a member of several wedding parties. Some had been simple ceremonies such as she was involved with now, and others elaborate affairs in which she marched down the center aisle of a crowded church to the thundering strains of organ music.

None had affected her as this wedding did. It must be because it was Gary and Erin marrying, Clare decided, when an unexpected lump filled her throat. It had to be that.

As the justice of the peace spoke, the urge to cry increased. Each wedding she attended had touched Clare in some way. The very nature of the ritual was compelling and rendering to the heart.

Moments earlier she'd spoken to Reed of Erin's concern, but if anyone was threatening to break into sobs, it was Clare herself.

As Erin's soft voice rose to repeat her vows, Clare's gaze was drawn back to Reed's. Their eyes met as if guided by some irresistible force, and locked. This awareness, this fascination she felt toward him flowered…no, it was much stronger than flowering, it *exploded* to life. Tears, which had been so close to the surface, filled her eyes until Reed's tall figure blurred and swam before her.

Whatever was happening, whatever was between them, was so powerful it took all her strength not to move to his side. He felt it, too, she was certain of it. As powerfully as she did.

Her lips were moving, Clare realized, although she wasn't speaking. With her eyes locked with Reed's, she found herself repeating the same wedding vows as her friend. *To love, to cherish, always…*

When it became *Gary's* turn to repeat his vows, his voice was strong and clear with no hint of nervousness. By holding her gloved finger beneath her eye, Clare was able to drain off the tears. Reed's gaze remained locked with hers and he, too, mouthed the words along with Gary. Clare was vividly aware of how intimate their actions were. Reed was silently beseeching her, echoing her own thoughts and needs.

Suddenly the vows had been said. Even though Clare didn't want the moment to end there was nothing she could say or do that would prolong it. Gary embraced Erin and kissed her, and Clare, desperately needing to compose herself, lowered her eyes. Her breathing was shallow, she noted, and her pulse pounded wildly against her breast.

Clare had only started to collect her emotions, when Erin turned and gave her a tearful kiss. "You're crying," she said, laughing and weeping herself.

"I know. Everything was so beautiful...you and Gary are beautiful." She didn't dare look in Reed's direction and was grateful to realize he was occupied with Gary. It was uncanny that a Las Vegas ceremony could evoke such a wellspring of emotion.

She found it impossible to believe that she'd mouthed the vows along with her friend. Then it hit her. She was so anxious, so eager to be a wife herself that an uncontrollable longing had welled up inside her. She yearned to share her life with a man whose commitment to her was as deep as hers was to him. It was this promise of happiness that had kept her locked in a dead-end relationship for three barren years.

Reed turned to her after all the congratulations had been spoken, and reached for her hand, tucking it into the warm curve of his elbow.

"Are you feeling all right?"

Words eluded her, so she tried smiling, and nodded,

hoping that would satisfy him. He was frowning at her, and she realized she'd made an utter fool of herself in front of him.

He raised his hand and gently traced his finger down the side of her face. "We'll talk more later."

His words raised a quiver of apprehension that raced up her spine.

He smiled, and to the best of her knowledge it was the first time she'd ever seen him reveal amusement.

"Don't look so worried," he told her, gently patting her hand.

They were walking side by side, her hand in his elbow, Clare obediently allowing herself to be led, although she hadn't a clue where they were headed. Not that it mattered; in those moments Reed Tonasket could have been escorting her to the moon. As a matter of fact, she was halfway there already.

The wedding dinner was a festive affair. Gary ordered champagne, and the sparkling liquid flowed freely as they dined on huge lobster tails and the best Caesar salad Clare had ever tasted.

The evening was perfect, more perfect than anything she could remember. As dinner progressed, she felt the tension slip away. By the time they feasted on a slice of wedding cake, Clare felt relaxed and uninhibited. The terrible anxiety that had been her companion most of the day had vanished, and she laughed and talked freely with her friends.

With eyes only for each other, Gary and Erin excused themselves, leaving Clare and Reed on their own.

"I can't remember a wedding I've enjoyed more," Clare said, looking over to Reed. Perhaps it was the simplicity, or her special relationship with the couple.

Whatever the reason, their love had tugged fiercely at the strings of her heart. "I think it was the most beautiful wedding I've ever attended."

She half expected Reed to challenge her words, but he didn't. Instead he reached for her hand, gently squeezed her fingers and said, "You're right, it was beautiful."

It might have been her imagination, but Clare had the elated sensation that he was speaking about her and not the wedding ceremony. Reed made her feel beautiful. She couldn't remember experiencing anything like this with any man. He was so different than what she expected, so gentle and concerned. With Reed she felt cherished and protected.

"We have several hours yet— Is there anything you'd like to do?"

Clare didn't need to give the question thought. "I'd love to gamble." They were, after all, in Las Vegas.

"Have you ever been to Vegas before?"

"Never," she admitted. "But I can count to twenty-one and if that fails me, there's a roll of quarters in my purse."

Reed chuckled. "You're sure about this?"

"Positive." She beamed him a wide smile. Rarely had she felt less constrained. It was as though they'd known each other for years. She experienced none of the restraint toward him that she had earlier. Looking at him now, smiling at her, she wondered how she could have ever thought of him as aloof or reserved.

"You'll need a clear head if you're going to gamble," he said, and motioning for the waiter, he ordered two cups of coffee.

"I only had one glass of champagne, but you're right,

I want to be levelheaded about this ten dollars burning a hole in my purse."

The waiter delivered two cups of steaming coffee and Clare took her first tentative sip. "How long have you and Gary been friends?"

Reed shrugged. "A few years now. What about you and Erin?"

"Since high school. I was the bookworm and Erin was a cheerleader. By all that was right, we shouldn't have even been friends, but we felt drawn to each other. I guess we balance one another out. I knew she should never have married Steve—I wish now I'd said something to her, but I didn't."

"I didn't meet Gary until after his divorce, but he's talked about his first marriage. His wife left him for another man."

"Steve didn't know the meaning of the word *faithful*. Sometimes I think I hated him for what he did to Erin. She moved back to Tullue when they separated and she was so thin and pale I barely recognized her." The outward changes couldn't compare to what Steve had done to Erin's self-esteem. Her self-confidence had been shattered. It had taken her friend years to repair the emotional damage.

"I remember when Gary first met Erin," Reed said thoughtfully. "He drove out to my place. I was working at the time, and he paced from one end of my shop to the other talking about Erin Davis, asking me if I knew her."

"Did you?"

"No."

"They took their time, didn't they?" It had been apparent to Clare from the beginning how well suited they were to each other. "Erin came to me in tears the night Gary asked her to marry him. At first I thought she was crying with joy, but I soon realized she was terrified." An emotion akin to what she'd experienced herself the night before when she'd first danced with Reed, Clare thought. She paused and guardedly glanced in his direction, unsure what had prompted the comparison.

"I wish I knew you better," she found herself saying. She inhaled sharply, appalled that she'd verbalized the thought.

"What is it you'd like to know?"

There was so much, she didn't know where to begin. "How old are you?"

"Thirty-six."

"We were never in the same school together." It was an unconscious statement. Naturally they wouldn't have been since he must have attended the reservation school. "I…we wouldn't have been in high school at the same time anyway… I'm four years younger than you." Avoiding his gaze, she sipped her coffee. "I guess I know more about you than I realized."

"Oh."

"You enjoy reading." She knew that by the frequency with which he visited the library, although she couldn't recall any single category of books he checked out more than others.

"My reading tastes are eclectic," he said as if he'd read her thoughts.

"How do you do that?" she asked, gesturing wildly with her arms.

"Do what?"

"Know what I'm thinking. I swear it's uncanny."

Reed's dark eyes danced mischievously. "It's an old Indian trick."

"I'll just bet." She reached across the table and picked the uneaten strawberry off his plate. After popping it into her mouth, she was amazed that she would do anything so unorthodox. "Do you mind, I mean... I should have asked."

He studied her more closely. "Are you sure you only had one glass of champagne?"

"Positive. Now are we going to the gaming tables or not? I feel lucky."

"Come on," he said with a laugh, "I hate to think of those quarters languishing away in your purse."

Clare smiled and, linking her hand with his, they left the restaurant.

Reed led her first to the blackjack tables. She was short and had trouble perching herself upon the high stool, so without warning, he gripped her waist and lifted her onto the seat.

The action took her by surprise, and she gasped until she realized it was him, then thanked him with a warm smile. After all her reservations, she discovered she enjoyed Reed's company.

"You betting, lady?" the dealer asked, breaking into her thoughts.

"Ah...just a minute." The table was a dollar minimum bet, and Clare exchanged a twenty-dollar bill for chips. She set out two chips and waited until the dealer had given her the necessary cards.

"You're not playing?" she asked, looking to Reed.

"Not now, I will later."

Clare won her first five hands. "I like this game," she told Reed. "I didn't know I was so lucky."

He said nothing, but stood behind her, offering her advice when she asked for it and keeping silent when she didn't. His hands were braced against her shoulders, and she felt comfort and contentment in his being there.

By the end of an hour there was a large stack of chips in front of her. "I'm going to wager them all," she said decisively, pushing the mounds of chips forward. To her way of figuring, gambling money was easy come, easy go. Her original investment had been only twenty dollars, and if she lost that, then she considered it well worth the hour's entertainment.

"You're sure?" Reed whispered close to her ear.

"Absolutely positive." She may have sounded confident, but when the cards were dealt, her heart was trapped somewhere between her stomach and her throat. The dealer busted, and she let out a loud, triumphant shout.

It required both hands to carry all her chips to the cashier. When the woman counted out the money, Clare had won over two hundred dollars.

"Two hundred dollars," she cried, and without thought, without hesitation, looped her arms around Reed's neck and hurled herself into his arms.

Three

Stunned, Reed instinctively caught Clare in his arms.

"Two hundred dollars," she repeated. "Why, that's ten times what I started out with." She smiled at him with a free-flowing happiness sparkling from her beautiful brown eyes. Reed couldn't help being affected. He smiled, too.

"Congratulations."

"Thank you, oh, thank you."

It wasn't until the man behind them cleared his throat that Reed realized they were holding up the line in front of the cashier's cage. Reluctantly he released Clare, but needing to maintain the contact with her, he reached for her hand.

"Where to now?" he asked.

Clare tugged her hand free from his and slipped her arm around his waist, leaning her head against his shoulder. "How about the roulette table? I'm rich, you know."

Reed wasn't quite sure what to make of the woman in his arms. He had trouble believing this was the same one who sat so primly behind the front desk of the Tullue library, handing out lectures for overdue books. Her eyes were bright and happy, and for the life of him, he couldn't look away.

It was doubtful Clare was drunk. She'd claimed to have had only one glass of champagne and he couldn't recall her having more. If anyone was drunk, it was him, but not on alcohol. He was tipsy on spending this time with Clare, of touching her as though he'd been doing so for years.

"Clare," he asked, pulling her aside and leading her away from the milling gamblers. His eyes searched hers; he was almost afraid this couldn't be happening.

She smiled up at him and blinked, not understanding the question in his eyes.

He didn't know how to voice his concern without sounding ridiculous. It wasn't as though he could ask her if she realized what she was doing. This wasn't the woman he'd loved from afar all these years.

The amusement drained from her eyes. "I'm embarrassing you, aren't I?"

"No," he denied quickly.

"I…shouldn't have hugged you like that? It was presumptuous of me and—"

"No." He pressed his finger over her lips, stopping her because he couldn't bear to hear what she was saying. He'd dreamed of her in exactly this way, gazing up at him with joy and happiness. He had yearned to hold her, kiss her, make love to her, but never thought it possible.

She pressed her hand to her cheek. "I don't know what came over me… I seem to be doing and saying the most nonsensical things."

Reed could think of no way of assuring her and so he did what came naturally. He kissed her.

Reed had longed to do exactly this for years, and

now that the dream was reality, it was as though he'd completely lost control of his senses.

His lips didn't court or coax or tease hers, nor was he gentle. The need in him was too great to bridle, consequently his kiss was filled with a desire so hot, so earthy he feared he'd consume her.

Taken by surprise, Clare moaned, and in an instant her lips parted to him. Dear heaven, she was even sweeter than he ever imagined. Kissing her was like sampling warm honey. She opened to him without restraint, holding nothing back. Her tongue met his, tentatively at first, as though she were unaccustomed to such passionate exchanges, then curled and shyly mated with his. Reed was convinced she hadn't a clue as to how blatantly provocative she was.

It cost him everything to break off the kiss. When he did, his breathing was labored and harsh.

Clare's eyes remained closed, and her sigh rolled softly over his face like the lazy waters of a peaceful river.

"Is…is kissing you always this good?" she asked softly, her lashes fluttering open. She gazed up at him with wide, innocent eyes. Reed couldn't find the words to answer.

"The rumors must be true," she said next, under her breath.

"What rumors?"

From the way her gaze widened and shot to him, it was clear she hadn't realized she'd spoken aloud.

"Tell me," he insisted.

"They say…women can't resist you."

Reed didn't know whether to laugh or fume. It was equally difficult to tell if Clare meant it as a compliment or an insult. His indecision must have revealed itself, because she stood on her tiptoes and planted a soft kiss across his lips. "Thank you."

"For what?"

Surprised, she glanced up at him. "For showing me how good kissing can be."

She didn't know? That seemed utterly impossible. His mind was reeling with a long series of questions he longed to ask, but before a single one had taken shape on his lips, Clare was moving away from him, passing through the crowd and heading for the roulette wheel.

Reed found the noise and the cigarette smoke in the casino irritating. He wasn't overly fond of crowds, either, but he gladly endured it all for the opportunity to be with Clare.

By the time he reached her, she was sitting at the table and had plunked down two twenty-five-dollar chips, betting on the red.

When she won, she whirled around to be sure he was there. Reed grinned and, collecting her winnings, Clare dutifully stuffed the chips into her purse.

"What else is there?" she said, looking around. "I feel so lucky."

"Craps," he suggested, although he wasn't certain he could explain the various rules of the game to her within a short amount of time.

It was a complicated but fun game. Clare was much too impatient to be delayed with anything as mundane as instructions on how to play.

There was plenty of room at the dice table, so Reed decided to play himself, thinking that would be the best way to help Clare learn.

It took a few moments for them to exchange their cash

for chips, and Reed noticed how Clare's eyes gleamed with excitement. If she continued to look at him like that, he'd have trouble keeping his mind on the action. Unfortunately craps was one game that required he keep his wits about him.

He placed his bet and Clare followed his lead. They managed to stay about even, until it became Clare's turn to roll the dice. She hesitated when she noticed Reed had placed a large wager.

"I thought you said you felt lucky," he reminded her.

"I know, but..."

"Just throw the dice, lady," said an elderly gentleman holding a bottle of imported beer. "He looks like he knows what he's doing."

"He might, but I don't," she muttered, and threw the dice with enough force for them to bounce against the far end of the table.

"Ten, the hard way," the attendant shouted.

Players gathered around the table and the money was flowing fast and furiously. Reed could see that Clare was having trouble keeping tabs on what was happening. She amazed him. She hadn't a clue of what she was doing, yet she ladled out her chips without a qualm, betting freely as though she were sitting on a fat bank account. He would never have guessed that she could be so carefree and unbridled by convention.

As he suspected, Clare was a natural, and within the next several rolls, she had every number covered. Soon the entire table was raking in the chips. The shouts and cheers caught the attention of the other gamblers, and shortly afterward there wasn't a single inch of available space around the table.

"How much longer?" Clare asked, looking anxious.

"As long as you can keep from rolling a seven," Reed told her. He didn't know how much money they'd won, but he ventured a guess that it was well into the hundreds.

"Don't even say it," the same older man who'd been drinking a beer chastised him. "She's making us money hand over fist."

"You mean everyone is winning?" Clare said, looking down the table. It seemed everyone was staring at her, waiting expectantly.

"Everyone," Reed concurred.

"All right." She tossed the dice and let out a triumphant cry when she made her point. Chips were issued by the attendants, and Clare wiped her hands against her hips before reaching for the dice again.

"I like this game."

"We love you, sweetheart," someone shouted from the other end of the table.

Clare hesitated, then blew her admirer a kiss before rolling the dice once more. Even before Reed could see what she'd tossed, there was a chorus of happy shouts.

"I can smell money," a man said, squeezing his way into the table, tossing down five one-hundred-dollar bills.

A cocktail waitress came by, taking orders, but everyone seemed so caught up in the action that no one seemed to notice. There was apparently some hullabaloo going on with the pit boss. Clare had held the dice for nearly thirty minutes and it went without saying that the casino was losing a lot of money.

"How am I doing?" she asked, looking to him, her eyes bright and clear. "Oh, heavens, I'm thirsty. Could I get something to drink...something diet."

Reed got the cocktail waitress's attention and ordered a soft drink for himself while he was at it.

On Clare's next roll she hit a seven. After a low murmur of regret she was given a round of hearty applause. Grinning, she curtsied and with her drink in her hand turned away from the table.

"Clare," Reed called after her.

She turned at the sound of his voice. "You forgot your chips."

Since he'd been collecting them for her, it wasn't unreasonable for her to think she'd won for everyone else and not herself. The attendant had colored up the chips for them both and Reed handed her nine black chips.

"I only made nine chips?" she asked, bewildered.

"The black chips are worth a hundred dollars."

For a moment, her mouth opened and closed as though she'd lost the ability to speak. "They're a hundred dollars *each?*"

Reed didn't know it was possible for a woman's eyes to grow so wide. He nodded.

"In other words, I just made *nine hundred dollars?*"

Reed smiled and nodded again. He'd won considerably more, and there were others at the table who'd walked away with several thousand dollars.

"Nine hundred dollars," she repeated slowly, pressing her one hand over her heart and fanning her face with the other. "I need to sit down. Oh, my goodness… all that money."

Reed slipped his arm around her waist and, realizing she was trembling, steered her toward the coffee shop.

"Nine hundred dollars," she continued repeating. "That's almost a thousand dollars. I made almost a thousand dollars throwing dice."

The hostess seated them and Reed ordered coffee for them both.

Clare glanced anxiously around her. "Do you think we should place this in a safety deposit box? I remember reading something about the hotel having one when we registered. Nine hundred dollars…oh, my goodness, that doesn't even include the two hundred I won earlier at the blackjack table. Oh… I won at roulette, too. If we didn't have to leave in the morning, I'd be rich."

Reed enjoyed listening to her enthusiasm. He enjoyed everything about Clare Gilroy. He fully intended to savor every minute, knowing it would need to last him all his life.

"Let's go for a walk," he suggested once they'd finished. He needed the fresh air, and the crowds were beginning to get to him. Clare would enjoy walking the Strip and it would do them both good.

She followed him outside, keeping her handbag close to her body, conscious, he was sure, of the large amount of cash she was carrying with her.

Reed had never known a time when the Strip wasn't clogged with traffic. Horns honked with impatience, and cars raced through yellow lights. Although it was well after the sun had set, the streets were bright with the flickering lights of the casinos. The sidewalks were crowded with gamblers aimlessly wandering from one casino to another like robots.

It seemed natural for Reed to slip his arm around Clare's waist and keep her close to his side. She might believe he was doing so to protect her from pickpockets, but Reed knew better. If he was to have only this one night with her to treasure, then he wanted to make the most of every minute. He wasn't fool enough to believe she wouldn't return to Jack Kingston the minute they were back in Tullue.

* * *

The evening was bright and clear and the stars were out in an abundant display. A hum of excitement filled the streets as they strolled along, their arms wrapped around each other. Neither one of them seemed to be in a rush. Reed had lost track of the time, but he imagined it was still early.

"I love Las Vegas," Clare said, looking up at him with wide-eyed wonder. "I never knew there was any place in the world like this."

Reed loved Vegas too, but for none of the reasons Clare would understand. For the first time he could hold and kiss the woman he loved.

"Where are we going?" she asked, after a moment.

Reed smiled to himself, then unable to resist, bent down and kissed her nose. "I'm taking you to my favorite volcano."

Reed hadn't been kidding. He did take her to see a volcano. It was the most amazing thing Clare had ever seen in her life. They'd stood outside The Mirage, a huge hotel and casino, in front of a large waterfall adorned with dozens of palm trees in what resembled a tropical paradise. After a few moments Clare heard a low rumbling sound that was followed by a loud roar. Fire shot into the sky, and she gasped as the flames raced down the rushing waterfall and formed a lake of fire in the pool in front of where they were standing. It was the most extraordinary thing Clare had ever seen.

Speechless to explain all she was feeling, Clare looked up to Reed and was surprised when she felt twin tears roll down her cheeks. She wasn't a woman given easily to emotion. One moment she was agog with wonder, and the next she was unexplainably weeping.

Reed studied her, and a frown slowly formed. She wished she knew what to tell him, how to explain, but she was at a loss to put all she was feeling into words. "It's just all so beautiful," she whispered.

Reed's eyes darkened before he slowly lowered his mouth to hers. She wanted him to kiss her again from the moment he had earlier. She needed him to kiss her so she'd know if what she'd experienced had been real. Nothing had ever been so good.

The instant his mouth, so warm and wet, met hers, she had her answer. It didn't get any more real than this. Any more potent, either.

Clare couldn't very well claim she'd never been kissed, but no one had ever done it the way Reed did. No one had ever evoked the wealth of sensation he did. She felt as though she were the volcano at The Mirage just moments before it erupted, just before the rumblings began. If he continued, she'd soon be on fire, too, the heat spilling over into a fiery pool.

His mouth moved over hers, molding her lips to his with a heat and need that seared her senses.

A frightening kind of excitement took hold of her, yet she wasn't afraid. Far from it. In Reed she found the man her heart had hungered to meet all these years. A man who generated romantic dreams. In her heart she knew Reed was a man of honor and he would never purposely do anything to hurt her. Nor would he take advantage of her.

She opened her mouth to him, pressing her tongue forward, wanting to participate in the delicious things they'd done earlier. Their tongues met and touched, and she responded shyly at first, then after gaining confidence, more boldly. Their mouths twisted and angled against each other, as they sought a deeper contact.

Reed's breathing came hard and fast as the kiss deepened and demanded more of her. She gave freely, unable to deny him anything. Clare's heart was banging like a huge fist against her ribs. Her own breathing was becoming more labored and needy.

"Clare…" Reed groaned and broke away from her as if he needed to put some distance between them.

"I'm…sorry," she whispered, burying her head against his shoulder. She'd never been so brazen with a man, and she couldn't account for her actions now. It was as if she were living in a dream world, and none of this was real.

His breathing was harsh as it had been earlier, his hands buried deep in her hair.

"Say something," she whispered desperately. "I need to know I'm not making an idiot of myself. Tell me you're not sorry… I need to know that."

"Sorry," he repeated gruffly. "Never…there'll be plenty of time for regrets later." With that he kissed her again with a hunger that left her stunned.

They were kissing on a busy sidewalk and no one seemed to notice, no one seemed to care. People walked around them without comment.

Clare's shoulders were heaving when they broke apart. She raised her hand and her fingers traced the warm, moist seam of his lips. "I'll never regret this, I promise."

His gaze narrowed as though he wasn't sure he could believe her. Not until then did Clare realize that he assumed she was still involved with Jack. A cold chill rushed over her arms as she thought of the other man.

He seemed a million years removed from where she was now. It seemed impossible that she'd been involved with him. Reed was everything she'd ever wanted Jack to be.

"It's over between Jack and me. I told him before we left that I didn't want to have anything more to do with him again, and I meant it."

Reed's eyes hardened.

"I've squandered three years on him, and it was a waste of precious time. I'm never going back…the only way for me to move now is forward." She looped her arms around Reed's neck, unwilling to waste another moment talking about Jack. She was in his arms and nothing had ever felt more right.

"Clare, then this is all because of your argument with Jack. You're…"

"No. This is because of you. I can't believe you were there all along and I was so blind. Kiss me again. Please, just kiss me."

His hands gripped her wrists as though he intended to break away from her, but he hesitated when their gazes met. "It's true? It's over with Jack?"

She nodded. "Completely."

"Then that explains it."

"Explains what?"

He didn't answer her question with words. Everything she'd ever heard about Reed claimed he was a man of deed, and in this case the rumors were right. He wrapped his arms around her waist and lifted her from the ground until their faces were level with each other. Clare met his gaze evenly, confidently.

Clare had anticipated several reactions from him, but not the one he gave her. He closed his eyes, and she noticed how tense his jaw went, as though he were ter-

ribly angry. Before she could ask, he set her firmly on
the ground and backed away from her.

"What's wrong?" she asked, her voice barely above
a whisper.

He stared at her for several seconds.

"Reed?"

His shoulders slumped as though he were admitting
defeat before he gently took her in his arms and rubbed
his chin across the top of her head. "You don't want to
know."

"But I do," she countered, not understanding him.
At first he appeared angry and then relieved. Wanting
to reassure him, she locked her arms around his waist
and squeezed. The sweet pleasure she received from
being in his arms was worth the risk of his rejection.

"Clare…"

"Tell me," she pleaded.

"All right," he said, bracing his hands against her
shoulders and easing himself away from her. "Since
you're so keen to know, then I'll tell you. You tempt me
too much." He said the words as though he were confessing a crime, as though he hated himself for even
having admitted it. Having said that, he turned and
moved away from her.

"But I want you, too," she said as she rushed after
him. She blushed as she said it, knowing it was true,
but desperate not to have him block her out. She'd never
admitted such a thing to a man in her life. Reed had
stirred awake dormant needs, and she wasn't going to
allow him to walk away from her. Not now. Not when
they'd found each other.

Reed hesitated and glanced down on her. Before,
she'd been so confident he was experiencing everything

she was, now she wasn't certain of anything. This feeling of separation was intolerable. She couldn't bear it.

"What is it you want from me?" he demanded, his jaw tight and proud.

Clare hadn't had time to give the matter thought. "I… I don't know."

"I do."

"Good," she said, sighing, "you can tell me. All I know is I feel incredible…better than I have in years. I'm not the same person I was a few hours ago and I like the new me. I've always been so practical and so proper, and when we're together I don't feel the need for any of that."

"If I didn't know better I'd swear you were drunk."

"But I'm not."

"I know."

He didn't sound pleased. If anything, he was weary, as if he weren't sure he could trust her, let alone himself. To Clare's way of thinking, paradise beckoned and nothing blocked the path but their own doubts and inhibitions.

Then it dawned on her, and the weight of her discovery was so heavy that she nearly sank to the cement. She'd always been the good girl. Reed didn't want to become involved with someone like her, not when he could have his pick of any woman in town. She was dowdy compared to women he'd known. Dowdy and plain.

"Whatever you're thinking is wrong," he commented with his uncanny ability to read her thoughts. "Tell me what it is, Clare."

She could feel his frown even with her eyes lowered. "I know what's really wrong…only you didn't want to tell me. I'm… I'm nothing like the women you're accustomed to being with. I'm the bookworm, the do-gooder."

His scoffing laugh effectively denied that.

"Then why are you looking at me like that?" she demanded

"We have nothing in common," he said, once his sharp laughter faded away.

"We share everything," she countered. "We're close in age...we were raised in the same town."

"Different school, different cultures."

Clare wasn't about to let him negate her argument. "We both like to read."

"You live in the city, I'm miles out in the country."

"So? It's a small town. You make Tullue sound like a suburb of New York. We know the same people, and share friends."

"Gary is my only Anglo friend."

"What about Erin? What about me?"

He grinned as though he found her argument silly, and that irritated Clare.

"You're talented and sensitive," she continued.

"You don't know that."

"Ah, but I do."

And he *was* talented and sensitive. He'd known she was suffering from a headache, and been gentle and concerned. He'd been aware of her pain when no one else was aware she was suffering. As for the talented part, she didn't want to admit she hadn't seen any of the totem poles he'd carved, but Erin had told her he was exceptionally talented, and she was willing to trust her friend's assessment.

Reed's eyes, so dark and clear, remained expressionless, and Clare knew that he'd already made up his mind about them, and it wasn't likely he'd budge. To Reed, they were worlds apart and would always remain so. He was right, she supposed, but in this time together, in this town, they'd managed to bridge those differences. If it happened in Vegas, they could make it happen in Tullue.

There was something else, something she hadn't considered, something Reed hadn't said but insinuated. Her heart started to beat heavily. Her cheeks filled with color so hot her skin burned.

"Clare?"

She whirled away from him and pressed her hands to her face, unable to bear looking at him. Never had she been more embarrassed.

"What is it?"

"You think…" She couldn't make herself say it.

"What?" he demanded gruffly.

Dear heaven, it was too humiliating to say out loud. Reed guided her away from the pedestrians, and they stood in the shadow of a streetlight next to one of the casino's massive parking lots.

"Clare," he repeated impatiently.

"You think… I'm looking for casual sex…that I'm after a one-night stand." It made her sick to her stomach to voice the words. Even worse it seemed that all the evidence was stacked against her. She'd been nothing less than wanton.

It had started earlier at Gary and Erin's wedding ceremony. Clare hadn't been able to take her eyes off Reed. Later when they'd first gambled, she'd practically thrown herself into his arms. She kissed him back, seeking more and more of him until she experienced an achy restlessness.

After the things she'd done, after the things she'd said, Clare would never be able to look Reed in the eyes again. He must think terrible things of her, and she wouldn't blame him.

"No, Clare," he said softly, "I wasn't thinking anything of the sort."

She chanced to look in his direction, unsure if she could believe him. She suspected he was only saying that to be kind.

"You're attracted to me?"

"I'd say it was a whole lot more than attracted," she said, having trouble finding her voice, and even more trouble believing he was so amazed. "It isn't just being a part of Erin's wedding, either. I felt it when we were dancing... I knew then...you were going to be someone important in my life. I feel it now even stronger than before. I've been waiting for you all my life, Reed."

"Clare, don't."

No one bothered to listen to her, no one bothered to allow her to voice her thoughts, and it angered her that Reed would be like all the rest. "Would you kindly stop interrupting me?" she said sharply.

He straightened as if caught unprepared for her small outburst of temper. "All right. Go ahead and finish what you want to say."

Now that she had his full attention, she wasn't sure she could. "You think that because I'm here for my best friend's wedding that my head's in the clouds and I don't have the sense the Lord gave me, but you're wrong."

"I'd call it a temporary lack of good judgment."

"I happen to believe otherwise...and my judgment's sound, thank you very much," she continued, fuming. "I'm as sane and sober as the next man." No sooner had the words escaped her lips than a man stumbled out from between two bushes, obviously drunk. Clare blinked and shook her head.

"As sober as the next man?" Reed teased.

"You might think it's because I've won all this money… I bet you do. You might even think I've lost touch with reality. I'm carrying over a thousand dollars in my purse and I'd hand it back to the casino in a heartbeat if you'd listen to me."

"I don't advise you to make the offer."

She was amusing Reed, and that infuriated her. "Maybe we can talk when you take me seriously. I'm baring my soul here and you seem to find it amusing. Let me assure you, Reed Tonasket, I'm not pleased."

He grinned then, and Clare swore she'd never seen a broader smile. He leaned forward and kissed her nose and edged away slowly, as if he wanted to kiss a whole lot more of her.

"My proper librarian is back," he said.

"I'm serious, Reed. I'd gladly give all the money I won tonight if…" She hesitated.

"If what?" His eyes were dark and serious, and she was so enthralled with him that she sighed and held her hand against the side of his face.

"Never mind," she said, turning away from him, walking purposely down the sidewalk. He wouldn't understand, and she couldn't bear to say it.

"Clare, tell me." His long-legged stride quickly outdistanced her. Soon he was walking backward in front of her.

She lowered her eyes, close to tears because it was impossible to explain what she meant in mere words.

He stopped abruptly and caught her by the shoulders. His eyes, so dark and serious, studied her. "Tell me."

Her teeth gnawed at her lower lip. "I waited three long years…thinking, hoping Jack was the one. I was so stupid, so blind to his faults, and all along you were there and I didn't know. And now…" She stopped, unable to continue.

"Now what?" he coaxed.

"It sounds so crazy. You'll think I've gone off the deep end, and maybe I have, but I don't want to lose what we've found. I'm afraid everything will be different in the morning, and more so when we return home. I couldn't bear that, and the only way I can think to keep hold of this is to…" She hesitated again.

Reed exhaled and brought her into the warm shelter of his arms. "I don't want to lose this, either. If you know of a way for us to keep this feeling, tell me."

Clare's fingers caressed his jaw line, lingering there. "It's crazy."

"It's been that kind of day."

"People will think we've gone nuts."

"Folks have been talking about me for a long time. Gossip doesn't concern me."

"Really?" She raised hope-filled eyes to him.

"Really," he assured her.

"Then I have the perfect solution."

"Oh?"

Her heart felt as if it would burst wide open. "You could marry me, Reed Tonasket."

Four

Clare hadn't watched for his reaction, but he stood frozen, as if she hadn't spoken. A long moment of hushed, perhaps shocked, silence followed her words.

"That's the reason you were mouthing the words along with Erin," he stated softly. "You want so desperately to be married."

"No," she said, and shook her head. If he were to accept the validity of her words he had to know the full truth. "You're the reason."

"Me?" He sounded incredulous.

"I know it sounds crazy... I can imagine what you're thinking, but I swear it was you. It was dancing with you, sitting on the plane next to you for two solid hours, and feeling peaceful for the first time in weeks. It was seeing you with Gary outside the wedding chapel and realizing I was going to fall in love with you. I've never felt anything like this before, and... I don't know how to explain it. Something happened during Gary and Erin's wedding, I felt it so strongly, and I thought you must have too."

Reed remained silent.

"You mouthed the words along with Gary," she said in gentle reminder.

"Clare…"

"If you're going to argue with me, then I don't want to hear it. Just listen, please, just listen. When we danced… it was as if we'd been together all our lives. You can't tell me you didn't feel it… I know you did."

"I don't think either of us can trust what we're feeling."

"I trust it. I trust you."

He didn't say anything, and Clare suspected he shared her faith in what was going on between them, only he wasn't willing to admit it.

"It's because you've broken up with Jack," he challenged. His eyes hardened as he mentioned the other man's name. "You're feeling insecure and lonely."

Although she knew Reed was sincere, she couldn't keep from laughing. "I've never felt more confident of having made a right decision in my life. I don't want to marry Jack. I want to marry you, Reed Tonasket. If it were in my power I'd do so this very night."

"Clare…"

"Shh, take me back to the hotel."

Neither of them said a word as they walked back. Clare was collecting her thoughts, collecting her arguments. She felt almost giddy with love. Reed must think she was crazy, and she couldn't blame him; she felt completely and totally unlike herself. Normally she was cautious, carefully studying each action, analyzing situations and events before making a move. This time with Reed felt completely right. Her judgment wasn't shadowed by a single doubt, she knew with a clarity that defied definition what she wanted—and she wanted him. Not for this one night, not for these short hours, but for always. Everything she'd ever longed for from Jack was in Reed.

They entered the hotel and by tacit agreement walked side by side through the casino and headed for the elevator. Neither of them spoke, but the instant the doors closed, Clare was in Reed's arms. She didn't know who reached for whom. Their hunger was explosive, their kisses urgent and crazed.

A bell chimed as the elevator stopped and the doors noiselessly glided open. "Where are we going?" Clare asked. Her question came between heavy breaths as she struggled to regain her equilibrium.

At first it was as if Reed hadn't heard her. He sighed and then said, "My room." He studied her as though he expected her to argue.

Swallowing her disappointment, she nodded.

But he didn't leave the elevator. "If we do go to my room, we're going to end up making love." His gaze narrowed as though he anticipated his words would alter her decision.

Again she nodded, unsure that she could verbalize her agreement. "I want to make love with you," she said, after a moment. "Someday...perhaps soon, I'd like to have children with you."

Reed froze, and she realized she'd told him the wrong thing. The worst thing she could have possibly said. He wasn't looking to make a commitment. He was looking to satisfy their physical need for each other.

"Don't worry, Reed," she whispered, feeling wretched. If she was honest it was what she wanted too. "You don't have to marry me."

He studied her, his eyes dark and unreadable.

"I understand," she said, having trouble maintaining her composure. After waiting three fruitless years for Jack, she should have realized no man would be willing to commit himself on the basis of a two-day relationship.

Decisively Reed stepped forward and pushed the button that closed the elevator doors. Without a pause he pushed another, then he turned back to her and reached for her hand.

"You're sure this is what you want?" The question was gruff, as though he were angry.

She nodded, although she hadn't a clue what she was agreeing to. "Wh-where are we going?"

His gaze shot to her as if he suspected she were joking. "To the wedding chapel. If we're going to have children, they'll have my name even before we set out creating them."

Clare must be out of her mind, Reed reasoned. Clare nothing, he was the one who'd gone stark, raving mad. He couldn't help believing he was taking advantage of her. She wasn't drunk, but she wasn't herself, either. She wasn't impulsive and while he wanted to believe she was sincere, he strongly suspected this was a reaction to her break-up with Jack.

There were a hundred reasons why they shouldn't marry and only one possible excuse why they should. He loved her and he was far too weak to turn down what she was offering. By all that was right he should escort her to her room, give her a peck on the cheek, and put an end to this lunacy.

In the morning, he knew as sure as anything, she'd regret what they'd done. Not so much a doubt crossed his heart. By noon she'd be pleading with him to quietly divorce her. Even knowing what was bound to transpire, it didn't matter.

If he was battling with doubts about marrying her, his feelings were muddied by his earlier intentions. He fully expected to make love to her when she agreed to go to his room. He hadn't hidden his intentions, nor had he disguised them. He'd been as open and forthright as he knew how to be. But when she'd agreed to make love, he'd witnessed the flash of pain move in and out of her eyes. He was treating her the same way Jack had, using her, taking advantage of her vulnerability.

Loving her the way he did, it wasn't in Reed to hurt her. Even acknowledging their marriage was doomed wasn't enough to turn his course. One thing alone had cemented his determination—the look of love in Clare's eyes. Her gentle acceptance of him forged his resolve. She'd been willing to give herself to him without asking anything in return. She'd even gone so far as to tell him she wanted his children.

Earlier that evening Reed had listened to Gary mention his feelings about starting a family. His friend had claimed he went mushy inside every time he thought about Erin carrying his baby. At the time, Reed had listened and found himself mildly amused.

He understood his friend's feelings now. Having Clare mention a child, their child, had a curious effect upon his heart. He wasn't a man given to sentimentality. Nor was he visionary, but the thought of Clare, her belly swollen with his child, had done incredulous things to his heart.

He wanted this baby, who had yet to be conceived,

more than he'd thought it was possible for a man to want anything.

His feelings were tempered, he realized because he'd never known what it meant to be a part of a traditional family. That privilege had been denied him almost from birth. He recalled almost nothing of his life before he'd gone to live with his grandfather, a widower.

The opportunity to give to his own child what he'd been denied was more than he could resist. This child who was nothing more than his heart's desire. He'd love this baby Clare would give him with the same intensity with which he loved his wife.

His wife.

Reed's mind faltered over the words. Perhaps fate was playing a cruel trick on him, leading him to believe there was hope Clare would ever come to love him. He wasn't fool enough to believe she did now. It wasn't possible—she was in love with an idea, a dream. He happened to be conveniently at hand. Knowing that, though, wasn't enough to deter him from the marriage.

Las Vegas was set up for quick, convenient marriages, but it took over an hour to make all the necessary arrangements. Reed, who was normally a tolerant man, found himself growing impatient. Although Clare was the picture of tolerance, Reed couldn't make himself believe she wouldn't change her mind later. By tomorrow at this time they'd be back in Tullue, and he knew to the bottom of his soul that everything would be different.

"It won't take much longer," Clare assured him, smiling peacefully at him as he paced the chapel.

The ceremony itself was only a formality in Reed's mind. As far as he was concerned, they'd stated their vows earlier with Gary and Erin. The service was necessary for legal purposes. Without realizing what he'd done, he'd married Clare in his heart a few hours earlier.

After the wedding was completed, Reed gently kissed Clare. They'd never spoken of love, and yet they'd each vowed to love each other for as long as they lived. They'd never spoken of the future, yet promised to spend it together. Reed feared their lives were destined to be filled with ironies.

Reed hadn't a clue where this relationship would lead him, but looking down on Clare with her eyes bright with joy, he realized he was willing to fight to the death to give her the happiness she deserved.

"I'll buy you a wedding ring later," Reed promised after the ceremony.

It seemed to take hours before everything could be arranged, but Clare hadn't minded. While Reed had impatiently paced the chapel, she'd been content, knowing they had the rest of their lives.

When it came time to exchange rings Reed had given her a large turquoise ring as a wedding band. One he'd worn himself. He'd slipped it onto her finger and it was so large, it threatened to fall off her hand. Clare had loved it immediately.

"Would you mind terribly if I had this one sized instead?" she'd asked.

"Wouldn't you prefer a diamond?"

Smiling, she looked to him and slowly shook her head. "No, I'd like to keep this ring…that is if you don't object to my having it." The ring was obviously designed for a man, but Clare saw a delicate beauty in it. Since there was little that was traditional about this marriage anyway, she didn't feel obligated to submit to convention with a diamond.

"All I have is yours," Reed assured her.

"And all I have is yours," she echoed, finding serenity in his words. Tears gathered in the corners of her eyes. She didn't know what was the matter with her, why she would give in to the weakness of tears when her heart felt as though it would burst wide open with a joy so strong it seemed impossible to hold inside.

"Shall we celebrate?" Reed asked as they left the chapel. "Champagne? Anything you want."

"Anything?" she teased, holding his gaze. "All I want is you, Reed Tonasket," she whispered.

His eyes brightened as he leaned down and kissed her. His kiss was gentle, with none of the urgency or hunger of their exchanges earlier, almost as if he were afraid of hurting her.

She'd always found it difficult to read him, but Clare had no trouble now. Reed was incapable of hiding how much he wanted to make love, but at the same time he restrained himself as if he were afraid of frightening her with the strength of his need.

"My room or yours?" she asked, her voice as soft as satin.

"Mine" came his decisive reply.

Reed led the way to the elevator, but he didn't kiss her. It was as though he were unwilling to cloud her judgment. After he opened the door to his hotel room, he turned and effortlessly lifted Clare into his arms.

She smiled up at him, feeling a bit shy and shaky, but never more confident.

His gaze held hers. "I'll always be who I am," he said in a low, almost harsh voice. "There'll be people who'll look down on our marriage, people who'll make snide remarks about you marrying a Native American. If you want out, the time is now."

Her arms circled his neck and she angled her mouth over his, kissing him with a thoroughness that left her grateful she was supported by his arms. "I'll always be who I am," she answered, choosing to echo his words. "There'll be those who'll disapprove of you marrying outside the tribe. If you're going to change your mind, I suggest you do it now, because after tonight there'll be no turning back."

Reed's chest lifted in a sharp intake of breath, and she took advantage of the moment to kiss him once more. From that point forward their kisses were no longer patient or gentle, but fiery and urgent, as if they had to cram a lifetime of loving into a single night.

Clare couldn't remember Reed setting her on the bed, but he had. His large hands were having difficulty with the tiny satin-covered buttons that stretched down the front of her dress.

"I'll do it," she promised, even as she worked at the fabric of his shirt. They kissed, their mouths straining against each other while she struggled to get out of her dress and finally abandoned the effort.

Reed grew impatient. "Clare, dear heaven, let's get out of these clothes first," he said, reluctantly breaking away from her. He sat upright on the mattress, his shoulders heaving. She offered him a slow, sweet smile as she kicked the shoes from her feet.

"Be careful, Clare, I'm having a hard time slowing this down." His hands worked frantically at the buttons of his shirt. Mesmerized, Clare was incapable of doing anything more than study him, although she was as eager to dispense with her clothes as he was to have her out of them.

"That's the most romantic thing anyone's ever said to me," she whispered. Reed made her feel beautiful and desirable, and for that she loved him with all her heart.

She shouldn't be wasting this time, but she found far more delight in watching her husband.

Her husband.

Her heart swelled with pride and love. She had no regrets for the time wasted with Jack, not when it had led her to this man and this moment.

His shirt came off first, revealing a powerful torso. Until that moment, Clare hadn't realized how muscular Reed was. He wasn't like other men, who made a point of revealing their brawn.

Reaching out, she ran the tips of her fingers across his broad shoulders, reveling in the powerful display of strength. His skin was hot to the touch, and she flattened her palm against the smooth texture and exhaled sharply, wanting him.

"Do you need help?" he asked, turning questioning eyes to her. The room was illuminated by a soft light. Clare would like to have believed it radiated from the moon, but more than likely it was generated by the brilliant lights that decorated the Strip.

Not waiting for her reply, he bent over her and kissed her deeply, while she impatiently worked free the last of the maddening buttons.

Reed helped her to sit up, then peeled the dress from her shoulders, carefully setting it aside. Clare removed her camisole and the rest of her underthings herself, revealing none of the care Reed had with her clothing. Soon she was completely bare before him. She half expected to feel shy with him, but the thought was pushed from her mind when she read the appreciation and awe in his eyes.

His hands were gentle when he reached for her. His kiss was gentle, too, and incredibly sweet. He pulled back the sheets and gently placed her atop the mattress and then looked down on her, his gaze filled with warmth and love.

Clare's heart felt like it would explode with love. She could think of no way of telling him all that she was feeling.

He inhaled, his eyes holding her. "I don't want to frighten you."

"You couldn't," she whispered, stretching her arms up to him.

He came down on the bed beside her, and gently brushed the hair from her face. "You're so incredibly beautiful."

Clare briefly closed her eyes to the heady sensation his words produced. "You are, too," she whispered.

He kissed her then with such intensity that she felt her breasts tighten. "Reed," she pleaded, not knowing, even as she spoke, what she was asking.

He brought his mouth back to hers and kissed her again and again with a hunger that fueled their need. She was hot, feverish with desire until she whimpered, needing him so desperately. "Please," she begged, "don't make me wait any longer."

His lovemaking brought her such keen satisfaction that she thought she would faint with the sheer intensity of it. She ran her hands over his face, whimpering softly. They were both silent as though they no longer needed words in order to communicate. He kissed her several times, soft kisses, a gentle meeting of their lips, and gathered her fully in his arms.

Clare nestled her face in his neck and closed her eyes, unbelievably tired, unbelievably content. Everything within her life was complete. She'd found love, a love so strong it would withstand everything. She had found her home at last.

Reed lay awake long after Clare slept. He held her in his embrace, not wanting to miss one precious moment of this incredible night.

Idly he ran his chin across the top of Clare's crown, his thoughts traveling at lightning speed into the future and what it would hold for them. Closing his eyes, he decided not to court trouble. They would face that soon enough.

Reed had always lived on the fringes of acceptance in Tullue. The town and he'd maintained something of an armed truce with one another. That was bound to change now because of Clare. If they were going to make their marriage work, something he badly wanted, then he was going to need to make his peace. But that peace would have to be made with himself first, and it was a commodity he'd always found in short supply.

Reed slept, waking sometime later. He couldn't see what time it was without disrupting Clare, and he didn't want to risk that. She slept contentedly in his arms in the sweetest torture he'd ever experienced. His first thought was that he wanted to make love to her again, then chastised himself for being so greedy. They had time, to make love before they left for the airport. He would let his wife sleep.

His wife.

Reed felt a smile touch the edges of his mouth. He liked the sound of the word.

Clare amazed him. She was warm and generous and more woman than he'd ever hoped to find. Unable to resist, Reed kissed her forehead, and pushed aside her tousled hair.

Clare's eyes fluttered open and she yawned, stretching her arms above her head. "What time is it?" she asked with half-closed eyes.

"I don't know," he whispered, "your head is on my watch arm."

She scooted closer to his side and Reed bent his elbow so that he could read the dial. "A little after three," he told her.

"Good," she whispered, lifting her head so their eyes met in the dark.

"Good?"

The room was dimly lit, but Reed had no trouble reading the heat in her gaze. Slowly she lowered her mouth to his and kissed him until his breath was quick and shallow.

Their need for each other was as great as it had been earlier, which surprised Reed. He'd never felt more drained, or more complete than with Clare. That his body would be so eager for her again was something of a surprise.

When they'd finished, Clare's mouth sought his in a gentle, heady exchange. "Thank you," she whispered.

Reed didn't understand. She was the one who'd un-selfishly *given* to him, yet she was the one offering appreciation. His puzzlement must have shown in his eyes because she traced her finger down the side of his face.

"For loving me...for showing me how beautiful love-making can be."

He went to move, to find a more relaxed position for Clare.

"No," she pleaded, stopping him. "Stay where you are." She purred, closed her eyes and smiled. Within moments she was asleep and Reed found himself dozing off, as well.

This was an incredible woman he'd married.

This was an incredible man she'd married, Clare mused as she stirred awake. Reed was sprawled across the bed, his arms draped from one side of the mattress to the other.

Silently she slipped from the covers and glanced around the room. Her clothes were tossed from one side to the other in silent testimony to their lovemaking. Clare sighed and headed for the bathroom. A long, hot soak in the tub would do her a world of good, and when she was finished, she'd find a special way of waking her husband.

She closed the bathroom door and ran the water, hoping the sound of it wouldn't wake Reed. The hotel didn't offer bubble bath, which Clare would have found heavenly at the moment, but a soak in a tub filled with steaming water was indulgent enough.

She sank gratefully into the tub and was resting her head against the back when a solid knock sounded against the door.

"Come in," she called out lazily.

"I've ordered us some coffee. It's late."

"Late?" Their flight was due to leave at eleven. She hadn't bothered to look at the time. Only on rare occasions did she sleep beyond eight. She'd always been a morning person.

"It's almost nine."

"Oh, my goodness," she said, sitting upright so abruptly that water sloshed over the edge of the tub. "How could we have slept so long?"

The sound of his chuckle came from the other side. "You don't honestly expect me to answer that, do you?"

She reached for a towel and wrapped it around her. "I can't very well wear that dress on the plane.... I'm going to have to get my suitcase from my room."

She came out of the bathroom in a tizzy, gathering her clothes against her stomach as she progressed across the room.

"Relax," Reed said, stopping her. He gripped her by the shoulders and turned her around to face him.

Clare did a double take, startled by the man who stood before her. Reed had dressed, and he wasn't wearing his tuxedo. His hair was combed, not as it had the day before, but into thick braids that flaunted his Native American heritage.

She wasn't expecting to see him like this. Not so soon. And giving a small startled cry, she leaped away from him.

Five

"What's wrong?" Reed demanded.

"N-nothing…you startled me is all. I'll get dressed and be gone in a moment." She was jerking on her clothes, with little concern to how she looked. Her hands were trembling as she hurried about the room, her head spinning. Something was very wrong, and she didn't know how to make it right.

It would have helped if Reed would say something, but he remained obstinately silent. Once she was presentable, she glanced at this man who was now her husband. "I'll need to go to my room."

He nodded, and the dark intensity of his eyes held her immobile.

"I did more than startle you." His words were ripe with incrimination.

Clare froze and closed her eyes, her heart pounding like a sledgehammer against her ribs. "You looked different is all… I wasn't expecting it," she whispered, turning her back to him. She'd always been a little afraid of him. Now, here he was, looking at her the same way he did when he walked into the library. Aloof and bitter. Their marriage, and even more important, her love, hadn't fazed him. Their night together had been a moment out of time. He didn't intend it to last.

"I am different, Clare," he said. "I'm Native American—and that's not going to change."

"I know, but…"

"You'd forgotten that, hadn't you?" His words were softly spoken, so low she had to strain to hear him. He wasn't angry, but there was a certain resolve she heard in him. A certain conviction, as though this was what he'd expected from her from the first.

"It's not what you're thinking," she told him, hearing the panic in her voice. "I don't regret marrying you…. I went into this marriage knowing exactly who you are."

"Did you?" he demanded.

"Yes…of course I did. Can't we talk about this later?" There wasn't time to discuss it, not now when she was barely dressed and they had to rush to catch a flight home. Later they could talk this out rationally when they'd both had time to think matters through. She wanted to kiss Reed before she left, but hesitated. He was tense and she was flustered. It seemed impossibly wrong that so much could have changed between them in so short a time.

"I'll meet you in the lobby," she said, and quietly left the room.

She was grateful their hotel rooms were only two floors apart. Clare didn't meet anyone in the elevator, and when a couple passed her in the hallway, she kept her gaze lowered, certain they must know she'd spent the night in another room.

Her hands wouldn't quit shaking and she had trouble inserting the key card into the lock. Once she was inside the room, she sank onto the end of the crisply made bed and buried her face in her hands.

Everything was so different this morning, so stark. Reed was cold and seemed withdrawn, and Clare feared it was all her fault. Her mind was crowded with all the if only's.

Where had the time gone? While lazing away in the tub, she'd imagined them sitting down to a leisurely breakfast and making necessary plans for their future. A multitude of decisions needed to be made, and Clare was eager for all the changes marriage would bring into their lives.

Now, however, there wasn't time to collect her thoughts, or for that matter anything else. Forcing herself into action, she quickly changed clothes, then hurriedly packed her suitcase, slamming drawers open and closed in her rush to stuff everything back into her suitcase.

Reed was waiting for her in the lobby when she arrived. He took the key from her and set it on the front desk, then removed the lone suitcase from her hand. "The taxi's waiting," he announced without looking at her.

Clare was convinced when they finally arrived at the airport that they'd missed their flight. Most of the passengers had boarded by the time they reached the departing gate. Because they were late, nearly all of the seats had been assigned, and Clare was deeply disappointed to discover they wouldn't be able to sit together.

Everything was going wrong. It wasn't supposed to work out this way. She'd endured the terrible tension between them in the taxi, knowing they'd have a chance to talk later. If nothing more, she could reach for his hand and communicate her commitment to him in nonverbal ways while on the plane. Not being seated together was another mini-disaster in a day that had started out so right and then gone very wrong.

The flight was scheduled to take two hours, and Clare was convinced they'd be two of the longest hours of her life. She was seated by the window, four rows ahead of Reed, making it impossible to see him or communicate with him.

Her thoughts remained confused, and try as she might, she was having trouble naming her fears. She married Reed, but she felt no misgivings over that. She'd known exactly what she was doing when she'd married him and would gladly tell him he owned her heart.

Something had changed that morning when she'd first seen him, and she needed to discern her reaction to him. This wasn't the man she'd married. Overnight he'd turned into the brooding man who'd frequented the library. The one who'd intimidated and confused her. The man she'd fallen in love with and married was sensitive and gentle. He had little in common with the one who wore a bad attitude like a second skin.

Clare looked out the small window of the Boeing 767 to the harsh landscape far below. All that came into view were jagged peaks.

"Did you win anything?" asked a delicate-looking older woman with white hair, seated next to her.

"Ahh…" At first Clare was uncertain the woman was speaking to her. "Yes, I did," she said, feeling a burst of enthusiasm well up inside her. She'd nearly forgotten she was carrying a thousand dollars in winnings in her purse. In cold, hard cash no less. Remembering, she edged her foot closer to her stash, just to reassure herself it was still there.

"I did, too," the spry older woman claimed excitedly. "Five hundred dollars, on bingo."

"Congratulations."

"I generally win at video poker, but not this time. I wasn't going to play bingo. I can do that any time I want at the Senior Citizen Center, so why fly to Vegas to play there? But my eyes gave out on me on poker and I decided to play bingo for a while. I'm certainly glad I did."

"My…husband and I played craps." It was the first time she'd referred to Reed as her husband, and it felt good to say it out loud. "It was my first time in Vegas."

"I fly down at least twice a year myself," the woman continued. "It gives me something to look forward to."

"I imagine we'll be coming back ourselves." Clare would like it if they could plan their anniversary around a trip to Vegas. It seemed fitting that they would.

A smile touched her heart when she realized for the first time that she shared the same wedding day as Erin and Gary. The four of them could make an annual trip out of it.

"I thought you must be traveling alone," Clare's new-found friend added conversationally.

"No, my husband and I overslept. We're lucky to have even made the flight, but unfortunately they didn't have two seats together." *Husband* definitely had a nice ring to it, Clare decided. Before the end of the trip she was going to sound like an old married woman.

The friendly stranger seemed eager to talk, and Clare was grateful to have someone turn her thoughts away from her troubles. It helped pass the time far more quickly. When they landed, Clare was anxious to talk to Reed and clear away the misunderstanding.

Heaven knows they had enough to discuss. They were married, and yet hadn't made the most fundamental decisions regarding their new status. Where they'd live had yet to be decided, although Clare hoped he'd agree to move into town with her. The Skyute reservation was several miles outside of Tullue and would require a lengthy commute for her. She'd feel out of place living there, too, and hoped Reed would understand and accept that.

The plane landed in Seattle shortly after noon. The sky was overcast, the day gray and dreary. Las Vegas had been clear and warm, even at ten in the morning.

Because Clare was seated several rows in front of Reed, she was able to disembark ahead of him. Not wanting to cause a delay to the other passengers, she walked out the jetway and waited just inside the terminal.

"It was nice talking to you," the elderly woman said as she came out of the jetway. She was using a cane and moved much slower than the others.

Reed came out directly behind her, and Clare looked to him eagerly, drinking in the sight of him as though it had been days instead of hours they'd been separated. His eyes met hers, his expression closed, his chiseled features proud and dark.

"How was your flight?" she asked, stepping forward and linking her arm with his.

"Fine," came the clipped response.

From the corner of her eye, Clare caught sight of the older woman who'd sat next to her on the plane. She was staring at Clare and Reed, and her friendly countenance had altered dramatically. The smile had left her eyes and she glared with open disapproval at the two of them.

Clare couldn't believe a look could reveal so much. In the woman's hostile eyes she read prejudice and intolerance. She appeared openly shocked that Clare had chosen to marry a Native American. Never had Clare had anyone look at her quite like that, and it left her feeling tainted, as if she'd done something wrong, as if she were something less than she should be.

Reed was looking down on Clare, and he turned, his gaze following hers. She felt him tense before he stiffly said, "I warned you. You can't say I didn't."

"But…"

"Ignore her. Let's get our luggage."

He was outwardly cool about it, outwardly unconcerned, but Clare knew better; she could almost feel the heat of his anger. Clare didn't blame him, she was furious herself. She longed to march up to the woman and demand an apology. How dare that woman judge her and Reed's love! Clare wanted to remind Reed that the woman's prejudices were long outdated but she could see it would do no good.

Reed remained uncommunicative while they waited at the luggage carousel. Clare was conscious every moment of the woman who'd been so friendly only moments earlier, who now blatantly ignored her and Reed.

It didn't help matters any to realize that within a short time she'd be facing her own relatives and friends with the news of her marriage to a man who was half Skyute Indian.

Her parents were wonderful people and she loved them both dearly, but when it came right down to it, Clare didn't know how they were going to react to Reed.

Her father had never made a point of asking her not to date Native Americans, but then there'd never been any reason for him to approach her with the subject.

Deep in her heart, Clare feared her father might disapprove of her marriage to Reed. He might not come right out and say so, but he'd make his feelings known.

That wouldn't be the case with her mother and her two brothers. They'd have no qualms about telling her what they thought. Her mother, in particular, would assume that Clare had grown so desperate to marry that she'd acted unwisely. She might even suggest Clare had married Reed as a means of getting back at Jack.

Jack.

She hadn't thought about him all day, hadn't wanted to think of him. Having her parents, especially her mother, regard him so highly could complicate the situation with Reed and her family.

Clare's last conversation with her mother burned in her mind. Ellie Gilroy had urged Clare to be more patient with Jack, to give him time to get his company on its feet before pressuring him on the issue of marriage. The landscaping business was only an excuse, Clare realized. There'd always be one reason or another Jack would find not to marry. It had taken her a long time to recognize that, much longer than it should have. But it was more than Jack's putting her off that was wrong with the relationship. It was much more.

It didn't matter what her family thought, Clare decided, tightening her resolve. This was her life, and she'd marry whomever she pleased and Reed Tonasket pleased her. Having concluded that, she was relieved. This marriage wasn't going to be easy. They knew it would require effort on both their parts to make it work.

Clare was willing, and she'd assumed Reed was, too. Now she wasn't so sure.

Their luggage arrived, and Reed silently lifted the two bags and walked away, leaving it for her to choose to follow him or not. His attitude irritated her, still she had no choice but to tag along behind him.

"I... I was sorry we weren't able to sit together," she said, rushing her steps in order to keep pace with his much longer stride. "There's a lot we need to talk about."

Reed gave no indication that he'd heard her. He was so cool, so distant, and that infuriated her even more. If he refused to slow down, then she wasn't going to trot along beside him like an obedient mare.

She deliberately slowed her pace, but it was apparent he didn't notice. If he did, he found it of no concern.

By the time she reached Reed's truck, he had loaded their luggage into the back and unlocked the doors. Once again he didn't acknowledge her.

"Will you stop?" she demanded, standing beside the passenger door.

"Stop what?" he asked in cool tones. Their gazes met over the hood.

"Acting like I'm not here. If you ignore me long enough I'm not going to disappear."

His steely eyes narrowed before he pulled his gaze from hers and jerked open the door. "I won't, either, Clare. This is what you wanted, remember that."

"What I wanted? To be ignored and frozen out? There're so many things for us to discuss, I don't even know where to begin. The least you could do is look at me."

He turned and glared in her direction. His stance, everything about him was tense and remote. She might as well have been pleading with the moon for all the impact her words had on him.

"Never mind," she said, climbing inside the cab and snapping her seat belt into place. She'd talk to Reed when he was ready to listen, which he obviously wasn't now.

He climbed in beside her. No more than a few inches separated them, but in reality they were worlds apart.

Reed had known it was a mistake to marry Clare. Even as he'd uttered his vows, he'd realized she'd soon regret the deed. He hadn't counted on it happening quite this soon. He'd assumed he'd encounter a few doubts in the morning, but knowing Clare, he expected her to show a certain resolve to work matters out. Clare wasn't the type of woman who'd take something as serious as marriage lightly. Even a Las Vegas marriage.

Her broken engagement had made her especially vulnerable, Reed mused. She'd come to Las Vegas to act as the maid of honor to her best friend when she'd desperately yearned to be a wife herself. Her generally good judgment had been clouded with visions of contented marital bliss. All her talk had been just that.

Talk. She meant well, but he knew better than most the path of good intentions.

It hadn't mattered who she married as long as she could say she was married. It salvaged both her pride and her honor to marry him, and he'd definitely been willing. Since he was the only one with a clear head, he should have been the one to put an end to this nonsense. Instead he'd gleefully taken from her all that she was offering.

Reed had called himself a fool any number of times,

but he'd never thought of himself as vindictive. He did so now. Because he loved Clare and had for years, because she represented everything unattainable to him, he'd taken advantage of her.

His reputation with women might have had something to do with her eagerness to marry him. She mentioned it herself. Perhaps by marrying him she was proving to the world that she was woman enough to handle him. Reed smiled grimly to himself. His reputation. What a laugh that was—and all the result of a lie Suzie Milford had spread several years back. For some odd reason it had followed him, enhanced by time.

Women were more stubborn than men and often had trouble admitting they were wrong. Reed had to find some way to convince Clare it was necessary before she could persuade him otherwise. His love for her had already eclipsed his judgment once, and he couldn't allow it to happen a second time.

An hour passed, and neither of them said a word. Tullue was almost three hours' distance from the airport, which gave him an additional two hours to sort through the problem.

"I need to eat something," Clare said just before they boarded the Edmonds ferry. Her hand was clenched around a brown plastic pill bottle she'd taken from her purse. "I need food in my stomach before I take the medication."

Her headache had returned, and Reed felt a rush of remorse. She was in pain and he'd been so caught up in self-recriminations that he hadn't noticed.

They drove aboard the Washington State ferry and parked. "Do you want me to bring you something back?" he asked, thinking it would be easier for him to climb the stairs up the two decks than for Clare to make the long trek when she wasn't feeling well.

"If you wouldn't mind. Please."

"What would you like?"

"Anything...a muffin, if they have one, and maybe a cup of coffee." He couldn't be sure, because it had been impossible to view Clare from where he was seated on the plane, but he guessed she'd forgone the snack the airline had served.

It was early afternoon and she hadn't eaten all day. She must be living on adrenaline and pain.

"I'll be as quick as I can," he promised.

She offered him a weak smile and whispered, "Thank you."

Once he was in the cafeteria-style galley, Reed bought them both turkey sandwiches, large blueberry muffins, drinks and fresh fruit.

Clare's eyes revealed her appreciation when he returned.

"Thank you," she said again and reached for the coffee. Peeling away the plastic top, she sipped from the paper cup, then, unwrapping the turkey sandwich, she ate several bites of that. When she'd finished, she removed the cap from the pill bottle and swallowed down a capsule.

Reed reached for the prescription bottle and read the label.

In a heartbeat, he understood. Everything made sense now, it all added up.

Clare hadn't been herself the night before and with good reason. She'd combined a glass of champagne with her prescription drug when the instructions on the bottle specifically advised against doing so. It hadn't made her drowsy or drunk as the warning claimed, but it had drastically affected her personality.

No wonder she'd gazed up at him with stars in her eyes and blown kisses to complete strangers at the far end of the craps table. He doubted she'd even realized what was happening to her,

"I'm sorry about this morning," she said after several minutes. "I didn't mean to offend you… I'm hoping we can put the incident behind us and talk."

"We can talk." Although he didn't know what there was to say. Everything was crystal clear in his mind. If he hadn't been so crazy in love with Clare he would have realized right away that something was drastically wrong.

He was a world-class jackass. The only option left to him was to try to undo the damage this marriage had caused, before it ruined Clare's life.

"First and foremost I want you to know I have no regrets," she said softly, sweetly and, to his remorse, sincerely.

Her words sent Reed's world into a tailspin before he realized she couldn't very well admit she wanted out. Clare wasn't the type of woman who would treat marriage casually. She wouldn't give up without a fight. Unfortunately she hadn't figured out what had prompted the deed. The issue was complex; her reasons for marrying him had been both emotional and physical.

"Aren't you going to say anything?" she asked, when he didn't immediately respond. "I can't stand it when you don't talk to me."

"What would you like me to say?" he asked. He'd never been a man who felt the need for a lot of words. This situation baffled him more than any other.

"You might tell me you don't regret being married to me. There are any number of things you might say that would reassure me that we haven't made the biggest mistake of our lives."

Reed felt at a complete loss.

"You're impossible— How do you expect us to make any worthwhile decisions when you refuse to communicate?"

"What type of decisions?"

She apparently didn't hear his question or she openly refused to answer it. "You certainly didn't have a problem talking to me last night. Compared to now, you were a regular chatty Cathy."

"Chatty who?"

"Never mind." She jerked her head away from him and glared out the side window. "The least you could have done was warn me."

"That I prefer to wear my hair in braids?"

"No," she fumed. "That you intended to change personalities on me. I thought… I hoped…" Her voice broke, and she hesitated.

"I'm not the only one who went through a personality change," he told her quietly, thinking it was best to get it out in the open now and be done with it. "I don't suppose you happened to read the label on your medication before you drank the champagne, did you?"

"No…" She reached for her purse and dug around until she located the bottle. After reading the warning, she raised her soft brown eyes to his. "The champagne… I didn't even think about it. But I wasn't drunk, I mean…"

"No, but you weren't yourself, either. You generally don't eat food off someone else's plate, do you?"

Clare went pale. "So that's what was different."

He was gratified to note she wasn't going to play word games with him. "No wonder you were so uninhibited, blowing kisses to strange men. What about the public displays of affection between the two of us," he continued. "I don't imagine you usually kiss men in the streets. If anyone changed, Clare, it was you."

Her head rolled forward, and she caught it with her hand.

"Marrying me was like everything else about our time in Vegas. Unreal. You no more want to be saddled with me as a husband than—"

"That's not true," she argued. "I want to be your wife, no matter what you say. But you're too…hardheaded, too macho to admit it, so you're trying to put everything on me."

Reed knew he dare not believe she was sincere about their commitment to each other. "Methinks the lady doth protest too much."

She went silent as they pulled into Kingston and drove toward Tullue.

"What do you want to do?" she asked after a time, sounding very much as though she were close to a physical and emotional collapse. Reed realized now wasn't the time to press the issue, although he preferred to have it over and done with. Later would be soon enough.

"I'll follow your lead," he told her when it was apparent she expected an answer. They were nearly to Tullue by then, and Reed was both regretful and, in the same heartbeat, eager for them to separate. He couldn't be near her and not want to hold her. Couldn't be this close and hide his love.

"My lead?"

"As far as I'm concerned, we can do this any way you want. I wasn't the one crossing prescription medication with alcohol." He didn't know why he continued to throw that in her face. Clare was confused enough. "You have every right to bow out of this entire episode," he concluded.

"Bow out?"

"It's a bit late for an annulment, don't you think?" The question had a sarcastic twist.

"You think we should get a divorce?" Her voice broke and wobbled before she regained control. "I'm probably the only woman in the world who can't manage to hold on to a husband for more than twenty-four hours."

Reed had no comment to make. A divorce wasn't what he wanted, but it wasn't his decision to make. After taking advantage of her the way he had, he couldn't allow his desire to dictate their actions.

"What if…if I'm pregnant?"

The subject had been foremost on his mind the night before, the prospect filling his heart and his soul with a profusion of happy anticipation. No more. A child now would be the worst kind of complication, torn between two worlds without the guardianship of parents who would offer love and guidance to an understanding and acceptance of his or her heritage.

"Is it possible?"

"Of course it's possible," she flared, taking offense at his question.

"When will you know?"

She shrugged. "I… There are the home pregnancy tests, but I've never used one before so I don't know how long I'll need to wait for an accurate reading."

They were in the outskirts of Tullue. Within a few

all-too-short moments he'd have her home, and they had yet to settle even the most rudimentary of the many decisions facing them. Everything hinged on what Clare decided to do about the marriage.

"I... I don't know what to do," she said, pressing her hands over her ears as though to block out all the questions that plagued her. "I can't think... I was so sure, and now I don't know what I feel."

"Sleep on it."

"How can you be like this?" she cried. "Don't you care what happens? We're talking about the rest of our lives and you make it sound so...so unimportant."

"It is the rest of our lives, Clare. It's much too important to answer here and now when your head aches."

"In other words, live my life in limbo, take all the time I need, but in the meantime what happens with us? Or would you rather I conveniently forgot our little... misadventure?"

"I'm not going to forget it."

"You certainly seem to be giving me that impression." Her eyes were bright, but Reed couldn't tell if she was holding back tears, because she gasped softly and went pale.

"What's wrong?"

She straightened and rubbed the heel of her hand under her eyes. "Nothing. Just...just pay attention to the road." No sooner had she finished speaking than Reed noticed a white pick-up truck pulling behind him.

Jack Kingston.

Reed tensed, welcoming the opportunity to confront the man, to make him pay for the misery he'd caused Clare.

"Don't look so worried," he said, grinning over at her.

"Please, Reed, don't do anything foolish."

"Like what?"

"Start a fight."

He was offended that she'd be so quick to assume he'd be the one looking for trouble. Then again, she might be worried he'd hurt her pretty Anglo boyfriend.

Reed heard Clare draw in several deep breaths as though she needed to calm herself. He noticed her hands were trembling and how she nervously wove a stray curl of hair around the outside of her ear.

The other man followed him for a couple of miles even when Reed slowed to a crawl.

"Reed, please." Clare sounded almost desperate.

"Please, what?"

"Just take me home."

"That's exactly what I intend to do."

"Ignore him, please," she begged, showing more life than she had in several minutes. "It's over between Jack and me. I don't want to have anything to do with him."

"Fine, I'll make sure he understands that."

"No." She sounded frantic.

"What are you so worried about? More importantly who?"

"Jack doesn't like you... He didn't like the idea of me flying to Las Vegas with you and I'm afraid he's looking for trouble."

"No problem, sweetheart, trouble's my middle name." He eased his truck to a stop in front of Clare's house and turned off the engine.

"Reed," Clare said, pressing her hand against her forearm, her eyes beseeching. "Just ignore him."

"Get out of the truck, Clare" came Jack's angry voice from behind her.

"Let's leave," she suggested. "There's no reason we have to put up with this."

"Leave?" Reed spit out the word. "Sweetheart, I've never backed away from a fight in my life, and I'm not about to start now."

Six

"Clare," Jack called a second time. "Get out of that truck."

Clare's mind was whizzing, as she tried to decide the best course of action. Reed seemed almost eager to fight her former fiancé, to prove his dislike for the other man, to defend her honor. She couldn't allow him to do that. Jack wasn't worth the effort.

"I'll never ask much of you," she said, trying hard to keep her voice even and controlled, "but I'm asking you now."

"What is it you want me to do?" Reed's steely gaze bored into hers.

"Don't fight Jack."

"That's up to him," Reed said matter-of-factly. He opened the door and stepped out onto the street.

Jack was out of the truck in a flash. He stormed across the lawn, jerked open the passenger door and offered Clare his hand, as though she required his assistance.

Clare ignored him and gathered her purse and sweater as Reed walked around to the bed of the truck. Jack's gaze moved from Clare to Reed and then back again.

"We need to talk," Jack said to her.

"No, we don't," she countered with a tired sigh. "Now if you'll excuse me I'm going inside. I'm exhausted and definitely not in the mood for company."

"I've done some thinking," Jack called after her, eyeing Reed malevolently, as if he found even the sight of him distasteful, as if he'd welcome the opportunity to prove how much of a man he was by challenging Reed.

Clare watched with a sick kind of dread as Reed carried her suitcase up the walkway leading to the front door.

Having no luck with her, Jack seemed to want to impress her by hassling Reed. He raced down the sidewalk, leaped in front of Reed and shouted, "Stay away from Clare!"

Clare gritted her teeth, not knowing what would happen. To his credit, Reed said nothing, sidestepped Jack and continued walking until he reached her front porch, where he deposited her suitcase.

Jack followed on Reed's heels, waiting for an opportunity to make trouble.

"Thank you," Clare said softly to Reed, when they met as he was returning to his truck. "For everything."

Reed's gaze met hers, and for an instant she detected a hint of a smile. "You can handle this jackass?" he asked.

She nodded. "No problem."

Reed studied her for an elongated moment. Clare wished they could kiss. They'd never had any problems communicating when it came to the physical aspects of their relationship. She'd been so certain marrying him was good and right and now she felt terribly confused. If he left now, she was afraid it would be the end, and she wanted so badly for them to find a way to build their lives together.

"Goodbye," she whispered, knowing it would be impossible for him to stay. "I'll be in touch with you soon."

"You won't have anything to do with Reed Tonasket," Jack flared angrily from behind her. "And that's final."

"Might I remind you, Jack," she said smoothly as she reached her front door and freed the lock, "you have no right to tell me whom I can and cannot see. If I chose to see Reed again, it's none of your business."

"Oh yes it is."

Reed was almost to his truck. If Clare could distract Jack long enough she might be able to prevent further confrontation between the two men.

"I'll make certain he knows it, too," Jack said, walking away from her.

"I might even choose to marry Reed," she said a bit louder. If she'd wanted Jack's attention, she had it then. For that matter she had Reed's, too. His eyes seemed to be warning her, but she chose to ignore the silent entreaty.

"Why is it," Jack demanded impatiently, "that everything boils down to marriage with you? That's what this is all about, isn't it? You think you're going to make me jealous. Well, I'm telling you right now, it isn't going to work."

"Frankly, Jack, I don't really care." Lifting her suitcase, she carried it inside the house and closed the door. She glanced out the window and was relieved to see Reed drive away.

Jack looked as if he didn't know what to do—follow Reed and have it out with him or take his chances with her. He took three steps toward his pickup, abruptly changed his mind and stormed back toward the house.

Clare turned on her radio and ignored him. She had run bathwater and put a load of wash in the machine before the pounding on her door ended. She wasn't going to speak to Jack Kingston. Everything had already been said. As far as she was concerned, the relationship was over. They were finished.

The following morning Clare woke more confused than when she'd gone to sleep. She needed to talk to Reed, before she could put order to her thoughts, but she didn't even know where he lived. Nor did she have his cell number.

She found it frustrating and irritating to be so ignorant about her own husband. He at least knew how to reach her and could come to her anytime he pleased.

Apparently he felt none of the urgency to set matters straight that she did.

If Clare was frustrated Monday, she was downright angry by Wednesday afternoon when Reed showed up at the library. Clare was busy at the front desk when he arrived. If she hadn't happened to glance up just then, she wouldn't have noticed he was there.

Despite her angry disappointment, her heart gladdened at the sight of him, but she took one look at his closed expression and her heart sank. Right away she knew nothing had changed.

It took several moments before she was free to leave the front desk. Reed had walked to the farthest corner of the library, the mystery section. No one else was within hearing distance. With swift, determined steps she followed him.

Reed was waiting for her, and she watched as his gaze moved over her, making her conscious of her appearance. She raised her hand to her head, distressed to note that several strands had escaped her chignon. She'd dressed carefully each morning that week, wondering how long it would take for him to make a showing. If she looked her best, then they might be able to recapture the magic they'd found in Vegas and then lost on their return.

"It took you long enough," she said with tart reproach, then immediately longed to jerk back the words. She'd been starving for the sight of him for days, needing desperately to talk to him.

With everything in her heart she prayed he'd come to offer her reassurances, to prove to her it hadn't all been a wild, impossible dream.

"Did Kingston give you any problems?"

"No. What about you?"

A half smile touched his lips. "I'd enjoy it if he tried."

"Oh, Reed, he isn't worth the effort."

He didn't agree or disagree. He kept his distance, she noticed, when she badly wanted to feel his arms around her. What she badly needed was the security of his embrace...of his love.

"Have you reached a decision?"

The abruptness of his question took her by surprise. "How could I?" she flared. "We have a lot to discuss, don't you think? I've felt so thwarted in all this. I don't even know how to get to your house. Nor do I have your cell number."

"I don't own a phone."

Clare had never known anyone without one, and blinked back her surprise.

"We can't talk now," he said, looking past her. Apparently someone had come into the library, and he didn't want them to be seen together. "I'll come to your house tonight."

"What time?"

He hesitated. "Late," he answered after a moment, "after dark."

"But why..." she began then realized he'd already turned away from her, "so late?" she finished lamely.

Reed had bided his time, waiting three days, hoping Clare would have accepted the reality of their mistake and be willing to take the necessary measures to put their lives back into order.

He was looking to protect her reputation from gossip. He feared his reputation and people's prejudices would tear her apart when it became public knowledge that she'd married him. News of Gary and Erin's wedding had been in the local paper, and Clare's name had already been linked to Reed's in the news piece.

He'd heard through the grapevine that Kingston wanted words with him. Apparently Clare's friend wanted to be sure Reed was going to leave "his woman" alone.

Reed had nothing to say to the other man. Clare had asked him to ignore Jack Kingston, and since there was little he'd be able to do for her, he'd decided to honor her one request. It seemed like a small thing to do for the woman he loved.

When he showed up at the library he'd been fairly certain he could count on them having a few minutes alone together. It wasn't until they were in the far cor-

ner of the building between Agatha Christie and Mary
Higgins Clark that he realized his mistake.

She'd stood beneath a window, and the light had fil-
tered down on her petite form. The sun, coming from
behind her, had given her a celestial look as though she
were a heavenly being. An angel, he imagined, but he
couldn't decide if she would lead him to heaven's door
or deposit him at the gates of hell.

Those few moments with her had knotted his insides
with a need so strong he knew he had to leave almost
immediately. It demanded every ounce of restraint he
possessed not to touch her. Before he could train his
mind, the vision of her on their wedding night flashed
before him. The sweet smile she wore as she raised
her arms to him left him weak in ways that were for-
eign to him.

The brief encounter at the library forced him to acknowledge how vulnerable he was when it came to
Clare. Something had to be decided, and quickly. Since
she had trouble knowing her mind, he'd make the decision for them both. A quick divorce wasn't what he
wanted, but it was necessary.

He couldn't be alone with Clare and not want to love
her. This evening presented an even greater challenge
than he'd originally anticipated. He didn't know how
he was going to keep from touching her. Nor did he
know how he was going to avoid making love to her.
He had to find a way to convince her to put an end to
this farce of a marriage without letting her know how
much he cared.

Reed liked to think of himself as strong willed. It
was his nature to close himself off from others. It had
also been necessary. He'd isolated himself from the

good people of Tullue by choice, preferring to think of himself as an island, needing no one, dependent only on himself.

Now it alarmed his sense of independence to realize how much he needed Clare. Not physically, although his desire for her clawed at him. This one woman, more than any other, was able to reach him in areas of himself he'd assumed were secure. There'd never been anyone in his life he felt as close to as Clare, other than his grandfather.

His relationship to his father's father had been unique. They'd been a part of each other, sharing blood and heritage. It had been his grandfather who'd guided his life, who'd trained him in the ways of the Skyutes. His grandfather had taught him what it meant to be Indian.

The harsh lessons about life he'd learned from the Anglos. Finding himself uncomfortable in both the Indian and the white man's world, Reed had forged one of his own. He'd isolated himself, finding solace in his art, fulfillment in his craft. He made certain he was completely self-sufficient.

For the first time, his hard-won serenity was being threatened. By Clare. She made him vulnerable in ways he couldn't protect. Marrying her had been the biggest mistake of his life. Having shared the physical delights of marriage with her had changed who he was, altered his spirit.

In the back of his mind, Reed had convinced himself that once they made love, this need, this vulnerability she brought out in him would leave.

He was wrong.

Loving her had created an appetite for her that left him physically frustrated and in a permanent bad mood.

His life had become a misery and all because of a slip of a librarian who refused to admit she'd made a mistake.

Clare waited impatiently, checking the front window every few minutes. She'd given up answering her phone, letting the machine pick up the messages, hoping to avoid being trapped in a conversation with Jack.

He'd called several times in the past few days, each time threatening to make it the last time he contacted her. In his last message he claimed he would wait until she came to her senses and phoned him.

Hell would freeze over first. She wanted nothing to do with him again.

Jack could continue to be a problem for her though. It'd be just her luck if he decided to show up the same time Reed did. She checked her watch again, wondering how long her husband was going to keep her waiting. It was already after nine, and she was growing anxious. Perhaps she'd misunderstood him. Perhaps he had meant he was coming the following night. His words were suddenly unclear in her mind.

She was looking out the front window for signs of his car when a knock sounded at her back door. Jack or Reed? Clare didn't care any longer. She hurried across the house to her kitchen and opened the door without looking.

"I was beginning to think you'd never come," she chastised Reed, wondering why she found it necessary to lash out at him each time they met. Especially when she longed to hurl herself into his arms and have him reassure her. Her heart fell as she looked at him. A single glance told her he wouldn't welcome her embrace.

She swallowed back the hurt and let him inside her home.

"Would you like some coffee…and really, it isn't necessary for you to come to the back door."

"It is if Kingston's parked outside."

"Jack's watching the house?"

Reed's eyes hardened as he nodded. "He's down the street. Don't marry him, Clare, the man's not good enough for you."

"How can I possibly marry Jack when I'm already married to you?" The idea was ludicrous. It seemed she couldn't make Reed understand it was over between her and Jack any more than she could make Jack accept her decision.

"We're going to straighten out this marriage business once and for all," he said pointedly, not wasting any time. He'd barely arrived, and already he seemed eager to leave. "It was a mistake. A big one. There's only one option left and that's to divorce."

"What do you mean? I… I haven't agreed to a divorce. I… I don't know what I'm going to do yet. I certainly don't appreciate you making my mind up for me."

Reed grinned as if her small outburst had amused him. He pulled out a chair and sat down, crossing his arms over his muscular chest as though he needed to do something to close himself off from her.

He seemed so bitter and hard, and Clare longed to force him to confront his anger toward her and toward life. He needed to put the past behind him. It would have to happen if they were ever to make a success of their marriage.

"I need to know what you're thinking," she said, sitting across from him. The coffee was forgotten. He didn't seem all that eager for a cup, and she didn't want to be distracted.

"I know an attorney in Seattle. I'll contact him and have him arrange for a quiet divorce."

Clare felt the blood run out of her face. It went against the very core of her being to give up on the idea of this marriage without either of them making a minimal effort. "Is...that what you want?"

He was silent for several earth-shattering moments. "It's for the best."

"How can you say that?" she flared. "Apparently you aren't interested in my opinion," she told him defensively, sarcastically. "You obviously want out of the relationship. It'll take...what, two or three months before everything is final?" She stood, and with arms cradling her middle, walked over to the stove. "Funny, isn't it, that the divorce will take longer than the marriage lasted."

"It's better this way, Clare."

"Better for whom?" she asked in a pain-filled whisper.

An eternity passed before Reed answered. "Both of us."

Clare had no argument. Reed clearly wanted out, and she had no option but to abide by his wishes. It cut deep to let go of the dream, just when she'd believed she'd finally found a man she could love.

"You'll let me know if you're pregnant?"

"How?" she asked automatically, remembering how frustrated she'd been with no means of contacting him. "I don't know where you live."

He gave her simple directions to his home, which she attempted to write on a yellow tablet she'd taken from her drawer. Because her hands were shaking so badly and because her heart was so unbearably heavy, she made a mess of it. Finally Reed took the pad from her hands and wrote everything out himself.

"I have some books due back at the library next week," he said, as if he wanted to warn her he'd be seeing her soon.

Clare nodded. There didn't seem to be anything more for her to say.

Reed opened the drawer and replaced the pen and tablet for her. "If Kingston gives you any problems, let me know."

She trained her gaze away from him, because it hurt too much to look at him, knowing he was about to walk out of her life and take all her dreams with him.

"I'm sorry it has to be this way."

"Right," she agreed. From somewhere deep inside she found the strength to smile. "I'll...be in touch."

He stood in front of the back door, ready to leave. Clare felt as though the entire state of Washington was bottled up inside her throat. Breathing had become almost impossible. Never had she felt more heartsick or more confused.

She couldn't look at him, certain he'd read the painful longing in her eyes. Pride demanded that she pretend it was as easy for her to let him go as it was for him to walk away from her. But standing there and saying nothing was the most difficult thing she'd ever done in her life.

Her hands folded around the back of her kitchen chair, her nails bending with the strength of her grip.

He opened the door, and suddenly her pride was forgotten. "Reed." She heard the aching inflection of his name in her own voice. It had demanded every ounce of courage she possessed to stop him.

He froze, his back to her. Clare trembled in confusion, raised her hand, then grateful he couldn't see the small entreaty, dropped it lifelessly to her side.

"Thank you for the most beautiful night of my life," she whispered through the pain she couldn't disguise.

Something broke in Reed. It was almost visible. His shoulders drooped, and he inhaled a deep breath and dropped his hand from the doorknob.

Within seconds she was locked in his arms; his mouth, hungry and hard, covered hers. The force of his kiss backed her against the wall and he held her there, urgently kissing her until a soft moan of pleasure eased from low in her throat.

"No more!" He groaned the words, lifting his head from hers. His eyes were squeezed shut as if he dared not look down on her.

"No," she cried in protest, seeking his mouth with her own. She caught his upper lip between her teeth and teased his mouth. A surge of power shot through her when Reed moaned and lowered his mouth to hers for a series of long, frenzied kisses.

Once more he jerked his head up. "This has got to stop. Right now."

"No." Her hands were in his hair, loosening his braids. Once they were free she locked her arms around his neck and angled her mouth over his to gently nibble at his lips.

He trembled, and she felt a surge of power at his need. "Make love to me," she whispered between slow, drawn-out kisses.

His hands stilled. Before she realized what was happening, a shudder went though him and he gently closed his fingers around her wrists and dragged them from his neck. "Our marriage isn't going to work," he said, his dark eyes glaring down on her own. "Pretending it will isn't going to change reality."

Without giving her time to react, he broke away from her and was gone, slipping silently out the door.

The doorbell chimed and, knowing it was Jack, Clare ignored the summons. Shaken, she lowered herself into a chair, her legs no longer capable of supporting her. She buried her face in her hands and drew in several head-clearing breaths.

All wasn't lost, she decided, with the sound of the doorbell buzzing in her ear. She experienced the first ray of hope since the morning after her wedding. She wasn't sure she could trust her instincts, but deep in her heart, she couldn't believe Reed wanted this divorce any more than she did.

"We don't do this often enough," Ellie Gilroy said as she lowered her menu early Saturday afternoon. "I hardly see you anymore," her mother complained.

Clare smoothed the paper napkin across her lap. "I was glad you called, Mom. There was something I wanted to discuss with you."

"I imagine it has something to do with Jack."

Although still young, in her early sixties, Clare's mother looked older. The past few years had been difficult for her parents, Clare realized. Her father had retired, and the two were adjusting to each other's full-time company. Ellie had been a housewife all these years and Clare summed up the problem as one of territory. Her father had invaded the space her mother had always felt was her own.

"I've broken off the engagement with Jack," Clare announced.

"Oh, dear," Ellie said on the end of a sigh. "I was afraid it was something like that. Jack called and talked to your father the other night. When I asked Leonard what Jack had to say, your father told me it was none of my business. You're not seeing a Native American by any chance, are you?"

"A Native American," Clare repeated, her heart in a panic. She would have willingly told her mother she'd married Reed Tonasket, but she couldn't see mentioning her marriage to her family seeing that Reed was planning to divorce her.

"Your father asked me if you knew Reed Tonasket."

"Oh, you mean Reed," she said, knowing she was a terrible liar. She'd never done well with pretense. "He was the best man at Gary and Erin's wedding."

"Ah, yes, I seem to remember something about that now. How was the wedding? Oh, before I forget, I have a gift for Erin and Gary at the house. Don't let me forget to give it to her when she returns. I don't suppose you happen to know when they'll be back?"

"In a couple of weeks."

If Clare had ever needed her best friend it was now. Erin had a way of putting everything into perspective.

"Tell me what's going on between you and Jack?" her mother continued.

"Nothing," Clare returned starkly, not wanting to ruin her day by discussing something so unpleasant.

"But I liked him, Clare. Both your father and I feel he'll make you a good husband."

"I'm sorry to disappoint you, but I don't want to have anything to do with Jack. He's out of my life, only he hasn't seemed to figure it out yet. Apparently he phoned Dad looking to make trouble."

Ellie settled back in her chair. "You know I think your father must have felt the same thing. I asked him about the call and he got short-tempered with me, then later he said he wasn't that sure Jack was the man for you after all."

"I spent a couple of days with Reed Tonasket," Clare said, hoping to sound nonchalant and conversational. "I like him very much."

Clare carefully watched her mother's reaction, but she read none of what she expected. Not concern, and certainly not anxiety.

"Isn't he the one who does such an excellent job of carving totem poles?"

"Yes," Clare answered quickly. "I haven't seen any of his work, but Erin says he's very talented."

"It seems I read something about him not long ago in one of those regional publications."

"Really?" Funny Clare hadn't seen the piece, especially since the library subscribed to several area publications.

"How would you and Dad feel if I were to start dating Reed?" Clare asked, diving headfirst into what she feared were shark-infested waters. Times had changed and so had attitudes. Her parents' generation had a difficult time adjusting to new attitudes.

Her mother's chin came up abruptly and her gaze clashed with Clare's. "You're not asking for my permission, are you?"

"No," Clare admitted honestly.

"Then it doesn't matter what your father and I think, does it?"

"No, but I'd like to know your feelings."

Her mother's sigh was deep enough to raise her shoulders. "You're over thirty years old, Clare. Your father and I finished raising you a long time ago. If you want to become involved with Reed Tonasket, that's your business. I just can't help thinking—" She stopped abruptly. "I'm not even going to say it."

Clare knew without her mother having to say it; nevertheless, she was glad to have aired the subject with her mother. She knew exactly where they both stood.

Needless to say, her family hadn't a clue that she'd done a whole lot more than date Reed. He was their son-in-law...at least for the present.

The lunch with her mother freed Clare. Afterward she felt jubilant that the groundwork for her marriage to Reed had been laid with her family. Clare didn't doubt for an instant that her mother would return home and repeat their conversation with Leonard. Within a week or less, everyone in the family would know she'd broken up with Jack Kingston. They'd also know she was interested in Reed Tonasket.

The urge to see Reed took hold of Clare when she left the restaurant. She stopped first at the house and grabbed the directions Reed had given her to his home, then took a leisurely drive into Port Angeles, where few people knew her.

By the time she turned onto reservation land, some of her bravado had left her. She'd been on the Skyute reservation countless times over the years. The tribal center there was one of the best in the Pacific Northwest and attracted a lot of tourist traffic.

The road twisted and curved beside the Strait of Juan de Fuca and the breeze blew in gently from the cool green waters. Colorful wind socks flapped wildly, and several Native American children played contentedly in the rows of homes that bordered the paved road.

Fishing nets were set out to dry in the warm afternoon sun. Clare noticed a few curious stares as she followed the directions Reed had written out for her.

His cabin, for it could be called little else, sat back in the woods, surrounded by lush green fir trees in what was part of a Pacific Northwest rain forest. Reed explained that he didn't have a phone, and from the looks of the place, she doubted that he had electricity, either.

The dirt road that led to his home was dry now, but Clare could only imagine what the rut-filled path would be like in the dead of winter, washed out by repeated rainstorms.

She parked her car next to Reed's truck, and after a moment or two, climbed out. Glancing around, she was relieved to find he didn't have a dog, at least none that revealed any interest in her.

No one seemed to be around. She stood next to her car for several minutes, thinking Reed would hear her and come, but that didn't seem to be happening.

Her knock against the rough wooden door went unanswered. After coming all this way, she didn't intend on being easily thwarted. They were married, after all, and as his wife, surely she had the right to go inside his—their—home.

The door was released with a twist of the knob. She let it open completely before she stepped inside. It took her eyes a moment to adjust to the dark, and what she found caught her by surprise. Reed's home was as modern as her own, perhaps more so, with large windows that looked out over the strait. Far in the distance she caught sight of Vancouver Island.

His sofa and chair were angled in front of a large basalt fireplace. A thick braided rug rested on the polished hardwood floor. Several oil paintings decorated the walls, and her gaze was drawn to them. She wondered if Reed was the artist.

The kitchen was to her left, the room huge and open. The bedrooms, she guessed, were down a narrow hallway that led from the living room.

It was apparent Reed was close, since there was a cast-iron kettle heating on the stove. Investigating, Clare discovered he was cooking some kind of stew. It smelled wonderful. Her husband was probably a better cook than she was.

Setting her purse aside, she decided to make herself at home. She reached for a magazine and sat in the deep overstuffed chair to wait for Reed.

It didn't take him long. She heard him even before he came through the door, his steps heavy on the wooden porch.

"Clare." He was inside the cabin in three strides.

He wasn't wearing a shirt, and his skin gleamed with a sheen of perspiration. He wore his hair straight with a leather band tied around his forehead. He looked all male, and Clare's heart stopped dead at the virile sight of him.

"Hi," she greeted with a warm smile. "I... I thought you might want to know if I was pregnant or not."

Seven

"Are you pregnant?" Reed asked. The vision of Clare carrying his child, her abdomen swollen with the fruit of his love, was deeply rooted in his heart. A vision he dared not entertain.

"I… I don't know yet. I bought one of those home pregnancy tests."

"In Tullue?" Reed's concern was immediate. With Clare living in such a small town, news of her purchase could create excess talk.

"No… I drove to Port Angeles, to a drugstore there. I didn't see anyone I knew."

"Good."

Her eyes flickered, and for an instant Reed thought he might have witnessed a flash of pain. If that was so, he didn't understand it.

"I read over the instructions," she said somewhat stiffly, further confusing him. "We'll know within a few minutes." She reached for her purse and took out a small brown bag. Inside was a test kit. "It only seemed fitting that we do this together."

"You're angry?" he asked softly.

The way her eyes widened revealed her surprise. "Not angry...nervous, I guess. I could have waited and let nature tell us in due course, but I wanted to know and I assumed you would, too."

"I do." Reed had difficulty identifying the wide range of emotions that warred inside him. His first thought was one of eager anticipation. But Clare bearing his child left his heart and his life wide open. He wouldn't be capable of hiding his joy or his love for her and their child.

If Clare was pregnant, Reed decided he'd move her here with him, shield her from the prejudice and small thinking that had haunted him most of his life. He'd do everything possible to protect her from outside influences.

If the test proved to be negative, he'd follow through with the divorce proceedings. He'd already left one phone message with the Seattle attorney, but he'd make another call on Monday morning.

"Are you ready?"

As ready as he was likely to get.

She hesitated, studying him. "I had lunch with my mother this afternoon," she said casually.

An odd inflection in her voice caught his attention. Either there was some meaning behind her words, or she was hiding her mother's reaction from him.

"Yes?" he prompted, when she didn't continue right away.

"I almost told her we were married, but I didn't, I couldn't...because you're so sure about this divorce thing. I'm happy to be your wife...and it's getting difficult to pretend you don't mean anything to me when you do."

"How much did you tell your mother?"

Clare's gaze fell to the floor. "I told her that I... I wanted to date you."

Reed stiffened. He could well imagine Mrs. Gilroy's reaction to that. It angered him that Clare had approached her family, knowing their approval meant a good deal to her. Needless to say, they wouldn't sanction him as a son-in-law.

"I know you'd rather I kept everything a deep, dark secret, but I've never been one to play games. We're married, and have been for a week now. I'm not going to conveniently forget it because you happen to have had a change of heart."

"What happened with your mother?" he asked again. Her purpose in coming to his home was clear to him now. The pregnancy test was an excuse. This visit had been prompted by the conversation with her mother.

"She said I was old enough to decide whom I dated and we left it at that."

"She wasn't pleased." Reed made the statement because there was no doubt in his mind of what had been left unsaid between mother and daughter.

Clare didn't answer him, and while she was preparing for the pregnancy test he went outside and stood on the porch. She joined him a few moments later.

"We'll need to wait a few minutes."

Reed had the impression they were going to be the longest minutes of his life.

And hers.

"It's beautiful out here," Clare said, wrapping her arm around the post and staring into the lush green growth of rain forest.

Reed glanced to the heavens. The clouds were rolling

in, darkening the afternoon sky. A squall would follow shortly. He'd best put his tools away, close up shop and keep Clare with him until after the storm.

Without explanation, he started to walk away from her and she called after him. "Where are you going?"

"To my shop. I need to do a few things."

"Can I come with you? Even a few minutes can seem like a long time when you're alone."

He nodded, knowing in his heart he would treasure every moment of her company the rest of his life. These were precious gifts not to be taken for granted. He hadn't meant to be rude, nor had he intended to exclude her. He simply wasn't accustomed to company, nor was it his way to announce his intentions.

Clare stood a little proud, a little unsure, a few feet from him.

"I'd like to show you my shop," he said, and was rewarded with a smile that seemed to come from the deepest reaches of her heart.

She slipped her hand into his, and the unexpectedness of the action caught him by surprise. He didn't have time to steel himself against her touch, and his hand automatically tightened around hers. He couldn't be with Clare and not want her physically. She'd be in his home several hours, from the look of those clouds, and he wondered how he was going to manage to keep from making love to her...especially if she was already nurturing his child.

"I didn't even know this building was back here," Clare said as they entered the large shop. The log had been cut only a few days earlier, and the scent of cedar permeated the air. Reed had been working on it most of the afternoon. It resembled little more than a long, slightly square red block at this point, but within a few weeks it would be shaped into an eight-foot thunderbird, bear and salmon. The city of Los Angeles had commissioned it for a park that was to be dedicated in early September.

Reed was pleased with his progress so far, although it revealed little of what the finished product would be like.

"I'm afraid I don't know very much about totem poles," Clare said, walking around the cedar log. Her fingertips glazed the ears, face and beak, which were partially shaped from the square wood.

"In our culture totem poles were a substitute for the written word," Reed explained. "Several hundred years ago they revealed the history of a man, his clan and any war victories or favorable events."

"And today?" Clare wanted to know.

"Today they decorate the entrances of parks."

"That's where this one will go?"

Reed nodded.

"What's it going to be?"

Reed carefully explained the design, pointing out the beak of the thunderbird, the shape of bear and the salmon.

"Do those mean anything?"

Reed gauged her question carefully, wondering if her interest was a polite curiosity or genuine. Her eyes met his and he realized her sincerity.

"The thunderbird is a guardian spirit, the benevolent protector of all Native Americans. The bear portrays immense strength and is capable of performing great feats of skill and daring."

"And the salmon?" she prompted.

"The salmon is the symbol of fertility, immortality and wealth." He mentioned several other of the more frequent symbols used by totem pole carvers. The raven, the owl, the loon, casually telling her of the totem poles he'd been commissioned to build through the years.

"I didn't realize how well-known your work has become. My mother mentioned reading about you in an article in *Washingtonian* magazine. I must have missed the piece."

As she spoke, Reed gathered his chisels and hammers and the other instruments that were strewn about the shop.

"I was surprised the local paper didn't pick up on the article and write one of their own." She frowned as she said it, as though irritated that Tullue would slight him.

"They asked for an interview. I declined."

"But why?"

Reed shrugged. "I'm known as a half-breed hellion in Tullue. I couldn't see any reason to correct their impression."

"But—"

"Shall we go back to the house?" he asked, interrupting her. This wasn't a subject he wanted to discuss. No amount of success would change Tullue's view of him. In the eyes of the town he was a troublemaker, and if that was what they chose to believe, he wasn't going to disillusion them with the truth.

Clare was strangely quiet as they walked back to the house. He wasn't sure what to make of her mood, and because he was uncertain, he quietly assembled the wood to build a fire.

"What's this?" Clare asked after a few moments. "I saw it earlier and wondered. It's so beautiful."

She held up a small totem pole he'd carved three years earlier, one made of black walnut wood. He'd carved a rainbow, an eagle and a salmon. The totem was rich with meaning because it represented Clare in his eyes. Laughing Rainbow.

"I carved that several years ago."

"A rainbow?"

"Yes," he said, squatting down in front of the basalt fireplace to build a fire. "You can keep it if you wish." Although the offer was made in an offhanded manner, it would mean a great deal to him if Clare would accept the gift. He'd made it with her in mind, spending several months on the intricate details of the carving. It seemed a small return for all that she'd given him. She continued to wear the ring he'd given her, and, despite his determination to go through with the divorce, he was pleased she had his ring.

"Reed, I couldn't keep this."

"Please. I want you to have it."

"Then I accept. It really is very beautiful. Thank you."

The flames were flickering hungrily at the dry kindling when Reed stood. "I'll only be a few minutes," he said, excusing himself. He needed to wash and put on a shirt.

By the time he returned, the living room had darkened considerably with the approaching storm. Clare was standing in front of the window, her back to him. He could tell even before she turned around that she was troubled.

"Clare?"

"The test…it's negative. I'm not pregnant."

Her voice was a low monotone, and when she didn't

immediately turn around, Reed went to her. She must have sensed he was behind her because she turned and wrapped her arms around his middle and buried her face in his chest. Instinctively he held her and he slowly closed his eyes, savoring the spontaneous way in which she'd reached out to him.

"Are you disappointed?" he asked softly, pushing the hair from the side of her face. The pregnancy test results left him with mixed feelings. He didn't have time to contend with those, not when Clare was snuggling in his arms. She was warm and delicate, and the feel of her caused his heart to beat slow and hard, building a heavy need within him.

"I...don't know," she answered with frank honesty. "Now isn't the time for me to be pregnant, especially when our marriage is so uncertain. It would have created a problem, but in other..."

"Yes," he prompted when she didn't immediately finish.

"It might have solved problems, too."

"How's that?"

"You might not be so eager to be rid of me." The hurt in her voice wrapped itself around him like new rope. She didn't understand and he couldn't explain. Every time he held her or kissed her made leaving her more difficult. He couldn't allow himself the luxury of becoming accustomed to her presence in his life.

"Let's sit down," he suggested, hoping that once she was out of his arms, his judgment wouldn't be clouded by the pleasure he received holding her.

Clare sat on the sofa and Reed joined her. They twisted to look into the fire, and before Reed quite understood how it happened, Clare was leaning back against him and his arms were around her. He couldn't remember either of them moving; it was as though they had gravitated naturally to each other. His hands stroked the length of her arms.

"Tell me about your parents?" she asked after several contented moments.

"My father was born and raised on the reservation," Reed explained. "He enlisted in the army and, from what I understand, did quite well. He died in a plane crash. I never knew him."

"And your mother?"

His memories of her were fleeting. Try as he might, he wasn't able to form a clear picture of her in his mind. From photographs he knew she was blond and delicate. And beautiful.

"She fell in love with my father when he was stationed back East. Her family disapproved of my father and wanted nothing to do with either of them when she married him."

"How sad."

"Apparently when my father died, she tried to contact them, but they refused to see her. I don't know what the death certificate says, but my grandfather told me she died of a broken heart. I came to live with him here on the reservation when I was four."

"Do you remember much about her?"

"Very little."

"She must have loved you very much."

Reed was silent. He'd learned a valuable lesson from his mother's life, the lesson of not crossing from one world to another, of the costly price of love.

In his heart, Reed was certain his father had carefully weighed the decision to marry an Anglo, but he'd miscalculated. His death had left Reed and his mother outcasts. No abject lesson could be more potent than what had happened to his parents. Yes, times had changed. Prejudice wasn't as prevalent now as when his parents married. Nevertheless it existed and he refused to subject Clare to such discrimination because of their marriage. Nor was he willing to risk bringing another child into a hostile environment.

The rain started then, in heavy sheets that slapped against the window. A clap of thunder was so loud, it sounded as though a tree had split wide open directly beside them.

Clare's startled gaze shot outside.

"It'll pass soon," Reed assured her. "You'll stay for dinner?"

She nodded. "The stew smells wonderful. I didn't realize you were an accomplished cook, but then there's a lot I don't know about you, isn't there?"

The question was open-ended, and Reed chose to ignore it. The more Clare knew about his life, the more vulnerable he became to her. He wished he knew what it was about her that affected him so deeply. When they were together, he felt intensely alive, profoundly calm, as though she brought him full circle, back to the love that had surrounded him while his parents had been alive.

"I'll check the stew," he said, needing to break away from her. Each moment she was in his arms increased the ache in his heart. He'd always possessed an active imagination, and sitting there with Clare in his arms, so content and peaceful, was slowly but surely driving him insane. The memory of their wedding night played back in his mind, tormenting him.

He wasn't a saint in the best of circumstances. Anyone reading his mind now would recognize he'd never be a candidate for canonization.

"I'll set the table," Clare offered, following him into the other room.

Reed stood in front of the stove, willing his body to relax, willing the graphic images of them together to leave his mind. Clare was either too busy to notice his predicament, or too innocent to realize what she was doing to him.

They sat at the table, across from each other, and it was all Reed could do to eat. The savory aroma from the stew should have appealed to him since he hadn't eaten much during the day. But his mind wasn't on dinner. He discovered Clare occupied his thoughts as keenly as she did when he was holding her.

"Tell me about your family," Reed requested, not because he was curious, but because he felt he should know more about her than he did. The attorney might need information Reed couldn't give him.

"I'm the youngest of three children. My brothers both live and work in Seattle. Danny's the oldest, and is an accountant. Ken's a salesman for a pharmaceutical company. He does a lot of traveling."

"They're both married?"

Clare nodded. "I have six nieces and nephews. Dad was in the logging business, but he's retired now."

"You were born and raised in Tullue?"

She nodded, tearing off a piece of bread.

"What about college?"

"I went to the University of Washington. It couldn't have worked out better. Mrs. Gordon was looking to retire as head librarian and waited until after I'd graduated."

"Why haven't you married?" He realized as he spoke that everything he'd asked her had been leading up to this one question. It was what he really wanted to know, needed to know about Clare.

She carefully set her fork beside her bowl. Reed had trouble reading her expression, but it seemed she stiffened defensively. "Do you want the long, involved story or the shorter version?"

Reed shrugged, leaving the choice to her. She looked very much the proper librarian now, her chin tilted at an angle that suggested a hint of arrogance. Her eyes were clear and her mouth, her kissable, lovable mouth was pinched closed.

"I'll give you the shorter version. No one asked." She placed one hand in her lap and reached for her fork.

"Are Anglo men always such fools?" he asked, amazed they had been blind to her beauty.

"White men are no more foolish than Native American men. Might I remind you, Reed, you seem mighty eager to be rid of me yourself. Don't be so willing to judge others harshly when you…when you're…" She left the rest unfinished.

Reed couldn't bear it any longer. Heaven help him, he'd tried not to kiss her, but the pain he read in her made it impossible.

He loomed over her, and she gazed up at him, her eyes wide and troubled.

"What is it?" she asked.

He hunkered down so their gazes were level. He studied her, wondering anew how anyone could be so oblivious to such warmth and passion.

Then Reed understood.

Others didn't see it because Clare hadn't recognized it herself. "You really don't know, do you?"

Confused, she slowly shook her head.

He tucked his arms around her waist and pulled her forward for a slow, deep kiss. Clare sighed, and her arms circled his neck as she melted against him. Reed went down on his knees, and Clare, who was perched on the edge of her chair, leaned into his embrace. He kissed her again, his mouth moving slowly, thoroughly over hers. Kissing Clare was the closest thing to heaven Reed had ever experienced, the closest he'd ever come to discovering peace within himself. Desire raged through him like wildfire, and he breathed in deeply, reaching blindly for something to hold on to that would give him the control he sought.

It was either stop now or accept that he was going to make love to her right there on his kitchen floor. Reed recognized that fact as surely as he heard the soft cooing noises she made.

When he hesitated, Clare kissed him, her mouth tentative at first, but slowly she gained confidence as she seduced him with her lips and soft murmurs of pleasure.

"Clare…" He groaned her name, needing to break this off while a single shred of sanity remained.

His breathing…her breathing went deep and shallow as she dealt with the pleasure his kisses brought her.

"Reed…please." She found his mouth with her own, and he felt in her the same painful longing he was experiencing. Only Clare, his beautiful, innocent wife, didn't feel she could say what she wanted. The realization had a more powerful effect on him than her kisses.

Reed pulled her forward until she was kneeling on

the floor in front of him. His hands stroked the gentle curve of her spine as his lips devoured hers.

"We have to stop," Reed groaned, tearing his mouth from hers. He was fast reaching the point where it would be impossible to control his needs.

"Why?" She found his ear and nibbled softly at the lobe. Desire shot through him like a hot blade.

"Because if we don't, we're going to end up making love," he told her frankly.

"We're...married."

"Clare, no." He reached for her wrists and pulled her arms free from his neck, breaking her physical hold on him. The emotional hold was far stronger and required more strength of will than he thought himself capable of mustering. His legs were trembling when he managed to stand and back away from her.

"I'll see to the fire," he announced, surprised by how weak he sounded. He walked over to the fireplace and added a dry log. The flames licked at the bark and greedily accepted this latest sacrifice.

Miserable, Clare sat back on her legs and waited until the trembling had stopped before she attempted to stand. Carrying their bowls over to the sink, she busied herself by rinsing their dirtied dishes.

"Leave that," Reed instructed.

"It'll only take me a moment," she countered. Occupying her hands with the dishes offered her the necessary time to compose her shattered nerves.

Once again she'd made a fool of herself over Reed. She'd practically begged him to make love to her. Not with words, she couldn't do that, not again. Pride wouldn't allow it, and so she'd used her lips and her heart to tell him what she wanted.

Once more Reed had rejected her.

How ironic that he could be telling her how foolish the men of Tullue were to have passed her over, while he was pushing her aside himself.

Tears brimmed just below the surface, and it was fast becoming futile to hold them at bay. Pride was a powerful motivator, however, and when she'd finished with the dishes, she walked into the living room and reached for her purse.

"I have to get back to town," she said, with little more than a glance in Reed's direction. He stood next to the fireplace, his back to her. "Thank you for dinner and for...the moral support with the test. Let me know what the attorney says." In any other circumstances Clare would have been pleased by how unaffected she sounded, unruffled by their fiery exchange, as if she often passed a rainy afternoon making love.

"You can't go," he said darkly. "The storm hasn't passed."

"It will in a few minutes."

"Then wait that long."

She didn't want to argue with him, but she wanted out before she made an ever bigger fool of herself. Despite superhuman efforts her bottom lip started trembling. If she uttered one more word, a sob was sure to escape with it. Clare couldn't risk that.

"Every time we touch we're playing with fire," Reed said angrily. "It doesn't help any having you look at me like that."

"Look at you?"

"One harsh word and you'll dissolve into tears."

"I'm in full control of my emotions," she shot back, furious that he could so accurately pinpoint her feelings. Her anger was what saved her from doing exactly as he claimed.

His smile was slightly off center, as if it were all he could do not to laugh outright. "Don't pretend you don't know what I'm talking about," Reed said calmly. "If we'd continued we both know what would have happened. We can't, Clare, not again."

His words hit her like a slap in the face. In one breath he was telling her the men in town were fools for not marrying her, and in the next he was quietly arranging to divorce her. She was married, but the opportunity to be a wife was being denied her. One night in bed together didn't constitute a marriage, but apparently that was all Reed had wanted. One incredible night.

She reached for the small hand-carved totem pole he'd given her and hurried outside. Pride urged her to leave it behind, but at the last second she took it, unwilling to forsake the gift.

The rain had stopped, although the sky remained dark and unfriendly, the air heavy and still. Fat drops fell from the trees and the roof as she bounded off the porch and headed toward her car.

"Clare." She heard the desperation in Reed's voice as he followed her.

"The storm's over," she called over her shoulder. "There's no reason for me to stay."

"Listen to me," he said, gripping her by the shoulders and turning her around to face him. His eyes were narrowed into hard slits, his control paper-thin.

"You needn't worry, Reed, I got your message loud

and clear, although I have to admit I'm a little surprised by your double standard."

"What are you talking about?" he barked.

"You don't want me as a wife any more than Jack did," she reminded him. The wind was whistling in the woods, a low humming sound, a groaning that seemed to come from the very depth of her spirit. "Don't worry," she continued, refusing to look at him, "you'll get your divorce."

His jaw went granite hard as he clenched his teeth. He looked away from her. His eyes, dark and haunted, burned with frustration. "You don't understand."

"But I do," she countered. "I understand perfectly."

He released her then, or at least his hands did. He didn't try to stop her when she opened her car door and climbed inside. He might not be clutching her physically, but his hold was as powerful as if he had been.

He'd wanted her as badly as she'd wanted him, but something more powerful than physical need was holding him back. Intuitively Clare recognized that whatever it was had restrained him most of his life. He couldn't allow any person to become important to him. He'd let her into his life as much as he'd dared, and now he was pushing her aside the way he had everyone else. She'd come as close as he would allow. He didn't want her, and she had to accept that and get on with her life.

By the time Clare pulled onto Oak Street, thirty minutes later, she'd managed to compose herself. The sky was clear and bright, sun splashing over the earth in vibrant renewal.

The first thing Clare noticed as she approached her home was Jack's truck parked outside. The frustration hit her in waves. She wasn't in the mood to deal with him now, but that option had been taken from her.

She parked her car. Jack was sitting on her front porch, looking beleaguered and defeated.

"Hello, Clare," he said, looking to her with a round, pleading expression.

"Jack." She prayed for strength and patience.

"Clare," he said, standing. "You win, baby, you win."

"I didn't know we were in a contest."

Jack didn't comment. "I can't go on like this. You want me to tell you how much I've missed you—all right, you deserve that much. I've missed you. You were right about so many things."

It wouldn't be savvy to disagree with him. Clare had never felt less right in her life, about anything or anyone. She'd wasted three years of her life on Jack, then married a man who couldn't wait to be rid of her.

"I'm pleased you think I was right."

"I love you, Clare. I've been miserable ever since we split up. It's made me realize I can't live without you." He got down on one knee in front of her, reached inside his pocket and took out a velvet ring case. "Will you marry me, Clare? Will you put me out of my misery and be my wife?"

Eight

Jack was serious, Clare realized. How often she'd dreamed of him coming to her, his eyes filled with gentle love, as he asked her to share his life. For three years she'd longed for this moment, and now she'd give anything if Jack could quietly disappear from her life.

"Well, say something," Jack said, holding open the jeweler's case for her to examine the solitary diamond. "I know you're surprised."

"Jack... I don't know what to say," she whispered. Not once did she doubt her answer. It amazed her that only a few weeks earlier she would have been overwhelmed, delirious with joy that she would have burst into happy tears. Now she experienced a regretful, embarrassed sadness, knowing his proposal had come far too late, and being so grateful that it had.

"That diamond's big enough to take your breath away, isn't it?" Jack reached for her hand, intending to place the engagement ring on her finger.

Clare lamely allowed him to hold her hand.

"What's this?" he asked, gazing down at the large turquoise ring Reed had given her on their wedding day. Clare hadn't removed it, not even to have it sized. Instead she'd wrapped tape around the thick band until it was snug enough to stay on her finger.

"It looks like a man's ring," Jack commented.

Clare closed her hand and removed it from his grasp. "Come inside, we need to talk."

"I'll say. There's a lot to do in the next few weeks. You might want to involve your mother and have her help you with the necessary arrangements. I imagine you'd like the wedding fairly soon, which is fine by me. You'd better snatch me up before I change my mind." He laughed lightly, finding humor in his own weak joke.

Clare led the way into her home, set her purse and the totem pole Reed had given her on the kitchen countertop. "Do you want something to drink?" she asked, standing in front of the open refrigerator. Her thoughts whirled like the giant blades of a helicopter, stirring up doubt and misgivings. The last thing she wanted to do was hurt Jack. "I've got iced tea made."

"What I want," Jack said, sneaking up behind her, "is a little appreciation." He grabbed her about the waist and hauled her against him, kissing her neck.

Finding his touch repugnant, Clare pushed away. "Not now," she pleaded.

For the first time Jack seemed to realize something was awry. "What do you mean 'not now'? You're beginning to sound like we're already married. You know, Clare, that's always been a problem with us. You've never liked me to touch you much, but, sweetheart, that's about to change, right?"

Clare recognized the truth of his words, and in the same heartbeat realized the same didn't hold true for Reed. She was anything but standoffish with him. The deep physical longing she experienced whenever they were together had been the cause of much consternation on her part.

"Jack, sit down," she instructed. From somewhere she had to dredge up the courage and the wisdom to explain she wouldn't marry him—and at the same time leave his pride intact.

She pulled out a chair and sat across the table from him. "We've been dating for a long time now."

"Three years," he returned brightly. "Which is good because we've gotten to really know each other. That's important in a relationship, don't you think?"

"Of course." Her fingers were laced atop the table as though she were sitting at attention in her first-grade class, shoulders square, eyes straight ahead. She tried to force herself to relax but found it impossible, especially when Jack's gaze drifted down to the bulky ring Reed had given her.

"Where'd you get that awful ring?" he asked for the second time. "I can't understand why you'd ever wear anything like that. It looks Native American."

Clare lowered her hands to her lap. "We need to discuss a whole lot more than my taste in jewelry, don't you think?"

His tight features relaxed as he nodded. "It's just that I'm eager to put this diamond on your finger." He removed the ring case from his pocket and set it on the table, popping it open. "I checked for clarity and color," he announced proudly. "I got a good deal, too."

"Let's talk about marriage."

"Right," Jack agreed, reverting his attention back to her. "We should set the date right away. Do you want to call your family now? No," he said, disagreeing with himself, "we should do that together. You want to drive over, surprise them?"

"No...let's talk."

"We are talking." His gaze narrowed. "It concerns me that we have so much trouble communicating. I thought you'd go wild when you saw this diamond. I don't understand what's wrong with you."

"I agree it's a beautiful ring," Clare murmured, experiencing a low-grade sadness at the sight of it. She wasn't disappointed to lose out on the diamond. The turquoise band Reed had given her appraised far higher in her mind, even though she realized she'd soon be returning it.

Her melancholy, she recognized, was a result of regret and self-incrimination that she hadn't faced the truth sooner. They'd never been right for each other, she and Jack, and never would be. Jack appreciated little about her and she about him. Their lives together would have been a constant battle of wills, of attempts to mold each person into the other's vision.

"You're darn right, it's a beautiful ring," Jack went on to say. "This half carat set me back a pretty penny."

"I'm pleased we dated for three years," Clare continued softly. "It was time well spent."

"I couldn't agree with you more." Jack relaxed against the back of the chair, confident and serene. "You kept pushing me and pushing me, but the time wasn't right and I knew it."

"I'm grateful for another reason, Jack," she said, her voice dropping, heavy with dread.

"Oh, why's that?" He picked up the ring case to examine the diamond more closely. When he looked up, he was grinning proudly, as if he'd mined the stone.

"I'm grateful for those years, because I've come to realize, I'm not the right woman for you."

Her words were met with stark silence.

"Say that again."

"This last week has—"

"You've got what you want," Jack flared, nearly shouting. "What more is there? I said I'd marry you."

"A marriage between us wouldn't work. You were right to wait, you were right to hold off making a commitment. I think you must have intuitively realized what it's taken me so long to accept. We simply wouldn't have made it as a married couple."

Jack shot to his feet and forcefully jerked his hand through his hair. "There's no satisfying you, is there? You want one thing, then you don't. It's the craziest thing I've ever seen in my life. You hound me for years to marry you, and then when I agree, you have this flash of lightning that says we're no longer compatible. Reed Tonasket has something to do with this, doesn't he?"

"I'm sorry, Jack," she said, meaning it, refusing to answer his demand.

Jack leaned forward, pressing his hands against the side of the table. "What happened, Clare? What changed?"

"I did," she admitted freely.

"This whole thing started when you were spitting mad because I wouldn't attend that stupid dinner party with you. Is that still what's wrong? You want your pound of flesh for that? It's because I missed that dinner that you've been throwing Reed Tonasket in my face, isn't it?"

Clare tensed. "This has nothing to do with the dinner party."

"Then what happened?" he demanded, stalking to the other side of the kitchen. His feet were heavy, his footsteps reverberating as they hit the floor.

"I...in Vegas I realized—" She stopped abruptly. Any further reference to Reed would be a mistake. She'd already wounded Jack's pride enough without revealing the full truth, although it burned within her. Keeping their marriage a secret was becoming more difficult by the minute.

"It all started when you ran off to Vegas with that troublemaker, didn't it?"

"Reed was Gary's best man," she reminded him. "And I was Erin's maid of honor. You could have come with us if you'd wanted to, remember?"

"Tonasket was with you when you returned," Jack said slowly, his eyes accusing her. "What happened, Clare?" he asked, strolling across her kitchen, his steps much slower now, as though he were dragging the weight of his suspicions with him. He paused in front of her countertop, where he reached for the totem pole. Clare watched as the side of his mouth lifted in a derisive smile.

"I think you should leave," Clare said stiffly, growing tired of this conversation.

"For curiosity's sake, where were you this afternoon?" he asked, looking at the totem pole and pretending to examine its workmanship. "Let me guess. You were with him, weren't you? Is he that good in bed, Clare? I've heard—"

"Get out, Jack."

"Not until I know the truth."

"The truth," she repeated, "is what I've been trying

to tell you for the last several minutes. I don't want to marry you...let's leave it at that."

"Oh, no, you don't, sweetheart. You've got some explaining to do."

Clare walked over to her telephone and lifted it from the receiver. "Either you leave now, or I'm phoning the sheriff."

"Threats, Clare?" His face was tight with anger, his eyes flashing with fury. "So you're screwing Reed Tonasket. I should have guessed long before now."

"Get out!" she yelled. "Before I have you arrested for trespassing."

It looked as if he would challenge her, but he changed his mind when she starting punching the numbers on her phone. He stalked across the room, jerked the diamond ring off the table and stormed out of her house.

The windows shook violently when he slammed the front door, but no more forcefully than Clare, who grieved for what she'd been too blind to recognize for three long years.

Reed carefully planned his trip into town. He waited until early Tuesday afternoon, hoping to catch Clare in the library during a slack time. He had information. The conversation with the Seattle attorney had resulted in several things he needed to pass along to her.

Clare had been right about one thing. The divorce would take longer than the marriage had lasted, which was a sad commentary on its own.

But what an adventure it had been. Reed felt honor-bound to follow through with the divorce, but he suffered no regrets over their brief marriage. His few days with Clare were more than he ever thought would be possible.

Reed hungered for the sight of Clare. She'd come to his home and spent an afternoon with him. Her leaving had left him alone in an empty house. He'd stood outside several moments after she'd driven away and experienced an ache that wrapped itself clear around his soul. The need for her had grown with each passing moment since.

Later that same day, he'd viewed, across the horizon, a multifaceted rainbow. He hadn't thought of Clare once since then without remembering the vibrant colors of the sundog.

It didn't help matters that they'd parted with so much left unsaid. Clare had been feeling foolish, with the sting of his rejection fresh in her mind. Although he'd wanted to ease her misery, he couldn't. In order to follow through with the divorce, Reed had to allow Clare to believe he was indifferent to her. Thus far he'd failed miserably, his actions contradicting his words each time they were together. The divorce was necessary because it protected her—and that was his biggest concern.

He drove past the library and noted several cars parked in the lot. Disappointed, he decided to wait an hour and try again. There were errands he needed to run, which would occupy him until then.

He spotted Jack Kingston when Reed came out of the hardware store, his arms loaded with his purchase. The other man parked his truck behind Reed's, blocking off his exit.

"Stay away from Clare," Jack shouted, leaning out of his cab. "I'm warning you, if you come near her again, you're going to be sorry."

Reed ignored him, opening the tailgate and sliding the stepladder onto the truck bed.

"Apparently you didn't hear me," Jack shouted.

Reed continued to ignore him and fished his keys from his jeans pocket. He half suspected Jack had been drinking, otherwise he wouldn't have the courage to face him.

"Clare isn't your squaw."

Reed paused in an effort to cool his rising anger. Jack could call him any name he liked, but he'd best leave Clare out of it.

Clare had asked him not to fight Jack. It was the only thing she'd ever requested of him, and although he could feel every fiber of his being tighten, Reed would honor her plea. Unless...

Jack climbed out of his truck and grabbed Reed by the shoulder, slamming him against the side of the truck, his face inches from Reed's.

Reed sighed. Jack was making this difficult.

In the back of her mind, Clare had told herself she'd probably hear from Reed by Tuesday. He'd told her he'd be in touch once he'd spoken to the attorney, which he seemed anxious enough to do. It made sense that he'd show up sometime soon to relay the pertinent information.

He didn't stop in at the library, and by the time she closed at six-thirty, Clare felt defeated and more than a little discouraged.

Erin and Gary were due to arrive back anytime, and Clare was anxious to talk to her best friend. Erin always seemed to know what to do in awkward situations.

Clare was headed home when she passed Burley's

True Value Hardware store. For a moment she was sure she saw Reed's battered pickup parked in the lot. It might have been her imagination, or simply because she was so anxious to see him again. Whatever the reason, she turned around and pulled into the lot herself.

It would take only a moment to see if he was inside and no harm would come of it. If he wasn't, she'd casually be on her way. If he was, she'd let him know she didn't appreciate the way he continued to keep her waiting.

"Evening, Mr. Burley," she greeted, smiling at the potbellied proprietor as she strolled past the checkout stand. She wandered down the aisles, pretending to be interested in a set of pots and pans.

"I tell you, Alice, I've never seen anything like it," a female voice drifted from the other side of the aisle. "Two grown men fighting like that right out there in the parking lot. Poor Mr. Burley ended up having to call the sheriff."

"What could they possibly have been brawling about in broad daylight like that?" Alice asked. She too sounded equally disgusted by the events of that afternoon.

Clare wandered down the row and glanced both ways, hoping to catch a glimpse of Reed.

"Reed Tonasket was involved."

Frozen, Clare listened.

"Were either one of them hurt?" the second woman asked.

"I couldn't tell how badly, but it seemed the other fellow took the worst of the beating. He got his licks in though. Reed was bleeding pretty bad."

Reed. Clare reached for the shelf when she realized the two women were talking about Reed and Jack. Without thinking, she reached for the carton of pots and pans and carried it to the counter where Ed Burley was working the cash register.

"I understand there was something of a commotion here earlier," she said breezily, drawing her debit card from her purse.

"We had a huge fight on our hands," Ed Burley confirmed. "I was afraid they were going to end up killing one another. I couldn't let that happen—I had to call in the sheriff. I hate to be the one to tell you this, Clare, but Jack was involved."

"*What* happened after that?" she prompted, needing to find out what she could.

"Not much. The sheriff's deputy hauled them both away."

Clare's gaze returned to the parking lot where Reed's truck was parked, and a sick kind of dread took root.

"That'll be $155.36," Ed Burley went on to say.

Clare stared at him blankly until she realized he was quoting her the price for her purchase. Quickly she handed him her debit card. She was halfway out the door when Ed Burley called after her.

"You forgot something," he said, handing her the oblong box of pans. By the time Clare reached her car, her legs were shaking so badly she needed to lean against the side of her vehicle. If she was to faint, folks would attribute it to the heat. The day was downright sultry. The hottest day of the year and much too hot for early summer.

But it wasn't the weather that had affected her so negatively. It was Reed. He'd been in a fight. No wonder he had a reputation as a troublemaker. If he was going to engage in violent behavior, he had only himself to blame.

Then she remembered how eager Jack had been to fight Reed the afternoon they'd returned from Las Vegas. Any excuse would do. It had bothered her then, and it did even more so now.

The two were destined to clash, she realized, but she'd hoped Reed would be able to avoid it. She feared he'd been as eager as Jack and that was what troubled her most.

That chip on Reed's shoulder was sometimes larger than the red cedar he used to carve his totem poles. It was as if he wanted to live up to every negative thing that had been reported about him. As if he found it his God-given right to feed the rumors.

Fine. He'd pay the price the same way Jack would. She certainly wasn't going to reward his uncivilized behavior by bailing him out of jail, even if she was his legal wife.

Clare realized she was too upset to be driving when she ran a stop sign. She pulled over to the side of the road and waited for her nerves to settle. But the longer she sat there, the more pronounced her feeling became.

Clare was rarely angry. It wasn't an emotion her family dealt with often. Anger was something to be corrected, or ignored.

Sifting through her emotions did nothing to ease her outrage. She was furious with Reed, more angry than she could ever remember being at anyone.

She tried to relax, to breathe in several deep, calming thoughts and exhale her frustration. But she soon discovered nothing would ease the terrible tension that held her as much a prisoner as Reed was in the local jail.

It was a minor miracle that she didn't get a ticket for a traffic violation as she drove home. She hadn't a clue of how many infractions she'd committed.

Parking in front of her home, she walked to the front door and hesitated. Heaven help her, she couldn't do it. She couldn't leave Reed in jail. With an angry, frustrated sigh, she turned around and marched back to her car.

She'd post Reed's bail, Clare decided, trembling. But he'd know beyond a shadow of a doubt how disappointed she was in him. He wouldn't like her going to the jail, but, by heaven, she was his wife—for now at least—and that entitled her to something.

Tullue's sheriff's office housed a holding cell where they kept those arrested until they could be transferred to larger Callam County jail in Port Angeles. Clare wasn't sure what the charges were against Reed. No doubt they were numerous.

She parked and hiked up the stairs of the sheriff's department as if she were attacking Mount Everest. A longtime family friend was sitting at the receptionist's desk, and Clare realized that news of her actions would undoubtedly reach everyone in town. But that did little to change her mind.

"Hello, Clare." Jim Daniels revealed some surprise at seeing her. "What can I do for you?"

"I understand a deputy brought in Reed Tonasket and Jack Kingston earlier."

Jim's gaze slowly rose to hers, his dark eyes questioning. "Reed Tonasket is here."

"What are the charges?" She removed her wallet from her purse.

"Disturbing the peace, but he may get aggravated assault thrown in. From what I understand, Jack Kingston's at the hospital now."

"Any priors?" How efficient she sounded, as though she were an experienced attorney on a routine call. As if she knew what she was talking about when in reality she knew next to nothing.

"One."

"Has the bail been set?"

Jim named off a figure, and Clare opened her wallet and handed over her credit card.

"You're posting bail?" Jim asked as though he were sure he misunderstood her intentions even now.

"Yes," she returned primly.

"This is going to take a few minutes," Jim continued, sounding ambivalent. "There's some paperwork that needs to be completed first."

"I'll wait here."

Still Jim hesitated. "You're certain about this, Clare?"

"Positive." Her words were stiffer this time. She didn't appreciate his concern, nor was she going to accept his censure. She was over thirty years old, and if she chose to bail someone out of jail that was her business.

Clare's back was rigid as she sat in the waiting area, her hands folded in her lap. Jim returned a few minutes later and announced it would take a couple of moments longer, then sat down at his desk. He glanced up at her once or twice as if seeing her for the first time.

Until she'd married Reed, she'd never done anything the town could consider the least bit improper in her life. Everything about her was predictable. Her entire life had followed a schedule with few deviations, a predetermined outline of events.

The one area she'd failed in had been marriage. She'd

assumed, that by a certain age she'd have settled down with a good, upstanding man and produced the required 2 or 3 children, the same way her brothers had.

The door opened and an officer escorted Reed into the reception area. Clare's gaze was instantly drawn to his. Before she could help herself, she gasped in dismay. His left eye was swollen and there was a deepening bruise along the side of his face. His nose looked as if it had taken the brunt of the attack. Although she didn't know much about this sort of thing, she feared it might be broken. Dried blood was caked just below his bottom lip.

Reed didn't say a word as the handcuffs were removed. He rubbed his wrists as if to restore the circulation to his hands. The officer said something to Reed, who nodded and moved toward Clare.

She remained silent until they were outside the sheriff's office. Tears blurred her vision.

"What are you doing here?" Reed demanded.

"Me?" she cried. "I'm not the one who got myself tossed into the clinker for disturbing the peace."

"Who told you?" He held himself rigid, his stare as cold as she'd ever seen it.

"Does it matter?" She hadn't expected gratitude, not exactly, but it hadn't occurred to her that he'd be so coldly furious with her.

"Did you post Kingston's bail, too?"

Clare whirled around so fast she nearly toppled down the flight of stairs. "I'm not married to him. You're the one who concerns me."

Reed didn't answer her. He marched down the steps and onto the sidewalk.

Clare raced after him. "Why'd you do it? You...
promised me you wouldn't. You said—"

"I promised you nothing."

Clare's entire life felt as if it had been nothing more
than empty promises. Empty dreams. Reed walked
away from her, but she refused to follow him.

"You shouldn't be here any more than you should
be married to me," he told her, holding himself stiffly
away from her. How unyielding he looked, unforgiving.

"You're...right on both counts," she cried, swallowing a sob. Tears streaked her face and forcefully she
brushed them aside, even more furious that he would
see her cry.

"I didn't ask you to come down and bail me out. It
would have been better if you—"

"I couldn't leave you there."

It was as though he didn't hear a single word she
said. He worked his jaw for a moment, then rubbed his
hand along the side of his face to investigate the damage. Clare could see that nothing would get through the
thick layer of pride he wore like a suit of armor, so she
gave up. He wasn't in any mood to listen to her, nor was
he seeking her help. There was nothing left for her to
do but go. He'd walk back to his truck and seek her out
when he was ready...if he ever was.

Not once did she look back as she drove away. Not
once did she allow herself to mentally review her marriage. In another couple of months their relationship
would be over; until then she'd try to forget Reed Tonasket meant anything to her.

It sounded good. Reasonable even. But it didn't work.
She couldn't stop thinking about Reed, couldn't make
herself forget his blackened eye and how swollen his

nose was. He should never have fought Jack, she told herself. No matter what he said, he'd promised her he wouldn't.

Technically he was right, he hadn't said it with words. He'd promised with his eyes the afternoon they'd returned from Vegas as he'd carried her suitcase to the front door. Even then it hadn't been easy for him to ignore Jack's verbal attacks, but he had, and he'd done it for her.

Clare might have been able to settle her nerves if it wasn't so blasted hot. Hoping to generate some cross ventilation, she opened both the front and the back door and then lounged on the sofa, waiting for the worst of the heat to pass.

It seemed impossible, but she must have fallen asleep. When Clare stirred some time later she was surprised to find the room dark. It was as though someone had lowered a black satin blanket over her.

Sitting up, she stared into the empty space, her heart heavy.

She hadn't eaten, hadn't changed out of her work clothes. The room was dark, but much cooler than it had been earlier. Silently she moved into the kitchen, her heart and thoughts burdened. She stood alone in the dark.

The night was rich with sound. June bugs chirped in the distance, the stars were out in brilliant display. Not knowing what drew her, Clare moved to the screen door and gazed into the raw stillness of the night.

Her eyes quickly adjusted to the lack of light. It was then that she saw him. Reed. He couldn't have been standing more than ten feet away.

They stared at each other through the wire mesh.

All the anger she'd experienced earlier, all the fear and the outrage vanished.

He stood there silent and still for several moments. Distance and the night prevented her from reading his features. In her mind it seemed that he was waiting for something, some sign, some word.

With her heart in her hand, Clare answered him.

She stepped forward and held open the screen door.

Nine

Reed didn't understand what had brought him to Clare's, nor did he question the powerful, unrelenting need he experienced for her. He walked toward her, his eyes holding hers. As the distance narrowed, he could see every breath she drew. His gaze was mesmerized by the small, even movements of her chest as it rose and fell.

His body was hard, tight, coiled with tension. For now this woman was his wife, and he was through denying himself what he yearned for most. He was through denying what Clare had asked to give him.

She stood in the moonlight waiting, silent, holding open the screen door for him. Words weren't necessary. They would have distracted him from his purpose.

He paused in front of her; their gazes locked. They stood no more than a few inches apart, reading each other. Clare sighed and, whether she meant to or not, she swayed toward him. He caught her by the waist and gently drew her forward. She came with a soft sigh, and slipped her arms around his neck.

Their kiss brought him pain, but the small discomfort

was far outweighed by the pleasure he received holding Clare. His face was sore, his eyes and mouth battered, but it would take far more than a few well-placed punches to keep him from his wife.

Lovingly, Clare raised her hands to his face, her fingertips lightly investigating the swelling around his eye. Her troubled gaze found his. "Why?" she whispered.

Reed shook his head. It wasn't important now.

"I...need to know."

Reed hesitated, then said, "He insulted you."

Clare's eyes drifted closed and when she looked to him again, he noted tears and a weary sadness. Her hands gently cupped his face as she raised her mouth to his, her lips tenderly moving over his, as though she were afraid of causing him even more pain.

"Clare." His fingers covered hers as he diverted her from her gentle ministrations. "I'm sorry," he breathed. It was why he'd come to her, he realized. To seek her pardon for his anger when she'd risked so much on his behalf.

"I am, too," she whispered on a half sob. The question must have shown in him, because she elaborated. "For having doubted you...for being so angry."

He kissed her again, and it was a cleansing, a pardon for them both. They were inside the darkened kitchen now, although Reed couldn't recall moving from the back stairs. He knew with a certainty that they were going to make love, and in some deep, unexplainable way that troubled him.

He wanted Clare; his desire for her had been an ever-present torment since Vegas. Yet he resisted her, refused himself, his reasons legitimate and sound, lined up like a row of righteous judges in his mind.

He'd convinced himself it was important for both their sakes to avoid anything physical, especially since a divorce was inevitable. He realized now he was only partially right. His reasons for backing out of the marriage were far more complex than he could acknowledge, deeply rooted in emotions he was only beginning to understand.

When he made love to Clare, he was completely vulnerable to her, his soul was laid bare. Loving her cost him dearly. He lost the ability to hide behind the barrier of indifference. He couldn't love her and remain passive. Marrying Clare had been the most exhilarating experience of his life, and at the same time the most revealing. Because of Clare he could no longer hide.

The desire to run from her vanished, overpowered by his rapidly increasing need. He kissed her again and again, tentative, light kisses in the dark. Her trembling body moved against him, and soon unabated desire seared through them both.

Making soft cooing sounds, Clare broke away from him, her shoulders heaving with the effort. Then, taking his hand, she led him down the darkened hallway to her bedroom.

Moonlight dimly lit the neat, well-kept room, and Reed smiled, remembering the careless way in which Clare had discarded her clothes the night they'd exchanged their vows. He hadn't known her well enough then to appreciate how eager she'd been for him.

He knew her now. Understood her. Heaven help them both, he loved her, and where that love would lead them, he could only speculate.

Clare smiled up at him, and Reed swore her look cut clear through him. Her unselfishness, her generosity had deeply affected him. He kissed her again, taking more time, savoring each small kiss, each sigh. Together they lay upon the mattress, their breathing growing more labored. Reed trembled with impatience.

They sighed in harmony as his mouth locked over hers. Reed found it impossible to refuse her anything, least of all what he wanted most himself. Again his lips claimed hers in a lengthy, deep kiss. By mutual, unspoken agreement, they parted long enough to remove their clothes. Reed's hands shook with the urgency of the task, finishing before her. He turned to help her and soon discovered that his fumbling hands impeded the process.

Clare smiled at him in the moonlight, her eyes eager and happy. The love he felt for her in that moment was nearly his undoing. A yearning, deep and potent, gripped him. He discovered he could wait no longer— his need was too great. He wanted to explain, apologize, but he found himself incapable of doing more than steering her back toward the bed.

Afterwards neither of them spoke. Reed had never been one for words, and he found them impossible now. He needed Clare. He loved her, but he couldn't have said it, couldn't have managed it just then.

Nestled in his arms, she seemed encompassed in lassitude and close to sleep. The same way Reed was himself. He closed his eyes, content and satisfied and she nestled into his embrace and they both slept.

Shortly after dawn, Reed woke. The sun shone through a narrow slice between the drapes. Clare remained in his embrace, and the wealth of emotion he experienced being there with her produced an odd, intense pain in his heart.

He'd never known a woman like Clare. She looked small and fragile, but she had the heart of a lion and a bold, unflinching courage. There'd never been anyone in his life like her.

He wrapped his arm around her shoulders and kissed her crown, savoring her warmth and her softness. She smelled warm and feminine and his body ached with his need for her.

In an effort to divert his mind, he allowed his thoughts to wander in an attempt to judge their future together. He loved Clare more than he had dreamed it was possible to love.

The thought of anyone looking down on her because of him, of calling her the names Jack had, produced a fierce protective anger.

He'd promised himself he wouldn't touch her, vowed he'd do the right thing by her, then broken his own word. When he'd seen her at the jail, he'd wanted to grab her and shake some sense into her. Didn't she realize what she was risking by posting his bail? She opened herself up to speculation and possible ridicule and everything else Reed was looking to protect her from. She'd done it for him. She'd do it again, too. Their lives together would demand a long list of forfeits, and he wasn't sure what she had to gain.

He frowned as he carefully weighed the cost in his mind. A sense of alarm filled him, alarm that she would carry the burden of speculation because of him. He knew she'd do so willingly, without question, with the same courage and generosity that he'd witnessed in her earlier.

He couldn't do it, Reed realized in the next heartbeat. He couldn't drag her into his world, that isolated island. She didn't belong there, and deserved much better. Nor could he join her in her world. He was who he was, and the ways of the white man had always bewildered him.

He had no option. He loved Clare, and because he did, he had to set her free.

Clare woke slowly, by degrees, more content than she could ever remember being in her life. Reed had come to her, had loved her, had spent the night with her. All night.

She had never known a man like him. They'd make love, sleep for an hour or so, then wake and make love again. It was by far the most incredible experience of her life. Clare found she could refuse him nothing. Each time they'd made love as man and wife had been different. Unique.

They hadn't talked. The communication between them had been made with sighs and moans. Quietly snuggled in each other's arms they'd lain utterly content and listened to the sounds of the night. A whispering breeze, an owl's hooting call. Clare's head had rested over Reed's heart, and she could hear the even, heavy thud of his pulse in her ear. She'd found such simple pleasure in being held by her husband.

Rolling onto her side, she scooted closer to him, intending to wrap her arm around his middle. After the tumultuous night they'd spent, she felt comfortable enough to freely touch him.

Only he wasn't there.

Clare opened her eyes, and even then she was surprised to find him gone. Surely he wouldn't have left her, not without saying something. Not without a warm goodbye. Surely he wouldn't do something so crass after what they'd shared.

She struggled out of bed, reached for her robe, and with quick steps ventured into the kitchen. Part of her was completely confident she'd find him sitting at her table sipping a cup of coffee.

Padding barefoot from one room to the next, she soon realized she was wrong. Reed was nowhere to be found. Her home was as empty as her heart.

One possible explanation piled on top of another. There could be any number of very good reasons why Reed had found it necessary to leave her.

Certain she'd missed something, she searched her home again, looking for a note, something, anything that would remove this terrible sensation of doubt and inadequacy.

Not sure what she should do, she brewed a cup of coffee and sat, holding the mug with both hands, while she collected her thoughts.

They were married. It wasn't as though he'd abandoned her, but if that was the case, then why did she feel so desolate, so...forsaken?

A glance at the clock reminded Clare that she didn't have time to lounge around her kitchen and sort through the uncertainties. Surely Reed intended to contact her at some point during the day.

She dressed, choosing a pale pink summer dress with a wide belt and pastel flowered jacket. It wasn't something she wore to work often, but dark outfits that had become her uniform looked stark and unfriendly. She kept her hair down, too, because she knew Reed liked it that way. He'd never told her so, but he seemed to take delight in removing the pins and running his fingers through its length.

All morning Clare looked for Reed. Her stomach seemed to be upset, but she wasn't sure if it was nerves or if she was coming down with something.

It wasn't Reed who stopped in to see her. Instead, it was her mother.

Clare recognized the look her mother wore immediately. The pinched lips, the beleaguered, weary sadness in the eyes that said Clare had done something to displease her.

"Hello, Mom," Clare greeted, forcing some enthusiasm into her voice.

"I need to talk to you."

"Go ahead," she said. She hadn't been very busy, and there wasn't anyone at the front desk who required her attention. She could listen to her mother's chastisement and return books to their proper slots at the same time.

"Your father had a call from Jim Daniels this morning."

It certainly hadn't taken the stalwart deputy long to make his report, Clare noted. She'd hoped it would take two or three weeks before word of her posting Reed's bail leaked to her parents.

"Do you have anything to say?"

"Yes," Clare answered calmly. "I'm a woman now, Mother. I'm not thirteen, or eighteen or even twenty-one. I'm not a young lady to be admonished for wrongdoing."

The pinched lips tightened even more. "I see."

"I mentioned to you earlier that I was dating Reed Tonasket. He's a friend…a very good friend."

"Do you have any other friends who get themselves thrown in jail?"

"No," she agreed readily enough. "He's the first."

"Then I hope to high heaven he's the last jailbird you date."

"Personally I don't think it was an experience he's looking to repeat, either."

"I should hope not," her mother said primly. Her black handbag dangled from her arm, and when she sighed, she looked older than her years and troubled. "I can't help being concerned about you, Clare. I'm afraid you're showing signs of becoming…desperate."

"Honestly, Mother." She tried not to, but she couldn't help laughing. In an effort to understand her parent's point of view, she added, "If the circumstances were reversed I'd probably be just as worried about you. All I'm asking is that you trust my judgment." Which was asking a good deal in light of her lengthy relationship with Jack Kingston.

"Your father doesn't know what to think."

"I imagine he's concerned, and I can't say that I blame either one of you. Perhaps it would help matters if I brought Reed over so you and Dad could meet him. Once you got to know him, I'm sure you'd feel the same way I do about him."

"You're serious about this young man, aren't you?"

Clare hugged a novel against her stomach and resisted the urge to laugh. "Very serious."

Her mother's eyes moved away from Clare. "I'll check with your father and get back to you with a time."

"Thanks, Mom." If they'd been anyplace else, Clare would have been tempted to blurt out the truth. She more than liked Reed, she was crazy in love with him. If they continued in the vein they had the night before,

Clare would be bleary-eyed from lack of sleep and pregnant by the end of the month.

Pregnant. The desire for children was no longer muddled in her mind. More than anything she longed to give Reed a child. Her feelings hadn't crystallized when she took the pregnancy test. She hadn't known what she felt when the results proved negative. She'd been a bit apprehensive, then later a little sad, her emotions too confused for her to judge her true feelings.

Clare was utterly confident about what she wanted now. At one time she'd been concerned about where they'd live. Details no longer interested her. Her needs were simple—she wanted to spend the rest of her life with Reed. If he opted to continue living on the reservation, then she'd be utterly content to be there, too. If he chose to move into town, all the better. As long as they were together, nothing else mattered.

Reed came into the library just before closing time, when she least expected to see him. The first thing she noticed was that the swelling had gone down around his eye. Other than a small bruise along his jaw line, it was difficult to tell he'd been in a physical confrontation.

He set several books on top of the counter and waited until he had her attention, which he'd had from the instant he walked in the front door. Unfortunately, Clare was occupied with a young mother and her two preschoolers, her last customers for the day.

Reed waited until they'd gone and Clare had locked the glass door behind them. She felt a little nervous with him. A little unsure.

She wanted to know why he'd left her that morning and why it'd taken him the entire day to come back, but she didn't feel she should make demands of him.

He had his reasons, and when it came time he'd let her know what had dictated his actions.

"Hi," she said, occupying herself with the last-minute details.

"You look different."

"Thank you." She wasn't entirely sure he meant it as a compliment, but she chose to accept it as such. She lifted a heavy stack of books from the counter, prepared to move them to the large plastic bin, when Reed silently stepped in and took them from her. It was then that she noticed his knuckles. They were scraped, bruised, the skin broken. In her concern about his face, she hadn't realized his hands had taken the brunt of the fight.

"Oh, Reed," she whispered, his pain becoming her own.

He raised questioning eyes to her. His gaze followed hers before he grinned. "Don't worry, it doesn't hurt."

"But I do worry. Jack…"

"He isn't bothering you, is he?"

"No… I haven't seen him since Saturday."

"What happened Saturday?"

"Nothing." She shook her head and resumed her task.

"Clare," he repeated softly, "what happened Saturday?"

"He…stopped by the house with a diamond ring and proposed."

Reed was silent for several moments. "What did you tell him?"

"I wanted to tell him I was already married, but I couldn't very well do that, could I?" she blurted out, growing impatient with his questions. They had a lot more important issues to discuss than Jack Kingston.

"What did you say?" Reed repeated.

Clare flashed him an irritated look, one similar to what her mother had given her earlier in the day. "I told him I wasn't the right woman for him and sent him on his merry way. He doesn't love me, you know. He might have convinced himself he does, but I know better."

A smile quivered at the edges of Reed's lips.

"What's so funny?" she demanded, reaching for her purse, ready to leave.

His smile became full-fledged. "You. I imagine you're able to quell whole groups of rebellious youngsters with that look of yours."

Clare didn't bother to pretend she didn't know what he was talking about. Arguing with him would have wasted valuable time.

"Unfortunately Jack saw the totem pole you gave me and guessed that I'd spent the day with you. He was angry when he left. In thinking over what happened, I'm sure he's relieved to be off the hook. Jack never was keen on marrying me until I wanted nothing more to do with him."

Reed didn't agree or disagree with her. "We need to talk about what happened last night."

"All right," she agreed hesitantly. As far as she was concerned there wasn't anything to discuss. She walked around the front desk and sat down at one of the round tables the library had purchased that spring. There wasn't any threat of someone interrupting them since the library was technically closed and she'd secured the lock.

He didn't make eye contact with her, and that troubled Clare. It bothered her enough for her to speak before he could.

"We can discuss last night—unless you plan to tell

me it was all a big mistake," she blurted out. "Because if that's why you're here, I don't want to hear it." If he attempted to trivialize their lovemaking, pass it off as unimportant, an error in judgment, then she would refuse to listen.

Reed didn't sit down. He walked past her, as if he needed time and space to form his thoughts. "You should never have posted bail for me. There's already talk."

"Talk's never bothered me. I knew when I went there what I was risking. It was my choice and I made it."

"Your parents—"

"Don't worry about them," she flared, growing impatient with him. "Stop worrying about what everyone else thinks."

"Your reputation's at stake."

"My reputation," she repeated with a small, humorless laugh. "I'm just grateful the good people in Tullue feel they have something to say about me. It's the first time in my life I've generated so much interest." This last bit was an attempt at humor, but she recognized right away that it was a mistake.

Reed's eyes darkened and his shoulders went stiff.

"I was just joking," she said, making light of her words.

"Your parents..."

"Already know," she finished for him. "Mom was in earlier this afternoon."

Reed's probing gaze searched hers. "You didn't tell her we were married, did you?"

"No, but I wish I had."

"Clare, no."

"Don't look so concerned," she said, frowning. "I

told her how important you are to me…much more important than a friend."

"This isn't good," he muttered.

"I'm not ashamed of being your wife. You might prefer to keep it some deep, dark secret, but I happen to—"

"You don't know what you're talking about," he bit off gruffly. He stalked away from her, and Clare realized he was removing himself from her emotionally, as well as physically.

"I told Mom I wanted to bring you over so she and Dad could meet you," she said after a moment, doing her best to keep her voice steady.

"I wish you hadn't done that."

"Why?" she asked innocently. "We're married, Reed, and they have a right to know. I'm their only daughter."

"They don't need to know."

"What is it you want me to do?" she flared back. "Do you want me to wait until we've moved in together before I tell them? Or do you want me to get pregnant first and then casually announce we've been married all along? Is that what you want me to do? Because I find that completely unfair to everyone involved."

"Pregnant." He said the word as though he'd never heard it before.

"Okay, I get it," she continued, "they aren't going to be leaping up and down for joy to know I got married behind their backs. That's going to cause some readjustment in their thinking, but they love me and in time they'll come to love you too."

Reed whirled around to face her, his look wild, almost primitive. His eyes were narrowed and pained. She could see him steel himself against her. Against her words, against her love.

When he spoke, his words were low and harsh. "I'm afraid you've assumed too much, Clare."

"What do you mean?"

An eternity passed before he spoke. "You're not moving in with me."

"Fine, you can come into town," she said brightly, giving a small, dismissive gesture with her hands as though to suggest it made no difference to her. "That'll save me the long drive from the reservation every day, so all the better."

Even as she spoke, Clare realized she was being obtuse. Reed was trying to tell her he fully intended on following through with the divorce.

"The attorney mailed me some preliminary papers for you to read over," he said, removing an envelope from his pocket. He set it on the table in front of her.

Mutely Clare stared at the envelope. It was a plain white one, not unlike thousands of others. This particular one had the name of the law firm printed on the upper left-hand corner. It amazed Clare that something so small, so simple, could be the source of so much pain.

Her heart felt as if it had stopped completely, then she realized it continued to beat, but it was her lungs that weren't functioning. Not until it became painful did she realize she wasn't breathing.

In the past, pride had saved her, granting her the impetus to pretend she was unaffected, unscathed, unconcerned. She could rely on it to carry her for several minutes, long enough, she prayed, before she broke.

"How embarrassing," she said with a frivolous laugh, trying to make light of it. "I've just made a complete idiot of myself, haven't I?"

"Clare..."

"Don't worry, I get the picture. Despite last night you don't want to stay married to me, but an occasional bout of good old-fashioned sex wouldn't be amiss."

He looked as if he wanted to say something, but held himself in check. "If you need me for anything…"

"Be assured I won't," she told him in clipped tones. The temperature would drop below freezing in Hawaii before she'd turn to Reed Tonasket for anything.

"If you're pregnant I'd appreciate knowing it."

"Why? Are you worried that might delay the divorce proceedings?"

"Don't, Clare," he whispered, and it almost seemed he was pleading with her.

She didn't realize how badly she was trembling until she attempted to stand up. "Please go…just go."

He hesitated, his face set and hard with determination and pride. Unfortunately, Reed Tonasket wasn't the only one with an oversupply of pride. It had carried Clare this far. Her heart was shattered, her dignity in shreds, but by heaven there was a shred of pride left in her and she clung to that the way a trapeze artist hangs on to the bar.

"You're right, I'm sure. This quickie divorce is for the best."

Reed's eyes were savage, but Clare was too busy concentrating on maintaining her control to pay him much heed. "I'll let you out of the library," she said, walking to the front door, her keys jingling at her side.

Reed walked out, and she stood there watching him through the glass door until he was out of sight. Somehow she made it home; only when she was parked outside the single-family dwelling did she realize where she was. She remembered nothing about the drive.

Her neighbors were out watering their flower bed, and Mrs. Carlson gave her a friendly wave. Clare returned the gesture, walked into her house, went straight into the bathroom and lost her lunch.

Someone rang her doorbell, but Clare was too distraught to care who it could be.

A short, impatient knock was followed by a small voice. "Clare, are you here? Your car's parked out front."

Clare hurried into the living room. "Erin," she cried, and burst into tears. "I'm so glad you're home."

Ten

Erin didn't seem to know what to do. "What happened?" she asked gently, then bristled. "Don't tell me, I already know. Jack's at it again, right?"

Clare laughed, not fully understanding why she found her best friend's words so amusing. Her life was far removed from Jack Kingston's now. He was a figure from her past, and although it had been only a matter of a couple of weeks, it seemed much longer.

Clare slumped onto her sofa and gathered her feet beneath her. She was feeling ill again and weepy, and detested both. Weakness had always bothered her, but never more than in herself.

"How was the honeymoon?" she asked.

Erin brightened, sinking into the overstuffed chair across from her. "Fabulous. Oh, Clare, marriage is wonderful."

The flash of pain was so sharp that Clare closed her eyes until it passed.

"Clare?" Erin asked softly. "Are you ill?"

Clare nodded. "I… I must have come down with a bug," she murmured.

"Then this doesn't have anything to do with Jack?"

"Not a thing. It's over between us."

"You told me that when we left for Vegas, but I didn't know if you were sure."

"Trust me, I'm sure. Now tell me when you got back and why you'd waste time with me when you've got a husband at home waiting for you."

Erin crossed her long jean-clad legs and smiled. "Gary told me to get lost for a few minutes. He's got some kind of surprise brewing. My guess is that he ordered new living room furniture and is having it delivered, but I'm not supposed to know that."

"I didn't think you were due back until Saturday." Clare had hoped that by then she'd have recovered enough both physically and mentally to welcome Erin and Gary home.

Clare couldn't ever remember seeing her friend more radiant. Love had transformed Erin's life. It had transformed her own, too, but not in the same way. Loving Reed was a mistake, she tried to convince herself. Another in a long list of relationship errors. But her heart refused to listen. If loving him was just another blunder, then why was she grieving like this? When she'd broken up with Jack, there'd been a sense of release, of freedom. She felt no elation now. Only a pain that cut so deep it was nearly crippling.

"How'd you and Reed get along after the wedding?" Erin asked conversationally.

Clare tensed. "Wh-what makes you ask?"

Erin paused, her leg swinging. "You two didn't get into an argument or anything, did you?"

Her lifetime friend had no idea how far the "or anything" had stretched. "No…we had a wonderful time together. I won a thousand dollars."

"Gambling!" Erin cried. "I don't believe it. Gary and I were in Vegas and I didn't so much as bet five dollars." She hesitated, and a shy, slightly chagrined smile lit up her features. "Of course we didn't leave the hotel room all that much."

The living room started to spin, and Clare scooted down on the sofa and pressed her head against the arm. "How was Boston?"

"Great. Gary's family is wonderful, which isn't any real surprise, knowing the man my husband is." She stopped abruptly and exhaled sharply. "My husband… I still can't get used to saying that. I never thought it was possible to find a man I'd love so much. I never thought it'd be possible to say the word 'husband' again and feel the incredible things I do."

Pain clenched at Clare's breast; how well she understood what Erin was saying. "Husband" was an especially amazing word to her, too.

"Then you and Reed had a chance to get to know one another a little better?" Erin continued.

For the first time that afternoon, Clare wanted to laugh out loud. "You might say that."

"Good."

"Why good?" Clare wanted to know.

"I like Reed. I never knew him very well—I don't think many folks around town do since he keeps to himself most of the time. Gary knows him about as well as anyone, and claims Reed's both talented and generous. I had no idea he was so actively involved with Native American youths. He's helped several of them over the years, kept them out of trouble, given them pride in their heritage. From what Gary said, Reed's taken in and been like a foster father to a handful of boys over the last several years."

Clare wasn't surprised, although she hadn't known that about him.

"I don't think anyone in town realizes how well-known his artwork has become all across the country, either," Erin continued. "Gary and I saw one of the totem poles he carved while we were in Boston."

"You don't need to list his virtues for me, Erin."

"I don't?" she asked, elevating her voice. "You like him?"

"Very much," Clare admitted.

"Then you wouldn't be opposed to the four of us having dinner together sometime soon? I don't want you to think I'm playing matchmaker here, but I was kind of hoping the two of you would be interested in each other."

Clare couldn't keep the sadness out of her smile. "I... don't think that would be a good idea."

"Why?" Erin returned defensively. "Because Reed's half Native American?"

"No," she returned, defeat coating her words, "because I sincerely doubt Reed wants anything more to do with me."

"That's ridiculous," Erin returned, shaking her head. "Gary said he thought Reed was attracted to you, and I absolutely agree. I saw the look in his eye right before the wedding ceremony. When a man looks at a woman like that, there's interest. In my opinion, Clare Gilroy, you should fan those flames."

"Trust me, Erin, they've been fanned."

"And?" Erin leaned forward expectantly.

"You don't want to know." Her friend was looking

at the world through rose-colored glasses. Clare didn't want to drag her back to earth with the sad litany of her own problems.

"Of course I want to know. I thought something was wrong," Erin said suspiciously, then stood and walked over to where Clare was lying down. Pressing the back of her hand against Clare's forehead, she asked, "This is a whole lot more than a flu bug, isn't it?"

"Not exactly, although it's much too soon to know if I'm pregnant."

"Pregnant," Erin repeated in a weak whisper.

"Don't look so startled...you don't need to worry—I'm married. Well, sort of married. No," she said, changing her mind once more. "If I'm married enough to get pregnant then I'm more than sort of married." Clare didn't know if her friend could make sense of her words or not.

Erin flopped into her chair. "Who? When... I did hear you right, didn't I?"

"You heard me just fine." Although she was feeling dreadful, Clare sat upright. "I'm just not sure you're going to find all this believable." She held out her left hand. "The ring belongs to Reed. He gave it to me in lieu of a wedding band. We...we were married a few hours after you and Gary, although it's going to be one of the shortest marriages in Nevada history. Reed's already arranged for a divorce."

Reed straightened and wiped the sweat from his brow with the back of his forearm. His muscles ached; the low-grade throb in the small of his back seemed to be growing more intense. Nevertheless he continued working. He welcomed the discomfort, because the physical pain balanced out what he was feeling emotionally.

It'd been three days since he'd last seen Clare. The temptation to drive into town and check on her had been nearly overwhelming. He was disciplined in every area of his life, by choice and by necessity. For both their sakes, he'd decided not to see Clare again until it was unavoidable. Until he could steel himself enough to hide his pain and ignore hers.

Clare was a survivor. She was hurting now, but that would pass, the same way his own pain would ease. Over time, prompted by pride.

They'd both needed to deal with several emotional issues, but knowing Clare, Reed was confident she'd find whatever good there'd been between them and cling to that. It was a trait he admired about her.

In the beginning he'd been amused by her Pollyanna attitude, but later he'd come to respect it as being a very special part of this woman he loved. She continually expected the best from others, and because she expected it, she often received it.

Their marriage was the exception, and that troubled Reed. She'd trusted him, believed him and given unselfishly of herself to him. His only comfort was that in the next few months, Clare would uncover something beneficial from their experience.

Reed had to believe that, had to trust in the strength of Clare's character or go insane knowing he'd hurt the one person he truly loved.

A sound of an approaching car caught his ear and he straightened, setting aside the chisel and hammer.

Coming out of his workshop, he noticed the blue sedan pulling into the parking space next to his house.

Gary Spencer.

He spied Reed about the same time, and an automatic smile lit up Gary's face. "Reed, it's good to see you."

"You, too." Marriage agreed with Gary, Reed realized immediately. "Welcome back."

"Thanks."

"Come inside and have something cold to drink." Reed led the way into the cabin, then pulled out a chair at the table for Gary to sit. "When did you get back?"

"A few days ago."

Reed opened the refrigerator and took out two cold cans of soda, tossing the first to Gary. "How's Erin?" he asked, straddling a chair himself.

"Busy, much too busy to suit me. I surprised her with some new furniture, which I'll tell you right now was a big mistake."

"How's that?"

Gary grinned. "Now she thinks the living room walls look dingy and insists we paint the room. The last few days of our honeymoon are going to be spent in the living room instead of the bedroom—the way I planned."

Reed pretended amusement. His own bride...he paused, forcefully pushing the memory of Clare sleeping in his arms from his mind. He had to carefully guard his thoughts when it came to his last evening with Clare. Indulgence came with a heavy price tag. He dared not remember the way she'd opened herself to him with generosity and love, or he'd find it impossible to stay away from her. Giving her time to heal and himself time to forget was essential for them both.

"I have to admit Erin was a good sport about it. She offered to do it herself, said she'd invite Clare Gilroy over to help. Apparently she helped Clare paint her kitchen sometime back and was going to ask her to return the favor. Unfortunately Clare's been sick, so it looks like I'm going to get stuck with the task." Gary raised the aluminum can to his lips and took a deep swallow.

Clare sick. Reed's mind raced. "Anything serious?" he asked, not wanting to reveal his immediate concern.

"I wouldn't know. From what Erin said it's some kind of flu bug. It's wiped her out."

"Has she seen a doctor?"

Gary shrugged. "I don't think so."

Reed relaxed, then tensed. He'd heard of women who suffered flulike symptoms throughout their pregnancies. His mind raced with fear and doubt. Maybe it was possible Clare was pregnant, but how possible, he didn't know. He'd hoped Clare would have the presence of mind to contact him, but in his heart he knew she wouldn't. If he wanted answers he'd have to ask.

Reed returned his attention to Gary, who was staring at him as though seeing him for the first time. His friend's shoulders sagged as he shook his head. "It's true, isn't it?"

"What's true?"

Gary hesitated, as if he were stunned and having trouble talking. "Erin came back from visiting Clare with this incredible story of the two of you marrying. Frankly, I didn't believe it."

Reed frowned. So Clare had told Erin. He wished she hadn't, but there was no help for it now.

"I don't know Clare that well," Gary continued, "but I know she's been under a lot of emotional stress over breaking up with Kingston. I thought she might have made the whole thing up."

"It's true," Reed said, standing. He walked over to the sink and looked out the window, blind to the lush green forest just beyond the house.

"The two of you were married in Las Vegas a few hours after Erin and me?"

"I said it was true." Reed's words were clipped and hard. Gary had waded into a subject Reed didn't intend to discuss.

"Why?" Gary asked incredulously.

The question angered Reed so much he stormed around to face his friend, hands clenched into fists at his sides. He didn't understand how other men could be so unconscious of Clare's beauty. She was a woman of strength and courage. Generous and loving. Was the whole world blind to the obvious?

Realizing he'd traipsed onto forbidden ground, Gary swiftly changed the subject. "I heard what happened between you and Kingston. I take it he got the worst of the beating. I don't know if you heard, but he has a busted jaw. His mouth had to be wired shut."

A fitting penalty after the things he'd called Clare. Reed had taken delight in making him retract each and every one. "He'll survive."

"That was one way of making sure he doesn't go near her again. What I don't understand," Gary continued, pausing long enough to take another drink of his soda, "is if you don't want her yourself, why you'd go out of your way to cause trouble with Kingston? From what I understand he intended to marry her until you got your hands on him."

"He isn't good enough for Clare," Reed muttered. He wanted to change the subject to something more pleasant, but he discovered a certain comfort in hearing about Clare and knowing Kingston wouldn't be around to bother her again.

"If you care for her, and you clearly do," Gary said with a hint of impatience, "then why are you so quick to divorce her?"

"That's my own business," Reed said harshly.

"If there's an ironic side to this situation," Gary continued, "it's that Erin and I had talked about getting the two of you together. Neither one of us is much of a matchmaker, but there was such a strong chemistry between you two. We both felt it."

"She didn't know what she was doing when she married me," Reed said, his words low and regretful.

"She was drunk?"

Reed shook his head. "She crossed some medication with alcohol."

Gary's eyebrows folded together as he collected this latest bit of information. "That could explain what prompted Clare," Gary murmured thoughtfully, "although I have a hard time picturing her doing something so out of character."

"She was caught up in the heat of the moment," Reed explained, excusing her actions.

"Maybe that's why Clare agreed to go through with the wedding. But you were stone sober, weren't you?"

Reluctantly, Reed nodded.

A satisfied gleam entered Gary's eyes. "Then tell me, what prompted you to agree to the marriage?"

Reed knew he wasn't going to be able to stay away from Clare any longer. Knowing she was ill, suspecting she was pregnant had hounded him ever since Gary's visit earlier in the afternoon. He should be more patient, bide his time, give Clare the necessary space before he went to her.

He couldn't now. He'd nearly worn a path on the kitchen linoleum worrying about her from the moment Gary mentioned she was sick. His friend was a clever character, Reed realized. He should have known Gary had an ulterior motive, dragging Clare into the conversation. He'd casually brought up Clare's name, then waited for Reed's reaction before questioning him about the marriage.

The fact Gary was able to read him so easily told Reed his feelings for Clare remained close to the surface. If he wasn't able to hide them from Gary, then it would be next to impossible to conceal them from her.

An internal debate had warred inside him the rest of the afternoon. It wasn't until he sat down for dinner, with no appetite, that he accepted the inevitable.

He would go to her.

The need, the urgency that drove him was an additional source of concern. He wondered how long his love for her would dictate his actions, drive him to do the very things he promised himself he wouldn't. The need to protect her, to look after her remained strong, and he couldn't imagine it changing.

Not now. Not ever.

Clare guessed this was more than a simple flu bug the second day she couldn't keep anything in her stomach. She would have called her doctor to make an appointment, but didn't for the simple reason that she was too sick to go into his office.

She felt dreadful, but blamed it on a combination of ailments. Her sinus headache, not surprisingly, was back, and she was suffering from all the symptoms of an especially potent form of flu. On top of everything else the man she loved was determined to divorce her.

It was enough to put a truck driver flat on his back.

When the doorbell chimed, Clare raised her head from her pillow and groaned. She wasn't in the mood for company; she especially didn't want to be mothered, coddled or bothered.

The temptation to ignore the summons was strong, but she realized her not answering would likely cause more problems.

Heaven help her if it was Erin again, dishing up chicken soup Clare couldn't keep down, along with aspirin and plenty of juice. Erin seemed especially worried about her, but Clare wished her friend would devote her attention to Gary and leave her in peace.

The doorbell chimed again and Clare groaned. There was no help for it; she had to get up. It surprised her how weak she was, how the room refused to hold still and how much effort it took to accomplish the simplest of tasks.

She reached for her robe while her feet groped for her slippers, then paused in the doorway, afraid for a moment she was about to faint. There was a good possibility she might get over this bug if people would kindly leave her alone.

"Who is it?" she asked, her hand on the dead-bolt lock.

"Reed" came the gruff reply.

Clare closed her eyes and pressed her forehead against the door. It felt cool against her skin and oddly soothing. "Would it be possible for you to come back another time?" she asked without unlatching the door.

"No."

Somehow she guessed that. With a good deal of reluctance she turned the knob and opened the door. If he hadn't already made up his mind about the divorce, seeing her now would erase all doubt.

Clare didn't need a mirror to know she looked dreadful. Her hair hung in limp strands about her face. She was pale and sickly, hadn't brushed her teeth, and she smelled like curdled milk.

"If you need me to sign some papers from your attorney, just leave them with me and I'll see to it later," she said. Her defenses were down and she didn't have the strength to fight him.

Clare wasn't sure what she expected from Reed. A lecture, a tirade, anger or love—she was beyond guessing anymore. But having him mutter curses under his breath, then lift her into his arms and carry her back into the bedroom certainly came as a surprise.

"How long have you been sick?" he demanded, gently placing her in the center of her bed.

"I don't know that it's any of your concern," she returned with as much dignity as she could marshal, which unfortunately wasn't much.

He picked up the bottle of pills on her nightstand and read the label. "Another sinus infection?"

"No... I don't know why you're here, but if it's because I'm sick, let me assure you—"

"What did the doctor have to say?" he asked, not allowing her to finish.

"Who told you I was sick anyway?" She had a few demands of her own, and one of those included privacy. "Don't answer that, I already know. It could only have been Erin."

"It wasn't. Now for the last time what did the doctor say?"

Clare remained stubbornly silent. She closed her eyes to block him out, hoping he'd take the hint and leave. When he did walk away, she opened her eyes and blinked back tears of disappointment.

Not until she heard his voice coming from her kitchen did she realize he hadn't left her after all. She squeezed her eyes closed and tried as best she could to listen in on the telephone conversation, but Reed's voice was too low for her to hear much. She couldn't figure out who he'd called or why.

He returned looking like someone from Special Forces on a secret mission. Methodically he opened and shut her closet doors, left and then returned a couple of minutes later with her suitcase.

"What are you doing?" she demanded, trying to sit up. If the room would stop spinning like a toy top she might have been able to pull it off.

Reed didn't answer her. Instead he opened several drawers, took out a number of personal items, not stopping until her suitcase was filled.

"Reed?" she pleaded.

"I'm packing."

That much was obvious. "Where am I going?" she insisted, then softly shook her head. "More important, why am I going?"

"You're too sick to be alone" came his brusque response. "I'll be taking you to your parents' house."

"You can't."

Reed turned cool black eyes toward her. "Why not?"

"They're on a camping trip."

"All right, I'll take you to Erin and Gary's."

Clare groaned inwardly. "Don't be ridiculous. I certainly don't want to pass on this germ to them, and furthermore, I'm not keen on sleeping in the bedroom next to a couple of newlyweds."

For the first time since he had arrived, Reed hesitated. She prayed to heaven he was listening, because she didn't have the strength to reason with him.

Unfortunately, he didn't pause long. Reaching up to the top shelf of her closet, he brought down a blanket. He laid it over her, then picked her and the blanket up in one swift, easy motion.

"Reed, please don't do this."

He ignored her as he had so often.

"I'm much better really... I want to stay in my own home, my own bed. *Please*."

He didn't hesitate, and the frustration beat down on her like war drums. She wanted to pound his chest and scream at him. He'd made it perfectly clear he wanted out of her life. Perfectly clear he regretted their marriage.

Clare didn't know what to believe any longer. She didn't know how he could hold and love her one night and casually mention divorce the next. He bewildered her, frustrated her.

At the moment, Clare's options were exceptionally limited. Despite her protests, Reed carried her outside, opened his car door and carefully deposited her in the passenger side. Before she could complain further, he went back to the house and returned with the suitcase and her purse.

"Will you kindly tell me where you're taking me?" she asked, her voice pitifully weak. He refused to answer her, his jaw as hard as granite. She might as well be reasoning with a statue for all the response he gave her.

"Reed...please tell me where you're taking me."

"Doc Brown's."

"His office has been closed for hours," she told him.

"I know. We're stopping off at his house."

"His house?" Clare couldn't believe what she was hearing. "You can't take me there. Reed, please, you just can't do that." Once again he acted as if he hadn't heard her. If she wasn't so weak, she would have cried.

"He's waiting for us."

"You talked to Dr. Brown? When?"

"Earlier. I let the library know you wouldn't be in for the rest of the week while I was at it." Each response he gave her was like a gift, Clare realized. She didn't understand why he was doing this, or why he appeared so angry. She hadn't asked him to come, didn't want his sympathy, nor was she interested in his pampering.

"You think I'm pregnant, don't you?" she asked after a few minutes. It all added up in her mind now. "It's... only been four days. I doubt I'd have this kind of reaction so quickly, so you can stop worrying."

Reed ignored her and continued driving until they reached the physician's residence.

He left her in the car while he went to the front door and rang the doorbell. Dr. Harvey Brown answered himself. Clare watched as the two men shook hands. Apparently they were acquainted with each other.

Reed returned to the car a moment later and carried Clare into the house, taking her through the entrance and down a picture-lined hallway to what she assumed was the doctor's den. Reed gently placed her in a black leather chair beside the desk.

"Hello, Clare," Dr. Brown greeted, his eyeglasses perched on the end of his nose as he gazed down on her.

"I understand you haven't been feeling well." Before she could answer him one way or the other, he stuck a thermometer under her tongue.

Reed stood in one corner of the room, with his arms crossed. The physician removed his stethoscope from his small black bag. Next he opened Clare's robe and gown enough to press the cold metal over her heart. He waited a few moments, and then, seemingly satisfied, he removed the instrument from his ears.

"I understand you're the one who shut up Jack Kingston," he said, glancing briefly to Reed.

Reed nodded. "We had a difference of opinion."

Dr. Brown grinned. "It's about time someone put that boy in his place."

Reed didn't respond, but Clare thought she detected a slight smile. She continued to watch the play between the two men. Meanwhile Dr. Brown continued his examination, then asked Clare a list of questions having to do with her symptoms.

"Does she need to be hospitalized?" Reed asked, after several moments.

"Don't be ridiculous," Clare flared. She had the flu, but she wasn't that sick.

"That depends on what kind of home care she'll be getting."

"Would you both stop it," she said, straightening in the high-backed leather chair. "If you want to give me your diagnosis, Doc, do so, but I'm not a child and I'd appreciate your talking to *me*."

Clare noted how Reed's gaze connected with that of the physician. They both seemed to find her small outburst cause for amusement.

"First of all," Dr. Brown said, turning to Clare, "I

want to know why you didn't come into my office earlier?"

"I couldn't," she told him a bit defensively. "I was too sick."

"Did you talk to my nurse?"

"No," she admitted reluctantly.

"Next time, young lady, you call in and talk to Doris, understand?"

To her mother she was a young lady, to Dr. Brown she was a young lady. Why did everyone insist upon treating her like a child when she was a woman? Even Reed seemed to think she needed a keeper.

"I'm mainly concerned about her keeping down fluids. She's…you're nearly dehydrated now. If that happens I won't have any choice but to admit you."

"I'll make an effort to drink more," Clare assured him. She hadn't realized she was so sick. She *knew* she was ill, of course, just not how ill.

"I don't imagine this bug will hold on longer than a couple more days. It'll take another week or more for you to regain your strength." Although he was talking to her, Dr. Brown was looking at Reed, which infuriated her even more when he'd completely excluded her from the conversation.

"I'll be a picture of health in another week or so," she announced tartly.

"I don't like the idea of her being alone."

"She won't be," Reed said without looking at Clare. "I'm taking her home with me."

Eleven

Clare was silent during the forty-minute drive to Reed's cabin, knowing it wouldn't do any good to argue with him. His mind was set and she'd bumped against that stubborn pride of his enough to know it'd be useless to try to reason with him.

Throughout the endless trip, Clare felt Reed's gaze upon her, but she paid no heed. Understanding this man was beyond her. She didn't know what to think anymore, and feeling as rotten and weak as she did, she wasn't in any shape to accurately interpret his actions.

Perhaps he felt responsible for her. Despite his best efforts to rush into their divorce, they remained legally married. Her guess was that he considered it his duty to nurse her back to health. Whatever his reason, Clare was past caring. He'd made his intentions clear enough. He wanted out of her life, out of their marriage, and had done his level best to be sure she understood.

Now this. Clare was more confused than ever.

When Reed pulled into his yard, he parked his car close to the house. Before she could do more than open the car door, he was there, lifting her in his arms as if she weighed no more than a child.

"I can walk," she protested.

He ignored her objection, as she knew he would, and carried her into his home. He paused in the entryway, seemingly undecided as to exactly where he should take her. After a moment, he headed into the living room and gently deposited her onto the thick cushions of the sofa.

Clare lay back and closed her eyes. Although she'd slept a good portion of the day, the jaunt into town to see Dr. Brown and the drive to Reed's home had exhausted her.

Before retrieving her suitcase, Reed brought her a thick blanket and a pillow. When he'd finished covering her, he stepped back. Her eyes remained closed, but Clare profoundly felt his presence standing over her, watching her. With anyone else she would have felt edgy and uncomfortable, but oddly, with Reed, it felt as if she were nestled in his arms.

Clare had learned more than one painful lesson trying to decipher Reed's actions. She dared not trust her feelings. He didn't want her. Didn't need her. Didn't love her.

With her heart crushed under the weight of her pain, Clare kept her eyes closed, not believing for a moment that she would sleep. Almost immediately she could feel herself drifting toward the beckoning arms of slumber. She resisted as long as she could, which was a pitifully short time, then surrendered.

She stirred later, not knowing how long she'd slept. The sun was low in the sky and the wind whispered through the trees in an enchanted chorus.

Her gaze found Reed in the kitchen, standing before

the stove, stirring a large pot. He must have sensed she was awake, because he turned and glanced at her.

For a moment their eyes met. Clare looked away first, fearing her unguarded glance would reveal her love. She was with him under protest and only because he felt some ridiculous responsibility to take care of her.

"How long have I been asleep?" she asked, struggling with the weight of the blanket to sit upright.

"An hour or so."

It had felt like a few minutes. She should have realized it was longer, since the sun was setting. Bronze rays of light slanted toward the earth, bouncing back.

"I'm making you soup."

The thought of food terrorized her stomach. "Don't. I'm not the least bit hungry."

It was as though she'd told him how excited she was at the prospect of dinner. He set a large bowl of the steaming soup at the table, along with a cup of tea and a glass of water and then came for her.

"I… I don't think I'll be able to keep it down," she confessed weakly.

"You can try." Tucking his arm around her shoulders, he helped her upright. At least he wasn't carting her to the table as if she were an ungainly sack of potatoes, granting her one small shred of dignity.

The soup was thick with vegetables, homemade and delicious. Clare was surprised by how good it tasted. After three days of being so violently ill, her appetite was practically nil, but she did manage five or six spoonfuls. When she finished, she placed her hands in her lap.

"Would you like a bath?" Reed asked. He stood beside her and brushed a thick strand of hair away from her face. His fingers were as light and gentle as his voice.

For the first time since he entered her home, he wasn't bullying and browbeating her. A part of Clare wanted to resist him at every turn, prove he wasn't the only one with an abundance of pride. He might insist upon nursing her, but by heaven she wouldn't be a willing patient.

"A bath?" she repeated slowly. Her strength to fight him vanished completely. "I'm a mess, aren't I? My hair…"

His eyes delved into hers. "No, Clare, you aren't."

It would take a better liar than Reed to convince her otherwise. As though reading her thoughts, he stood, cupped her face in his hands and gazed down on her.

"I was just thinking," he said, and his voice sounded strangely unlike his own, "that I've never seen a woman I've wanted more."

Clare turned her face from his, battling tears. Leave it to Reed to say something sweet and romantic when she looked her absolute worst. Emotions churned inside her and, sniffling, she rubbed the back of her hand under her nose.

"I'll see to your bath," he said, leaving her.

Taking time to collect herself, Clare gathered the blanket around her and moved down the hallway to find Reed sitting on the edge of the tub, adjusting the water temperature.

"I can get my things," she offered, "if you tell me where you put my suitcase."

"It's in the first bedroom on the right," Reed instructed, then stood to help her.

"I can do it," she assured him with a weak smile. "Don't look so worried."

He hesitated a moment, then nodded.

Clare traipsed down the hall, following Reed's instructions. Pausing in the doorway of the bedroom, she realized this wasn't the guest room, as she suspected it would be, but Reed's own. His presence was stamped in every detail, from the dark four-poster bed to the braided rug that covered the floor.

"I'll be sleeping in the guest bed," he explained, scooting past her. He lifted her suitcase onto the mattress and opened it for her, removing a fresh gown.

Clare didn't understand. It made no sense to her that he would give up his own bed. As if reading her thoughts, he explained. "It's more comfortable in here and closer to the bathroom."

"I know but…" Before she could finish, he left the room as if he were as bereft to explain why he'd opted to give her his own bed as she was to understand why.

Sighing, Clare wandered back to the bathroom. Reed was there, sorting through a cupboard. He removed an armful of fresh towels.

"Thank you," she said, and waited for him to leave. It soon became apparent he had no intention of doing so.

"Trust me, I can bathe myself," she informed him primly.

His returning smile was roguish. "You're sure about that?"

"Of course, I'm sure."

"You aren't going to show me anything I haven't seen before," he took delight in reminding her.

Clare felt the color seep into her cheeks. This seemed to amuse him, and, chuckling, he took her by the shoulders, kissed her softly on her cheek and left. The door remained open, but only a crack so he'd be sure to hear her if she were to call for him.

Clare undressed slowly, leaving her clothes in a heap

on the floor. The steaming hot water felt heavenly. Sighing, she sank down as far as she could, closed her eyes and leaned back in the tub. Clare didn't know how long she soaked.

"Need me to wash your back?" Reed asked from the other side of the door.

"I most certainly do not."

He chuckled, and she heard him walk away, leaving her to her pleasure. Sinking low in the tub, Clare rested her head against the porcelain base. Slowly a smile came to her.

Reed stood at the end of the bed, watching Clare, who was fresh from her bath. He knew he should leave her to rest, but found himself unable to walk away. She was small and incredibly fragile. And so beautiful she took his breath away.

He invented reasons to touch her, to stay with her, to make himself useful so he'd have an excuse for being there. She'd washed her hair and sat amidst a pile of pillows with a thick towel piled on top of her head.

"I can't remember when I've enjoyed a bath more," she said as she unwound the towel and set it aside.

She must have enjoyed it. Reed swore she'd been in the bathroom a solid hour. Every time he'd gone to check on her, she'd shooed him away, insisting she was fine.

Her hair was all tangled, and after attempting to free the strands with her fingers, she reached for her brush, tugging it through the length. He paused, wanting to offer to comb it for her, but hesitated, knowing she'd have trouble surrendering even the smallest task to him.

"I can do this," she assured him, but it became clear

to him after the first few strokes of the brush that the effort exhausted her.

"Let me," he volunteered readily, glad for the excuse to linger. He knelt on the edge of the bed. The mattress dipped with his weight.

After a moment's hesitation, Clare handed him the brush and then twisted so that her back was to him. Her hair was thick and tangled, and he painstakingly worked the brush through the matted strands, being careful not to hurt her unnecessarily.

His hand was steady and sure, but his thoughts were in chaos, tormenting him. It didn't take him long to realize that volunteering for this small intimacy had been a mistake. His gut knotted as desire flooded his veins. Clare was sick; it was lucky she hadn't ended up in the hospital. He cursed himself for his weakness and continued brushing, hoping she wouldn't guess his thoughts.

Clare's head moved in the direction of the brush as though her neck were boneless. When he heard her soft sigh, Reed knew she was enjoying this small intimate exchange as much as he was himself.

Every cell in Reed's body had stirred to life. He'd scooted further up on the bed than he intended, and Clare's back was pressed full against his chest. When he'd packed her suitcase, he'd purposely chosen a flannel nightgown, wanting to keep temptation at bay. He realized too late that even the sexless gown couldn't conceal her exquisite shape. His hand tightened around the brush as he struggled with himself. Reed had never thought of himself as a weak man. Not until he'd married Clare, that was.

The ache to touch her, to taste her, grew so intense Reed's hand stilled. "I think that should do it," he said.

He pulled away from her, although he'd never wanted to make love to her more as he did right then. The ache in him was physical, but he couldn't take advantage of her now when she was ill, despite the fact they were man and wife and she was sleeping in his bed.

"Thank...you." Clare's voice was small as she scooted down in the warm blankets. "I...feel better than I have in days."

Grumbling to himself, Reed left the room. She might feel better, but he certainly didn't.

Clare woke the following morning feeling greatly improved. After being so wretchedly sick, all her body needed now was time to recover. She realized she was hungry, and wondered if Reed was up and about. If not, she'd fix herself something to eat and him, too.

Her suitcase revealed a pair of jeans and a sweater, which she slipped on, grateful to be out of the flannel gowns that had made up her wardrobe the past several days.

The act of dressing weakened her, and, discouraged, she sat on the edge of the bed and regrouped before heading for the kitchen.

Reed was there, in front of the stove, cooking eggs. He smiled warmly when he saw her.

"Morning," she said a bit shyly.

"Did you sleep well?"

Clare nodded, almost embarrassed by how soundly she had slept. She didn't know where Reed had spent the night and felt mildly guilty that she had put him out of his own bed. And disappointed that he'd opted to sleep elsewhere instead of with her.

"You look like you might be feeling a little better," he said as he cracked an egg into a pan of simmering water.

"I feel almost human."

"Good. I've made you some tea and there's eggs and toast. Fruit, too, if you'd like some."

His thoughtfulness brought a curious ache to her heart. That he would so painstakingly care for her physically and think nothing of devastating her emotionally baffled Clare. He seemed to genuinely care for her, although it was difficult for her to judge the depth of his feelings. Every time she dared to hope, to believe he might want to keep their marriage intact, she'd been bitterly disappointed.

Clare was through second-guessing Reed. She'd take it one day at a time and wait him out, she decided.

"Sit down and I'll bring you breakfast," he told her.

Clare sat at the table and he carried over a plate with poached eggs on dry toast. The meal was heavenly. Sitting across from her with his own plate, Reed seemed to enjoy watching her eat.

"Will you be all right by yourself for an hour or so?" he asked when she'd finished.

"Of course."

"I need to run a couple of errands," he explained, carrying her dishes to the sink. "Do you need anything from town?"

She answered him with a small shake of her head.

It occurred to Clare that she should ask him to take her with him. It was apparent the worst of her malady had passed. She had no right to infringe on his hospitality longer than necessary, but he said nothing, and Clare didn't offer.

If he wanted her there with him, then she was content

to stay. No matter what it cost her later. There would be a price, Clare realized, but one she would willingly pay.

Reed left shortly afterward, after setting her up on the sofa in the living room. She sat for a time, content to read and enjoy the morning.

The sun came out, bathing the scenery in a golden glow. After having been cooped up inside for several days, Clare felt the need to breathe in the fresh scent of the morning. Although it was warm, she reached for Reed's light jacket and moved onto the front porch. She stood there for several moments, her arm wrapped around the post for support, surveying Reed's world. It was peaceful, still.

The morning was glorious, and before she even realized her intent, Clare moved off the porch and down the pathway that led to Reed's workshop. Continuing along the trail, she discovered a small lake. Sitting on a stump, she breathed in the beauty of the world surrounding her.

Clouds, like giant kernels of popped corn, dotted the sky, while an eagle lazily soared above her, the sun on its wing. Clare wasn't aware of how long she sat there; not long, she guessed. Time lost meaning as she closed her eyes and listened to the sounds of the forest. Squirrels chattered and scooted up the trees. Bluebirds chirped irritably and fluttered along the trail with gold finches and swallows.

"Clare." Reed's voice had a desperate edge to it.

"I'm here," she shouted back, surprised by how weak her voice sounded.

He came down the path, half trotting, and stopped when he saw her. His relief was evident and Clare realized she should have left him a note. She would have if she'd known where she was headed.

"It's so peaceful here," she said, not wanting him to be angry with her.

He moved behind her and cupped her shoulders. "I love it, too."

"I feel better for being here… I feel almost well."

She was improving each hour. Her body drank in the sunshine and fresh clean air the way a sponge does water. "Did you finish your business in town?" she asked, looking up at him.

Reed nodded. "I let Erin and Gary know you were with me and why."

Clare wondered if their newly married friends had offered to care for her themselves and guessed they hadn't. If anything, they seemed to encourage the romance between her and Reed.

"Let's get you back before you exhaust yourself."

Clare didn't want to leave this enchanted spot on the edge of the thick evergreen forest, but she realized Reed was right. He wrapped his arm around her as though he suspected she wasn't strong enough to make it all the way on her own. It amazed her how accurately he was able to judge her limited strength.

By the time they reached the house, she was shaking and fatigued, although it was only a short distance.

"I think I'll rest," she murmured, heading toward the bedroom.

Reed gave her a few moments, then came into the room. Her head was nestled in the thick down pillow. He laid his hand on her hair. "Sleep."

Clare smiled, doubting that she'd be able to stay awake much longer. Her eyes drifted closed. "Tonight… I'll sleep in the guest bed."

"You'll stay exactly where you are," Reed whispered.

"It's where you belong." He stayed with her until she was asleep, at least Clare assumed he did. Her fingers were laced with his and his hand brushed the hair from her brow until she became accustomed to the feel of his callused palm against her smooth skin.

When Clare woke, the house was quiet. She went into the kitchen and glanced at the clock, surprised she'd slept so long. Reed was nowhere in sight, but she guessed he was probably in his shop, working. Pouring them each a cup of coffee, she carried it to the outbuilding.

"Hello," she said, standing in the open doorway. She'd guessed correctly. Reed was working, his torso gleaming with sweat, his biceps bulging as he chiseled away at the thick cedar log. She found his progress remarkable. When he'd first shown her the project, she'd barely been able to make out the shape of the three figures. The thunderbird in particular caught her eye now. The beak and facial features of the creature were vivid with detail.

"You're awake."

"I feel like all I've done is sleep." Clare resented every wasted moment, wanting to spend as much time as she could with Reed.

"Your body needs the rest." He set aside his tools and took the mug out of her hand.

"Are you hungry?" he asked, sipping from the edge of the earthenware cup.

She shook her head. "Not in the least."

Reed leaned against a pair of sawhorses and drank his coffee, grateful, it seemed, for the break. Not wanting to detain him from his job, Clare took his empty

mug when he'd finished, and prepared to head back to
the house.

Reed stopped her, his gaze finding hers. Then he
bent over and found her mouth with his. The kiss was
as gentle as it was sweet, a brushing of lips, an appreciation.

When they pulled apart, Clare blinked several times,
feeling disoriented and lost. She must have swayed toward him, because Reed caught her by the shoulders
and smiled down on her with affectionate amusement.

It nettled her that she should be so unsettled by their
kissing when Reed appeared so unaffected. Confused,
she backed away from him. "I'll... I'll go back now,"
she said, and twisted around.

Clare was still shaking when she returned to the
house. Standing at the sink, she tried to put their kiss
into perspective. It had been a spontaneous reaction, a
way of thanking her for bringing him coffee. She dared
not read anything more into it than he intended; the
problem was knowing what that was. In clear, precise
terms, he'd assured her he meant to follow through with
the divorce. She had to accept that because she dared not
allow herself to believe he wanted them to stay married.

Clare was on the sofa, reading, when Reed came
inside the house a couple of hours later. She glanced
up and smiled, now used to seeing him shirtless and
wearing braids. It was as though he had stepped off the
pages of a Western novel. She recalled the morning following their wedding, how taken aback she'd been by
the reminders of his heritage. No longer. To her mind
he was proud and noble. She'd give anything to go back
to that first morning in Vegas.

"Gary's on his way," Reed announced.

Clare frowned. "H-how do you know?"

"I can hear his car. My guess is that Erin's with him."

It was on the tip of Clare's tongue to suggest she ride back into town with her friends. She was much improved. The worst of the flu had passed, and other than being incredibly weak, she was well. But she didn't offer, and Reed didn't suggest it.

Within a couple of minutes of Reed's announcement, Clare heard the approaching vehicle herself, although she wouldn't have been able to identify it as Gary's car.

Reed had washed his hands and donned a shirt, although he'd left it unbuttoned. By the time the sound of the car doors closing reached her, Reed had opened the front door and stepped onto the porch.

Erin came into the cabin like a woman scorned. "I told you you were sick," she fumed, hands on her hips. "But would you listen to me? Oh, no, not the mighty Clare Gilroy. Reed told me what Dr. Brown said... I should have your hide for this, Clare. You could have died."

Erin had always possessed a flair for the dramatic, Clare reminded herself. "Don't be ridiculous."

"You nearly ended up in the hospital."

"I know... I was foolish not to have made an appointment earlier. I certainly hope you didn't drive all this way just to chastise me."

"I wouldn't bet on it." Gary appeared in the doorway, grinning. "She's been fuming ever since Reed stopped by this morning."

"I'm much better," Clare assured her friend. "So stop worrying."

As though Erin wasn't sure she should believe Clare, she looked to Reed.

"She's slept a good portion of the day. Her fever is down and she ate a good breakfast."

Erin sighed expressively, walked farther into the living room and sat on the end of the sofa. "Your face has a little color," she said, examining her closely.

Clare didn't know if that was due to her improved health or the result of Reed's kiss. "I'll be good as new in a few days," Clare assured her friend.

Gary and Reed were talking in the background. Reed walked over to the refrigerator, took out two cans of cold soda and handed one to Gary.

"So?" Erin whispered, glancing over her shoulder. "How's it going with Reed?"

"What do you mean?"

"You know," Erin whispered forcefully. "Have you two…made any decisions about the divorce?"

Clare's gaze moved from Erin to the two men chatting in the kitchen. "No…it's up to Reed."

"He isn't going to follow through with it," Erin said confidently. "Not now."

"What makes you think that?" Clare dared not put any credence into Erin's assessment, but she couldn't help being curious.

"From the way he looks at you. He loves you, Clare, can't you see it?"

Frankly she couldn't. "Then why does he…"

"Think about it," Erin said impatiently. "Why else would he have hauled you to Doc Brown's house, then carted you home with him? It's obvious he cares."

"He feels morally responsible for me."

"Hogwash."

Erin and Gary stayed for a little more than an hour and then left. Clare walked out to the porch with Reed to see off the newlyweds. When Reed slipped his arm across her shoulders, she drank in his warmth and his strength and smiled up at him.

Reed's gaze narrowed as he studied her, and then without either of them saying a word, Reed took her in his arms. They kissed long and hard, drinking their fill, standing there on the front porch.

"I've wanted to do that all day," Reed admitted, burying his face and his hands in her hair.

"I've wanted you to kiss me, too."

His arm circled her waist, and as he lifted her from the porch, he brought her mouth back to his. Clare didn't need further encouragement. She looped her arms around his neck and sighed with pleasure.

"I need you, Reed," she whispered, running her tongue around the shell of his ear.

Reed shuddered. "Clare, no."

"I'm your wife."

He shook his head adamantly. "You've been sick."

"Make me well." Her hands framed his face as he brought his mouth back to hers. "I need you so much."

"Clare," he groaned her name.

She kissed him again and he moaned once more. "You don't play fair."

"Does that mean you're going to make love to me?"

"Yes," he whispered, his voice low and husky. He carried her into the bedroom, and Clare swore he didn't take any more than a few steps.

Their lovemaking was completely different than it had been at any other time in their relationship. When they'd finished, Reed held her close. Clare buried her face in his shoulder as she sobbed uncontrollably.

Twelve

Reed comforted Clare as best he knew how. He was at a loss to understand her tears, and not knowing what to say, he gently held her against him until the sobs had abated.

"Can you tell me now?" he asked, his voice a shallow whisper.

She shook her head. "Just hold me."

He rubbed his hand across her back, caressing her smooth, velvet skin, and waited. After several moments it dawned on him from the even rise and fall of her shoulders that Clare was asleep.

Asleep!

One moment she was whimpering and confused and the next she was snoozing. A smile came to him as he tucked her more securely in his arms and closed his eyes. Twenty years from now he doubted that he'd understand Clare. He'd thought he knew her, assumed...

Twenty years from now... The words echoed in the silent chamber of his mind. At some time over the past few weeks, he didn't know when, he'd accepted that their lives were irrevocably linked.

Only a fool would try to turn back now. Only a fool would believe it was possible to walk away from Clare.

Clare was his wife. At some point she'd ceased being Clare Gilroy, and he accepted that she was his future. The woman who filled the emptiness of his soul. The one who would heal his bitterness and erase his skepticism.

He didn't know how it would happen, but he trusted that his love for her and hers for him would make a way where his humanness found none.

The time had come for him to wipe out the past and start anew. To forgive those who had wronged him. The time had come for him to get on with his life. He couldn't love Clare and remain embittered and hostile.

Lying there with his wife in his arms, Reed felt as if the shackles were removed from his heart. He was free. Emotion tightened his chest as he recalled the time as a youth when he'd been passed over by the tribal leaders, his talent ignored by the elders. He recalled the incident as if it were only a few days past, and once again anger gripped him.

It was their rejection that had set the course of his life, that had cast his fate as an artist. From the tender age of fourteen onward he'd decided to resurrect the art of carving totem poles. He'd made a good living because of this one slight. His name was becoming well-known across the country, and all because Able Lonetree had received the award Reed had deserved.

Good had come from this unfairness, and for years Reed had been blind to that. He'd held himself apart from his tribe, the same way he'd held himself apart from his mother's people.

The local paper had wanted to write an article about

him after the piece had appeared on him in the regional magazine. Reed had declined, preferring to maintain his anonymity with the good people of Tullue.

His reputation as a rebel was the result of an incident that happened when he was nineteen. A fight. He'd stumbled upon two of the high school's athletes bullying a thin, pale-faced youth. Reed had stepped in on the boy's behalf. A fight had broken out, two against one. Eventually they were pulled apart, but when questioned, the youth Reed had been defending changed his story and Reed was arrested for assault.

No doubt the rumors about him would be fed by his recent confrontation with Jack Kingston. So be it. In time, he'd make his peace with Tullue, Reed decided. He wasn't sure how, but he imagined Clare would aid him in this area, too.

A sigh lifted his chest. He felt as though a great burden had been taken from him. He recalled his grandfather and the wisdom handed down to him as a boy. He didn't appreciate what his grandfather had told him about hunting until he'd fallen in love with Clare.

The man who'd raised him had taught Reed to trap and hunt. It was the way of the Skyutes, but each spring and summer they fished instead. Reed could hear his grandfather as if he were standing at the foot of the bed. There was no way in the world a man could mate and fight at the same time. Other than the obvious meaning, Reed had assumed his grandfather was also referring to trapping. Animals couldn't raise their young if they were being hunted. The logic of this was irrefutable, but Reed understood a greater wisdom.

He couldn't love Clare and maintain his war with the

world. He couldn't love Clare and live in isolation. He could no longer maintain his island.

As quietly as he could, Reed slipped from the bed, not wanting to disturb Clare. He dressed and wandered barefoot into the kitchen. His first inclination was to wake her and tell her of his decision. There were a large number of items they would need to discuss. First and foremost was her family.

The burden that had so recently left him came to weigh upon his shoulders once again. Clare had told him she'd spoken to her parents about him. At one point, she'd confessed to dating him. But Reed knew dating was one thing, marriage was something else again.

With a sick kind of dread he recalled the reaction his mother's family had had to his parents' marriage. Even in her greatest hour of need, her family had turned their backs on the two of them.

Reed sensed they might have experienced a change of heart following her death, but he wanted nothing to do with them. As a teenager he'd received a letter from the grandmother he'd never known, which he'd read and promptly destroyed. For the life of him he couldn't remember the contents of the letter. He hadn't answered, and she'd never written again.

The thought of Clare being forced to give up her family because of him troubled Reed. If bridges were to be built, he'd have to be the one to construct them. For Clare's sake he'd do it; for the sake of their children, he'd find a way to make their love acceptable to the Gilroys.

Their children. The two words had a profound effect upon Reed. He scooted a chair away from the table, sat down and pressed his elbows against the wood surface.

He'd barely become accustomed to the idea of marriage, and already he was looking into the future.

Children.

He wanted a son, yearned for this child Clare would give him. Frowning, he realized his attitude was chauvinistic in the extreme. When the time came for them to have a family, there was every likelihood that their love would produce a daughter.

The instant surge of delight that filled him with the prospect of a girl child came as something of a surprise. His mind envisioned a little girl, a smaller version of Clare, and Reed experienced the same intense longing as he had imagining a son.

The future had never seemed more right.

A sound from the bedroom told him Clare was awake. The water on top of the stove was hot and he brewed her a cup of tea, taking it into the bedroom with him.

Clare was sitting up, the blanket tucked around her front.

"Hello, Sleeping Beauty," he said, sitting on the edge of the mattress. He set the tea on the nightstand and leaned forward to kiss her.

He tasted her resistance, which took him by surprise. Clare had always been so open, welcoming his touch.

"Do you want to tell me what's wrong?" he asked.

With her eyes lowered, she shook her head.

Needing to touch her, he brushed the hair from her face. "I shouldn't have allowed us to make love," he said, blaming himself for any unnecessary discomfort he might have caused her. She was barely over her bout with the flu and he was dragging her into his bed, making physical demands on her. He couldn't be around Clare and not desire her.

Thirty years from now it would be the same. Reed wasn't sure how he knew this, but he did. He'd be chasing her down the hall of a retirement center.

"You're right," she said, emotion tattering the edges of her words. "That shouldn't have happened."

Regret? Was that what he heard in her voice? Reed didn't know. He scooted off the bed and aimlessly strolled to the far side of the room.

"I… I want to go home," she announced.

It was on the tip of his tongue to tell her that she *was* home, but intuitively he realized now wasn't the time. The determined, stubborn slant of her jaw assured him of a good deal more. They wouldn't be able to discuss anything of importance in her present mood.

"I'll pack my things. I'd appreciate it if you'd drive me back to Tullue."

Reed said nothing.

"If you'd leave I'd get dressed." It sounded as if she were close to tears, and not knowing what to say to comfort her, Reed left.

Reed felt at a terrible loss. He'd never told a woman he loved her, and he feared the moment he opened his mouth he'd blunder the whole thing.

Clare appeared a few minutes later, her suitcase in her hand. Once again her eyes refused to meet his.

Reed stepped forward and took the lightly packed bag out of her grasp. He had to say something before she left him. Nervously he cleared his throat. "My grandfather told me something years ago. I didn't realize the significance of it until recently. It had to do with the reasons our tribe fished during the summer months."

Clare cast him an odd, puzzled look.

Reed tensed and continued. "Grandfather claimed a man couldn't fight and mate at the same time."

An empty silence followed his words, and Reed realized he'd botched it just the way he'd feared. Clare continued to glare at him.

"We aren't fighting," Clare said.

"Not fight," he assured her quickly, "but talk."

Her eyes drifted shut, and after a moment she sighed and shook her head. "I don't know what more there is for us to say."

She was wrong, but Reed didn't know how to tell her that without invoking her wrath. He searched for a possible excuse to keep her with him. "Don't you think we should pick up another one of those test kits before you traipse back into town?"

"Test kits?" she asked, scowling. Pain flashed across her features. "Oh, I see you're afraid I'm pregnant."

"Afraid isn't the word, Clare."

"Terrified then."

"No," he countered. "I'd like it if we had children together. I was thinking about this while you were sleeping and I realized how very pleased I'd be if you were pregnant."

"Pleased," Clare cried. "Pleased! No doubt that would feed your pride if I—"

"Clare," he said, losing his patience, "I love you. I'm not looking to bolster my ego. Yes, I want children, but we'll only have them if it's what you want, too. It just seemed to me that as my wife…" He stopped midsentence at Clare's shocked expression. "Clare," he said her name gently, not knowing what to think.

She burst into tears and covered her face with both hands.

If he lived to be an old man, Reed decided then and there, he'd never understand women. He'd thought, he'd hoped this was what she wanted, too, to share his life, his home, his future.

He guided her to a chair and left her long enough to retrieve several tissues from the bathroom. Squatting down in front of her, he pressed the tissues into her limp hand. It was then that he noticed she'd removed the turquoise ring he'd given her the night they were married.

She'd been wearing it earlier that day. He found it interesting that she would continue to wear the bulky piece of jewelry when it was so obviously ill suited to a woman's hand. He had his mother's wedding band and he'd thought to give her that.

If she intended to stay in the marriage.

Perhaps Clare had experienced a change of heart and decided she wanted out. It would be just like fate to kick him in the face when he least expected it.

"You want me to be your wife?" she asked between sobs. Clenching the tissue in her fist, Clare leveled her gaze on him.

"You are my wife, or had you forgotten?" It was difficult to keep the frustration out of his voice.

"I've never forgotten…you were the one who contacted the attorney…who insisted from the very first that we take the necessary measures to correct the… mistake."

Their gazes held. Reed stood the full length of the kitchen away from her. "Was marrying me a mistake?"

"At first I wasn't sure," she admitted softly. "Everything seemed so right in Vegas. I felt as though I'd been waiting all my life for you."

"And later?"

"Later…the morning after, I didn't stop to think. It seemed to me, after we were married, the deed was done. I didn't once consider the right or wrong of it. It never entered my mind that a married couple would entertain regrets quite so soon."

"You didn't know what you were doing," Reed reminded her forcefully, regretting having brought up the subject of their wedding. Each time he did, he felt as though he'd taken advantage of her.

"But I did know what I was doing," she countered. "You make it sound like I was drugged or something. Let me assure you right now, I wasn't. No matter what you say about me crossing my medication with alcohol, I was fully aware of my actions. If I was behaving out of character there were…other reasons."

"Kingston," Reed muttered under his breath. Clare had ended a three-year dead-end relationship with the other man. Reed should have realized much sooner that had dictated her actions.

She must have been near giddy with relief to have Kingston out of her life and desperate that no one else would ever want her. A sickening feeling clawed at his stomach. Just when he'd squared everything in his mind, he found another excuse for Clare to want out of their marriage.

"Yes," she agreed hesitantly, "I think breaking up with Jack had something to do with it, too." Reed hadn't realized she'd heard him say the other man's name. "I've often wondered what you must have thought when I suggested we marry," she continued slowly. "Surely you knew I'd broken up with Jack. I was absolutely certain no man would ever want me again. If you're looking to fault me for anything, fault me for that."

He nodded and buried his hands deep in his pockets.

"I've never understood why you agreed to marry me," she said softly, smearing a trail of tears across her cheek. "You can question my motivation with good reason. But it doesn't help me understand why you agreed to marry me."

Reed went motionless. It was the same question Gary had posed the other day, the one Reed had skillfully avoided answering. He could steer around his friend's inquisitiveness, but not Clare's.

Reed was a proud man. He'd never given his heart to a woman, but it seemed to him that if he was willing to spend the rest of his natural life with her then he should be equally amenable to confessing the truth.

"Why'd you agree to marry me?" Clare asked him a second time.

"I loved you then just as much as I do now," Reed admitted stiffly.

His words were met with a stunned silence. "But we barely knew one another," Clare argued. "You couldn't possibly have loved me."

Reed lowered his gaze. "There's a library on the reservation, Clare. Every visit I ever made to the Tullue library was to see you, to be close to you, even if it was only for a few minutes."

Her eyes revealed her shock. "But you never said more than a few words to me."

"I couldn't. You were dating Kingston."

"But..." She stood, then sat down again as though she needed something stable to hold her. "Why? You didn't even know me... You don't honestly expect me to believe you were in love with me, do you?"

"It was your eyes," he told her softly, "so serious, so sincere. I saw fire there, hidden passion."

"You've since proved that to be true," she muttered, and her cheeks flushed crimson.

"I saw joy in you. Your spirit is fragile, it is even now. It was why I named you Laughing Rainbow."

"Laughing Rainbow," Clare repeated slowly, then looked to him once more. "The totem pole you gave me...the top figure is a rainbow."

Reed smiled, pleased that she'd made the connection. "I carved that some time ago because I love you. It helped me feel close to you."

"Oh, Reed." She pressed the tips of her fingers against her lips as though his words had brought her close to tears.

They moved toward each other. Reed closed his arms around her and he sighed with relief. He'd never experienced emotion so deep. He trembled at the depth of it, bottled up inside him for so many years.

He felt release as though he'd survived a great battle. Weak, but incredibly strong.

"I don't want a divorce, Reed," she told him. She planted her hands on the sides of his face and spread eager kisses over his features. "I want us to stay married. And...there'll be children. I want them so much." Her voice trembled with happiness.

His arms circled her waist, lifting her so he could kiss her the way he wanted, with her making soft whimpering sounds of need. She lifted her face from his and smiled slowly, her eyes laughing. Reed swore he could have drowned in the gentle love he found in her.

"I could already be pregnant," she whispered.

He longed to lose himself in her, yet when he came

to Clare he wasn't lost; instead he'd been found. Her love gave him serenity and peace. Her love was the most precious gift he'd ever received.

Reed promised himself he couldn't make love to her twice in one day, not when she was recovering after being so ill, but he felt powerless to resist. "You've been sick...weak." He tried to offer her all the reasons why they shouldn't, but one more kiss, one silken caress of her hand convinced him he was wrong. He lifted her in his arms and hauled her back to the unmade bed. She raised smiling eyes to him. "Conserve your strength," he told her, "because you're going to need every bit of it."

Clare laughed, and Reed swore he'd never heard a sweeter sound. "If anyone needs to conserve their strength it's you, my darling husband."

Clare woke early the following morning while Reed slept contentedly at her side. The drapes were open and the morning was gray and foggy. By midmorning the sky would be pink with the promise of another glorious summer day.

Clare had made her decision, and Reed had made his. They were man and wife. Her heart gladdened at the prospect of them joining their lives.

Reed stirred, and she rolled into his arms.

"Morning, husband," she whispered.

Reed's eyes met hers before he smiled. "Morning, wife."

"For the first time since we said our vows I feel married."

"Is that good or bad?" he asked.

"Good," she assured him, "very good."

"How are you feeling otherwise?"

Clare kissed his nose. "Wonderful, absolutely wonderful."

"What about the flu...we didn't..." He left the rest unsaid.

"I think we've stumbled upon a magical cure. I've never felt better and furthermore, I'm starved." They'd eaten dinner late that evening, close to midnight. Reed was ravenous and had fried himself a thick T-bone steak. Clare was content with soup, not wanting to test her stomach with fried foods.

Afterward they'd cuddled on the sofa and he'd entertained her with tales of adventures from his childhood. Stories of learning to fish with his hands, of hiking deep into the woods and finding his way home, guided by the stars, and what he'd learned from the forest. Before returning to bed, he placed a plain gold band—the band his mother had worn—on the fourth finger of her left hand.

"Do you want breakfast in bed?" Reed asked, tossing aside the blanket and sitting on the end of the mattress.

"Why? Do you intend on spoiling me?"

"No," came his honest reply, "but I'd like to pamper you."

"What if I decide I want to pamper you?" she asked.

A mischievous look came into his dark eyes. "I'm sure I'll think of something."

Clare reached for her robe to cover her nakedness and followed him into the kitchen. She sat in the kitchen and braced her bare toes against the edge of the chair. Her knees were tucked under her chin. "I want to ask you about something you said."

"Fire away." Reed dumped coffee grounds from the canister into the white filter.

"You said something about me having a fragile spirit. What did you mean?"

Reed hesitated. "It isn't a negative, Clare. You have the heart of a lioness."

"But my spirit's fragile? That doesn't make sense."

Reed took his time, seeming to choose his words carefully. "It's because the people you love mean so much to you. I'm afraid you're going to be in for a difficult time once your family learns we're married."

"They'll adjust."

"But in the meantime, you'll suffer because you love them. It hurts me to know that."

"If they make a fuss, then they're the ones losing out." Although she sounded strong and sure, she realized Reed was right. Her family's opinion was important to her. She'd always been the good daughter, living up to their image, doing things precisely the way they'd planned. But her love for her husband was strong and steady. Nothing, not her parents, public opinion, or anything else would give her cause to doubt. Clare was convinced of it.

While the coffee brewed, Reed told her the story of his own parents and how his mother's family had turned away from her following her marriage.

"My parents would never do that." Clare desperately wanted to believe it, but she couldn't be sure. "Times have changed," she continued, undaunted. "People aren't quite as narrow-minded these days."

"If it comes down to you having to make a choice, I'll understand if you side with your family."

Hot anger surged through Clare's veins. "You'll understand? What exactly does that mean?"

"If you're put in a position where you have to choose

between me and your family, I'll abide by whatever you want."

"What kind of wife do you think I am?" she demanded.

Reed didn't so much as hesitate. "Lusty."

"I'm serious, Reed Tonasket. You're my husband… my place is with you."

"Here?" He glanced around as if seeing the cabin for the first time, with all its faults. As he'd told her earlier, this was the only home he'd known since he was little more than a toddler.

"I'll live wherever you want," Clare assured him. "Here, Tullue, or downtown New York."

Although Reed nodded, Clare wasn't completely convinced he believed her. "I'm serious," she reiterated.

Reed kissed her, then silently stood to pour their coffee.

His words stayed with her that morning as Clare washed their breakfast dishes. When she squirted the liquid detergent into the water, her gaze fell to the gold band Reed had given her that had once belonged to his mother.

Clare wished she could have known Beth Tonasket. When she'd quizzed him about his mother, Reed hadn't been able to tell her much. His own memory of the woman who had given him birth was limited.

He'd gotten some pictures of her from a box stored in his closet, and Clare had stared at the likeness of a gentle blonde for several moments. Although her coloring was much lighter than Reed's, Clare could see a strong resemblance between mother and son. Of one thing Clare was sure—Beth Tonasket hadn't possessed a fragile spirit.

Clare wasn't sure why Reed's words had upset her so much. She feared it was because they were so close to the truth. Sooner or later she would have to face her parents. Soon the whole town would know she'd married Reed.

She recalled the look on Jim Daniels's face when she'd gone to the city jail to post Reed's bail. It had angered her at the time that this old family friend would be so quick to judge her. He certainly hadn't wasted any time in letting her parents know what she'd done. Her mother had shown up at the library the next afternoon flustered and concerned.

While Reed was busy working in his shop, Clare took down the box of pictures from the shelf, wanting to look them over, learn what she could of Reed's life.

Sitting atop the bed, she sorted through the stacks of old photos and found several that piqued her curiosity. One, a tall proud man in an army uniform, caught her attention. Clare knew immediately this must have been Reed's father.

Studying the photo, Clare felt a heaviness settle over her. How he must have hated leaving his wife and young son, knowing they would have to deal with life's cruelties alone.

"Clare."

"I'm here," she called.

Reed came into the bedroom, pausing when he found her. "I haven't looked through those in years."

"Are you in this one?" she asked, holding out a black-and-white photo of several Native American youths.

Reed laughed when he saw it. "I'm the skinny one with knobby knees."

"They're all skinny with knobby knees."

"There," he said, sitting next to her. He pointed to the tall one in the middle, holding a bow and arrow. "That was taken when I was about eight or so. The tribal leader had held a council and grandfather and I attended. I'd forgotten all about that."

"Will...you be taking our son to tribal councils?"

Reed hesitated. "Probably. Will that bother you?"

"I don't think so. He'll be Native American like his father."

"I'll be teaching all our children the ways of our tribe." He said this as though he expected her to challenge his right to do so.

"Of course," she agreed, though she wasn't sure what that would entail. Skills like trapping, hunting, fishing were often passed down from any father to son.

"I need to go into town sometime today," she told him. Her sick leave was about to expire and it was important that she make out the work schedule for the following week. Although she was much better, Clare wasn't ready to go back full-time. Even if she was, she would have delayed it a day or two so she could be with Reed.

"I'll drive you later. It might be a good idea if we checked in with Doc Brown while we're in Tullue."

"Reed, I'm a thousand percent better than I was when he first saw me."

"I don't want there to be any complications."

Clare grumbled under her breath, deciding it would be a waste of time to argue with him. She had the distinct feeling he was going to turn into a mother hen the moment he learned she was pregnant.

After this past month it would be a minor miracle if she wasn't. When Reed had described her as lusty he hadn't been far off the truth. It embarrassed her how much she wanted him. The future might hold several problems, but Clare was convinced none of them would happen in their marriage bed.

"Someone's coming," Reed announced, straightening. He climbed off the bed.

"Erin?"

"Not this time." He frowned. "It sounds like two cars." His uncanny ability to make out noises fascinated her.

Reed walked onto the porch, and Clare followed him. She was standing at his side when the two vehicles pulled into view.

One look down the narrow driveway and Clare froze. She felt as though the bottom of her world had fallen out from under her.

The first car was marked Sheriff. Clare recognized Jim Daniels. The second car followed close behind. Inside were her parents.

Thirteen

"Get inside, Clare," Reed said with steel in his voice.

"I don't think that's a good idea," she murmured, moving closer to his side. Her heart felt as though it were on a trampoline, it was pounding so hard and fast.

Clare fully intended to tell her parents she was married, but she'd hoped to do it in her own time, in her own way, when the conditions were right.

"Clare, for the love of heaven, do as I ask."

"I can't," she said miserably. "Those are my parents."

Reed was already tense, but he grew more so at her words. His eyes found hers, and in their dark depths Clare read his doubts and his concern.

"I love you, Reed Tonasket," she said, wanting to assure him and at the same time reassure herself. Reed had claimed she possessed a fragile spirit. At the time Clare had been mildly insulted. His words contained a certain amount of truth, but she wasn't weak willed. No matter what happened she'd stand by her husband.

The sheriff stepped out of the car. The sound of his door closing felt like a giant clap of thunder in Clare's ear.

"Good day, Officer," Reed said, appearing relaxed and completely at ease. "What can I do for you?"

"Clare, sweetheart," her mother cried, climbing out of the car. Ellie Gilroy covered her mouth with her hand as if she were overcome with dismay. "Are you all right?"

"Of course I am," Clare answered, puzzled. Blindly her hand reached for Reed's. They stood together on the porch, their fingers laced.

"Would you mind stepping away from Clare Gilroy?" Jim Daniels requested of Reed in a voice that sounded both bureaucratic and official.

"Why would you want him to do that?" Clare demanded defensively.

"He wants to be sure I haven't got a knife on you," Reed explained. He dropped her hand and placed some distance between them. A chill chased down her arms when Reed moved away from her.

"That's the most ridiculous thing I've ever heard in my life." Clare was outraged. Old family friend or not, how dare Jim Daniels make such a suggestion!

"This man is a known troublemaker," Jim insisted.

"That's not true." Clare was so angry she was close to tears.

"Are you here of your own free will?" Jim inquired in the same professional tone he'd used earlier.

He sounded as if he were reading for the part of a television detective.

"You don't honestly believe Reed Tonasket kidnapped me, do you?"

"That's exactly what we think." Her father spoke for the first time. His large hands were knotted into fists at his sides as if he were waiting for the opportunity to fight Reed for imagined wrongs.

Never having crossed the law herself, Clare wasn't familiar with legal procedure, but it seemed the deputy was sticking his neck on the chopping block. She wasn't entirely sure the sheriff's jurisdiction extended onto the reservation. Furthermore it seemed highly peculiar that he would drag her parents into what he believed to be a kidnapper's den.

"I came with Reed of my own free will," Clare explained as calmly as she could. She'd never had an explosive temper, but she feared that much more of these ridiculous accusations would change that.

"I don't believe her," her father said to his friend.

"There's not much else I can do, Leonard."

"Clare." Her mother's eyes implored her. "Are you ill?"

"Do I look sick?" she flared.

"I brought her to the cabin with me when she came down with a bad case of the flu," Reed explained in reasonable tones. "I intended to contact you, but from what I understand you were on a camping trip."

"I was worse off than I realized," Clare explained. Her mother had been in touch with her before they left for camping. Clare had been the one to insist they go. Her parents didn't get away nearly often enough and she would have hated to be the one responsible for ruining their plans.

"Clare was nearly dehydrated and close to being hospitalized," Reed added.

"But did she come of her own free will?" Jim demanded.

"I already said I did," Clare shouted, losing patience with the lot of them.

"She wasn't happy about it," Reed admitted, "but

there were few options available. She needed someone to take care of her, and…"

"She didn't need a jailbird doing it."

"Daddy!"

"The man was recently arrested for aggravated assault," her father stormed. "If he'd attack another man, what is there to say he wouldn't kidnap my daughter?"

Clare couldn't remember ever seeing her father so agitated. He'd always been a calm and reasonable man. She could hardly remember him raising his voice. He seldom revealed emotion of any form.

"Arrest him," Leonard insisted.

"On what charge?" Clare demanded. "I've already told you I'm here because I want to be. I can't believe you're doing this. Reed took me in, nursed me when I was ill and this is the way you treat him?"

"He didn't need to bring you here. There were plenty of other places he could have taken you."

"Dad, you're being unreasonable."

"He admitted himself that you didn't want to come."

Clare clenched her teeth to keep from saying something she'd later regret. "Why doesn't everyone come inside and we'll sit down and talk about this in a civilized manner?"

"That sounds like a good idea, doesn't it, Leonard?"

Clare could have kissed her mother. She started toward the front door, then realized she was the only one who'd moved. Reed, who stood with his arms crossed, hadn't budged. Neither had Jim Daniels or her father. Her mother took one tentative step forward, but froze when no one else moved.

The sound of another car barreling up the driveway diverted everyone's attention.

"Who else could be coming?" her father demanded.

"I think it would help matters a whole lot, dear, if you'd come off those steps and stand by your father and me," her mother suggested in low tones, as if she assumed speaking softly would coax Clare to leave Reed.

"It's Gary and Erin," Reed told her long before the car came into view.

Clare felt as though the whole world had descended on them at the same moment. Gary pulled in behind her parents' car and leaped out of the front seat as though the engine were on fire.

"What the hell's going on here?" he demanded, hands on his hips. Erin stepped out of the car, but held on to the door as she surveyed the scene around them. It was apparent to Clare that their friends had inadvertently stumbled upon the confrontation. Erin looked as shocked as Clare felt.

"It seems Deputy Daniels believes I kidnapped Clare," Reed explained.

"That's ridiculous."

"That's what I've been trying to tell them," Clare cried. "Why doesn't everyone come inside so we can discuss this situation rationally?"

Gary and Erin stepped onto the porch, but hesitated when no one else followed.

"What's the matter with you people?" Gary asked, glancing from one to the other. "Reed didn't kidnap Clare any more than he did me or Erin. He brought her here because she was ill. You should be grateful."

"That's my daughter he took—"

"Dear," Ellie Gilroy said softly, "I don't think it's fair to say Reed took Clare."

Her father glared at his wife but said nothing.

Knowing she would need to face her parents with the truth, Clare was hoping to soothe the waters as best she could before hitting them with the news of her marriage.

"I'll help you with the coffee," Erin said, taking Clare by the elbow and leading the way inside the cabin. Reluctantly Clare went inside, but not before casting Reed a pleading gaze. She wasn't sure what she expected him to do.

"Do they know?" Erin asked the instant they were inside the house. Clare didn't need for her friend to clarify the question. Her parents hadn't a clue she was married to Reed.

"No."

Erin sighed expressively. "I was afraid of that."

"Reed won't tell them, either." Of that, Clare was certain. Even if it cost him dearly, he wouldn't do or say anything that would place Clare in an awkward position with her parents.

"How'd they know you were here?"

"I haven't a clue, unless Doc Brown said something."

"That isn't likely," Erin muttered.

Clare went about assembling the pot of coffee. The temptation to walk back onto the porch and find out what was happening was strong, but it was more important to collect her thoughts.

Erin brought down several mugs and set them in the center of the table. Her father used sugar, so Clare brought over the sugar bowl, a couple of teaspoons and a handful of paper napkins.

"The coffee will be ready in a couple of minutes," she said, stepping outside. She rubbed her palms together as she cast a pleading glance to her parents.

Everything seemed to be at a standstill. No one was

speaking. They stood like chess pieces, reviewing strategy before making another move.

"Mom?" Clare pleaded.

Her mother glanced toward her father, but he ignored her.

"Jim, I appreciate you coming, but as you can see I'm in no danger."

Jim Daniels nodded, but he didn't reveal any signs of leaving.

"It might be best if you left," she said pointedly. "There are several things I need to discuss with my parents. Family matters."

"I want him here," her father insisted.

"Why?"

"That man's dangerous."

Clare was too angry to respond. "He's no more *dangerous* than you are!"

"I wasn't the one arrested for aggravated assault."

"That does it," Clare shouted, slapping her hands against her sides in a show of abject frustration. "Does anyone know why Reed and Jack fought? Does anyone care?"

"Clare." Reed's low voice was filled with warning.

"Reed doesn't want me to tell you, but I will." She folded her arms across her chest the same way Reed had and shifted her weight to her left foot. "I broke up with Jack for a number of excellent reasons."

"We know all that, dear," her mother said.

"What you don't know is that Jack started pestering me afterward. First he started bothering me with phone calls. It got so bad I had to unplug my phone. Then he sat outside my house, watched every move I made."

"You should have got a restraining order against him," Jim told her.

Clare agreed, but she hadn't thought of it at the time. "I... I don't know what led up to the fight, Reed never told me exactly what he said but Jack apparently insulted me. In my heart I know there was a very good reason. Jack learned that I was...dating Reed, and his ego couldn't take that. Jack never cared for me, but the thought of me having anything to do with another man was more than his petty ego could take."

"According to the statement we got from Kingston at the time of the—"

"Knowing Jack, it was a pack of lies," Clare interrupted. "It was bad enough having Jack hound me the way he was. I knew that once he discovered I was seeing Reed, matters would get much worse. Jack was determined to make my life a living hell. Yes, Reed got into a fistfight with Jack, but he did so to defend me. I haven't heard from Jack once since the fight and I have Reed to thank for that. Jack won't pester me again because he knows if he does he'll have Reed to contend with."

"And me," Gary chimed in.

"I wasn't aware there was a problem with Jack," her father admitted reluctantly.

"We had our suspicions though," Ellie mumbled. "He called shortly after you broke off your engagement, and it was clear to your father, that Jack was trying to make trouble."

"I don't think Jack was ever the man we thought he was," Clare said with a tinge of sadness.

"There's no need to do something foolish because of Kingston," her father said pointedly. "Getting involved in another relationship because you're on the rebound isn't wise."

"Especially with a Native American," Reed supplied, stating what had been left unsaid.

Her father's gaze connected with Reed's. Clare could only speculate what passed between the two men.

"Will you come inside now?" she asked softly.

"Come home with us, Clare," her father insisted, holding his arm out to her. "You've had a bad time. First this business with Jack, and then having to deal with the flu. Let's put all this behind us."

"I am home, Dad."

"Nonsense, your place is with us and—"

"Dad, you're not hearing me."

"Now listen here—"

"Dad," Clare shouted, her voice cracking. "Would you stop and for once in your life listen to what I'm trying to tell you?"

"Clare." Reed's eyes implored her. He seemed to be saying now wasn't the time, but she ignored his silent plea, refusing to put off the truth any longer.

"Mom and Dad," Clare said, moving to Reed's side. She slipped her arm around his waist. "Reed and I are married."

Fourteen

"You're married? You and Reed? Oh, dear." Ellie Gilroy pressed her hand over her heart. "I do believe I need to sit down."

Clare's father gripped his wife by the elbow and directed her inside Reed's home, his former hesitancy gone.

Jim Daniels would have followed right behind him if Leonard Gilroy hadn't turned and said, "We'll take it from here, Jim. We appreciate your time and trouble."

"No problem. Give me a call anytime."

By the time her mother was seated in the living room, Clare had poured her a glass of water and brought it to her. Ellie studied Clare as she sipped from the glass. She seemed to be judging the accuracy of Clare's announcement.

"I'm Reed's wife, Mom," Clare whispered, unsure her mother believed her.

Ellie nodded as though accepting the inevitable, then she curiously studied the room. "This home is very nice," she murmured. "Of course it needs a woman's touch here and there, but really I'm quite—"

"Ellie."

Her husband's voice cut off the small talk.

"It seems you four have lots to discuss, so I think Gary and I'll be leaving," Erin said, stepping just inside the doorway. She hugged Clare and whispered, "Everything's going to work out just fine."

Clare wished she felt half as confident as her friend.

A silence fell over the room after Gary and Erin were gone. Clare's mother sat on the sofa, her father stood at his wife's side. Reed was at the other end of the room, before the fireplace, and Clare was positioned close to the kitchen.

"Coffee, anyone?" she asked brightly.

"That would be nice, dear."

Clare looked to her father and Reed, but both men ignored her, concentrating instead on each other, as if sizing up one another. Clare sighed and disappeared into the kitchen long enough to pour her mother a cup of coffee.

"Is it true?" Her father's question was directed at Reed.

Rarely a man of words, Reed nodded.

"There's never been an artist in the family," Ellie said conversationally, as though nothing were amiss. "It might be a nice change, don't you think, Leonard?"

"As a matter of fact, I don't," Clare's father returned abruptly.

"Dad, if you'd only listen."

"How long have you known him?" her father demanded next, slicing her with his eyes.

Clare bristled at his tone. She wasn't a child to be chastised for wrongdoing. "Long enough, Dad."

Her father, who'd always been the picture of serenity,

rammed his fingers through his hair. His gaze skirted
away from hers. "Did...he take advantage of you?"

It would have been a terrible mistake to have laughed,
Clare realized, but she nearly did. "No." She couldn't
help wondering what her father would say if she confessed how often she'd asked Reed to make love to her.

"Do you love him?" His fingers went through his
hair once again.

"Oh, yes."

"What about you, young man? Do you love my
daughter?"

"Very much." Clare was grateful Reed chose a verbal response. Although he didn't elaborate on his feelings, the message was concise and came straight from
his heart.

"Do you make enough money to support her?"

Clearly her father had no idea how successful Reed
was, nor was he taking into account that she made a
living wage at the library. It was a question that could
have offended her husband, but it didn't.

"He's famous, Leonard," her mother answered before
Reed could. "Don't you remember there was that article about him in the *Washingtonian?* We both read it.
You even asked me about Reed then, wanted to know if
we'd ever met him. You seemed to be quite impressed?"

"I remember," her father muttered, but if he recalled
reading the article, he took pains not to show it.

Clare moved so she was standing next to Reed. He
slipped his arm around her waist and brought her close
to his side. Clare was convinced the protective action
was instinctive.

"Are you pregnant, Clare?" her father asked, his
voice low and a bit uncertain. Pregnancy and child-

birth were subjects that were uncomfortable to a man of his generation. His gaze studied the top of his shoes.

"I...don't know, but I'm hoping I am. Reed and I both want a family."

"You plan to live here?" was his next question.

"For now," Reed answered. "If Clare agrees I'd like to have another home built on this site within the next couple of years."

His arm tightened around her waist, and Clare pressed her head to his chest, drinking in his solid strength.

"I love Reed," she said softly, straightening. Reed's arms lent her courage to speak her mind. "I know our marriage came as a shock and I'm sorry for telling you the way I did, but you had to know sooner or later."

Her father said nothing.

"I really hope you'll accept Reed as my husband," she said, trying hard not to plead with her parents. "Because he's a wonderful man. I...realize you may not approve of my choice, but I can't live my life to please you and Mom."

"Of course we'll accept your marriage," her mother rushed to say, willing to do anything to keep the peace. "Won't we, Leonard?"

Her father seemed to be carefully weighing the decision.

"Reed Tonasket is a man of honor and pride. The happiest day of my life was when Reed agreed to marry me. That's right, Dad, I asked him. If you think Reed said or did anything to coerce me into this marriage, you're wrong."

"I see," her father said with a heavy sigh, and sat on the cushion next to his wife. The way he fell onto the sofa suggested his legs had gone out from under him.

"I don't think you do understand, Dad, and that makes me sad—because you should be sharing in my joy instead of questioning my judgment. You raised me to be the woman I am, and all I'm asking is that you rest on your laurels and allow me to practice everything you taught me." Clare felt close to tears and rushed her words, wanting to finish before her voice betrayed her emotion. "I've made my choice of a husband and I'm very proud of the man he is. If you can't accept that then I'm sorry for you both. Not only will you have lost your daughter, but you'll have wasted the opportunity to know what a fine man Reed is."

Reed's hand was at her neck, and he squeezed gently as if he, too, shared her emotion.

The silence that followed was so loud it hurt Clare's ears. She watched as her father slowly stood. It looked as if he were in a stupor, not knowing what to do.

Clare's mother remained seated and stared up at her husband. She opened her mouth as if she wanted to say something, but if that was the case, she changed her mind.

After a moment, Leonard Gilroy crossed the living room until he stood directly in front of Reed. The two proud men met eye to eye.

Her father stretched out his hand. "Welcome to the family, Reed, and congratulations."

Clare sniffled once and then hugged her father with all her strength. "I love you, Daddy."

"You make a mighty convincing argument, sweetheart," her father whispered. "If I was angry, it was because I've always looked forward to walking my little girl down the aisle."

"I think you should," Reed said, surprising them

both. "We were married by a justice of the peace. I wouldn't object to a religious ceremony and I don't think Clare would, either."

"You mean we could still have a wedding?" her mother asked excitedly.

"A small one," Clare agreed. "The sooner the better."

"I imagine we could pull one together in a few weeks." Ellie's eyes lit up with excitement at the prospect.

Clare nestled snug against her husband's side in the early-morning light. "You awake?" she whispered, rubbing her hand against his bare back.

She could feel Reed's grin since it was impossible for her to see it. "I am now."

"It went well with my parents, don't you think?"

"Very well," he agreed. Rolling onto his back, he reached for Clare, collecting her in his arms. "I was wrong about you, Clare Tonasket."

Clare agreed. "You made the mistake of underestimating me."

He chuckled. "Forget I ever said anything about you having a fragile spirit. You've got more tenacity than any ten women I know."

"You aren't angry I told them we're married, are you?" She lifted her head just enough to read his expression. From his small smile she realized he was teasing her. Her hair fell forward and he lovingly brushed it back.

"They had to find out sooner or later," he agreed. "I just wish you'd announced it with a bit more finesse."

"I'm through hiding the fact I'm your wife."

Reed slipped his arm around her waist and Clare leaned down and kissed him. "Talking about surprise announcements," she said, elevating her voice, "when did you decide you wanted to go through with a wedding ceremony?"

"It was a peace offering to appease your mother. Besides, your father had a good point. You're their only daughter and they didn't want to be cheated out of giving you a wedding."

"I don't feel cheated," she whispered. "I feel loved."

Reed slipped his hand to the small of her back. "We may have a daughter someday, and I'm going to want the privilege of escorting her to her husband."

"We may be proud parents sooner than either of us realizes if we have many more sessions like the ones recently."

Reed's eyes grew dark and serious. "Am I too demanding on you, Clare, because if I am…"

"You're not, trust me, you're not. Just don't let anyone know." She kissed his throat, working her way to his mouth. Reed groaned deep in his chest.

"Know what?" he asked breathlessly.

"What a shameless hussy your wife turned out to be."

"Sweet heaven, Clare, I love you. I never realized loving someone could be like this."

"I didn't, either," she admitted.

"My life was so empty without you. I couldn't go back to the way it was, not now." He buried his face in her neck. "The day will come when our children will marry. If it makes your parents happy to have us renew our vows so they can give us a wedding, then it's a small price to pay, don't you think?"

"I knew you were talented," Clare said, her lips scant inches above his, "I just didn't expect you to be brilliant."

"You've only scratched the surface of my many

skills." He wove his fingers into her hair and directed her mouth back to his. Their kiss was slow and thorough. When she raised her head from the lengthy exchange, Clare drew in a deep, stabilizing breath.

Dawn was breaking over the horizon, a new day, fresh and untainted, a celebration that Clare felt certain would last all the days of their lives.

* * * * *